W9-BJV-113

XOXO

AXIE OH

An Imprint of HarperCollinsPublishers

HarperTeen is an imprint of HarperCollins Publishers.

XOXO

Copyright © 2021 by HarperCollins Publishers
www.epicreads.com
ISBN 978-0-06-302499-1
Typography by Jessie Gang
21 22 23 24 25 PC/LSCH   10 9 8 7 6 5 4 3 2 1
❖
First Edition

For my smart, loving, and talented sister, Camille.

One

Jay's Karaoke sits at the center of a Koreatown strip mall between a Boba Land 2 and Sookie's Hair Emporium.

The door to the latter bursts open as I pass. "Yah, Jenny-yah!" Sookie Kim, owner and hairdresser, stands in the doorway holding a plastic bag and a flat iron. "Aren't you going to say hello?"

"Hello, Mrs. Kim," I say, then stretch my neck to look over her shoulder where three middle-aged women are seated in a row beneath hair dryers watching a K-drama on a wall-mounted TV. "Hi, Mrs. Lim, Mrs. Chang, Mrs. Sutjiawan."

"Hi, Jenny," they chorus back, waving at me briefly before returning their attention to the couple on screen who appear to be heading toward a K-drama kiss. The man leans his head one way, the woman the other, their lips touch and hold as the camera pans out with dramatic music soaring in the background.

As the credits start to roll, the ladies collapse back in their chairs with dreamy sighs. Well, two of them do.

"That's it?" Mrs. Sutjiawan throws her house slipper at the TV.

"Here." Ignoring the women, Mrs. Kim hands over the plastic bag she's holding, which on closer inspection appears to be food wrapped up in a H Mart grocery bag and knotted tight. "This is for you to share with your mother."

"Thank you." I adjust my tote on my shoulder and bow slightly as I take the offering.

Mrs. Kim clicks her tongue. "Your mother works too much! She should be at home more, looking after her daughter."

I'm almost certain my mother works the same amount of hours at the office as Mrs. Kim does at her own business, but I have a strong enough sense of self-preservation not to point this out. Instead, I continue to give off respectable-young-person-vibes and smile politely. It seems to be working because Mrs. Kim's face softens. "Your mother must be so proud of you, Jenny. A good student. And so gifted in cello! I tell my Eunice that good music schools only take the best, but does she listen?"

"Sookie-ssi!" one of the ladies calls from inside.

"Coming," she yells back. As she heads into her shop, I make my way next door.

Ever since Eunice and I started entering the same classical music competitions in seventh grade, Mrs. Kim has been comparing the two of us. With the compliments she's always giving me, I shudder to think what Eunice is receiving on the opposite end. Lately, I haven't seen her at any of the competitions. She wasn't at last Saturday's, the results of which are currently burning a hole through my jacket pocket. If Mrs. Kim were to read what the judges said about me, she wouldn't be so quick with her praise.

The bells above the door at Jay's Karaoke chime my arrival.

"Be right there!" Uncle Jay's voice travels from behind the curtain that separates the bar from the kitchen.

Edging around the counter, I drop my tote and open the mini fridge to stuff Mrs. Kim's Tupperware between bottles of soju.

Seven years ago, Dad and Uncle Jay bought this place in order to fulfill a dream they'd had since they were kids, to own and manage a karaoke business together.

Uncle Jay isn't related to me by blood, but he and my dad were like brothers. After my dad passed, it was Uncle Jay who asked my mom if I could come work for him after school. At first Mom was against it, worried a part-time job wouldn't leave enough time for school and orchestra practice, but she came around when Uncle Jay said I could do my homework during off hours. Plus I practically grew up here. I have memories of Dad behind the bar, laughing with Uncle Jay as he whipped up his latest concoction, not forgetting a special non-alcoholic drink just for me.

For years, I wasn't allowed in the bar—Mom was afraid it'd bring back memories—but so far it's been fun, and the memories, only good ones.

I spray the counter with cleaning solution and wipe it down, then move onto the tall bar tables. There aren't any customers in the main room, though a glimpse down the hall shows a few of the private karaoke rooms are occupied.

"Hey, Jenny, thought that was you." Uncle Jay emerges, holding two paper plates of steaming food. "Today's special is bulgogi tacos. Hungry?"

"Starving." I hop onto a barstool and Uncle Jay places the plate in front of me, two tacos with bulgogi marinated in his own special sauce, lettuce, tomatoes, cheese, and kimchi.

While I inhale my food, Uncle Jay turns on Netflix above the bar, scrolling through available movies.

This is our ritual. The bar doesn't get busy until later in the night, so we spend early evenings eating and watching movies, specifically Asian gangster films.

"Here we are," Uncle Jay says, landing on a classic. *The Man from Nowhere* also known as *Ajeossi*. An action thriller about an embittered ex-cop whose young neighbor is kidnapped and goes on a journey to bring her back home. It's like the Korean *Taken*, but better. Because it has Won Bin. Won Bin makes everything better.

Uncle Jay puts on the subtitles and we eat and watch the film, commenting on the believability that somehow Won Bin is an ajeossi, a middle-aged man, *at thirty-three*. When customers come in, he turns the volume down and leads them to their rooms. I keep an eye on the monitor that shows whether someone has pushed a call button, so that I can take the customers' orders and bring them their food while Uncle Jay handles their drink orders.

By the time nine o'clock rolls around, half the rooms are

filled and the movie is finished; instead, K-pop blares over the speakers. Every month, Uncle Jay streams YouTube compilations of the top music videos of the month on the TV in the bar. I watch as a group of girls in color-coordinated outfits performs a complicated and synchronized dance to a catchy electro-pop song.

Unlike some of the kids at my school, I never could get into K-pop, or any pop, really. A playlist of my life would include Bach, Haydn, and Yo-Yo Ma.

"Didn't you have an important competition this week?" Uncle Jay inspects a glass behind the counter, drying it with a rag.

My stomach sinks. "Saturday." I give him a bitter smile. "I got the results back this morning."

"Yeah?" He frowns. "How'd you do?"

"I won."

"What? Really? Congrats, girl!" He pumps his fist in the air. "My niece is a champ," he adds to the couple sitting at the bar, startling them from their tacos.

"Yeah . . ." I trace the letters of two sets of initials carved on the surface of the counter and linked by a heart.

"What's up?" He puts the glass and rag down on the counter. "Something's bothering you, I can tell."

"The judges left me feedback." I take out the paper from my pocket, which has been noticeably crumpled, then smoothed out, then folded into a square, and hand it over. "It's supposed to help me improve before the next competition."

As Uncle Jay reads the note, I replay the words I've already memorized.

While Jenny is a talented cellist, proficient in all the technical elements of music, she lacks the spark that would take her from perfectly trained to extraordinary.

Next year, hundreds of cellists just like me will be applying to the best music schools in the country. In order to get into one of the top schools, I can't just be perfect. I have to be extraordinary.

Uncle Jay hands the paper back. "Talented *and* technically skilled. Sounds about right."

I stuff the note deep into my pocket. "You missed the part where they called me a soulless robot."

He laughs. "I definitely missed *that* part." Though he must feel a tad sympathetic because he adds, "I can see that you're disappointed. But it's just critique. You get them all the time."

"It's not *just* that it's critique," I say, trying to put my frustration into words. "It's that there's nothing to improve upon. Emotion in music is expressed through pitch and dynamics. I'm great at both of those things."

Uncle Jay gives me a sidelong glance.

"They said I lack spark!"

He sighs, leaning against the bar. "I think it's more that you haven't found your spark yet, something that lights that fire within you to go after what you want. For example, your dad and me deciding to open up this karaoke bar, even though so many people told us it was a waste of money. Even your mom, though seeing as how she didn't grow up with much, I don't blame her. We knew it'd be hard and that we might not succeed but we still tried because it was our dream."

"But. . ." I say slowly, "what does any of that have to do with impressing music schools?"

"Here, let me explain it to you in Jenny-speak. You know that movie we watched earlier tonight? *Ajeossi*. There's a quote Won Bin's character says that roughly translates to, 'People who live for tomorrow should fear the people who live for today.' Do you know why that is?"

"No," I drawl, "but you're going to tell me."

"Because the people who live for tomorrow don't take risks. They're afraid of the consequences. While the people who live for today have nothing to lose, so they fight tooth and nail. I'm saying that maybe you should stop caring so much about your future, about getting into music school, about what'll come after, and . . . live a little. Have new experiences, make new friends. I promise you can get the life you want now, if you just live in it." The door chime jingles as customers walk into the bar.

"Welcome!" Uncle Jay calls out, leaving me to stew in my thoughts as he rounds the counter to greet them.

I think about texting Mom, except that I know what she'd say; I should practice more and maybe schedule additional lessons with Eunbi. Also not to listen to Uncle Jay. If Uncle Jay is all about living in the moment and following your dreams, my mom is much more practical. I can have a successful career as a cellist but only if I work hard and focus completely.

Anything outside of that is a distraction.

Though, it's not like I *haven't* been working hard—Mrs. Kim, and presumably Eunice, would know—and *still* I got that critique.

Maybe Uncle Jay has a point.

"Don't worry about it, kiddo," he says returning from helping out the customers. "You'll figure it out. Why don't you go home early, rest up? Bomi should be here soon." Bomi is the surly UCLA student who usually works the night shift. "Just check in on room eight before you do. The time ran out on their machine but they haven't left yet."

I sigh. "Okay." Slipping off the barstool, I trudge down the hall. Confronting customers is one of my least favorite tasks at Jay's. Why can't they just read the rules?

In most karaoke joints in the States, customers are charged at the end of the night, usually by the hour, and the customers are the ones who keep track of the time and how much they're spending. Uncle Jay runs his karaoke business like they do in Korea, charging in advance for a set amount of time that appears as a countdown clock on the screen inside the room. That way, people aren't overcharged. If they want to sing for longer, they can add more time to their room. Mom always says Uncle Jay doesn't really have a head for business.

The door to room eight is closed with no sound coming from inside, but that makes sense if their time has run out. I knock once, then open the door.

This is the VIP room, the largest in the bar that can hold up to twenty people.

I'm surprised to find a single person in the room. He's a guy around my age, seated in the corner with his back against the wall and his eyes closed.

I look for evidence of another person, but the long table is empty of food or drinks. If he's renting the room by himself, he must be wealthy. His clothes look expensive. A silky shirt clings to his shoulders, and his long legs are clad in smooth black pants. His left arm is in a cast, but a Rolex glints from his right wrist—and are those *sleeve tattoos*?

What teenager has sleeve tattoos?

I look back to his face, startled to see that his eyes are open. I wait for him to speak, but he remains silent. I cough to clear my throat. "Your time expired. If you would like to use the room longer, it's fifty dollars an hour. Otherwise, you need to leave."

That came out ruder than I intended. I blame the judges for putting me in a bad mood.

The silence that follows seems heightened with the strobe lights issuing from the disco ball on the ceiling.

Maybe he can't speak English? He might be *from* Korea. No American kid is this stylish.

I try again, this time in Korean. "Sigan Jinasseoyo. Naga-seyo." Literally, "Time's up. Get out." Though with honorifics, so *technically* I'm being polite.

"I heard you the first time," he says in English. His speaking voice is low and smooth. He has a slight accent, a sort of warm curl around his words.

I feel an inexplicable blush rise in my cheeks. "Then why didn't you say something?"

"I was trying to decide whether I should be offended."

I point to the large laminated book at the center of the table that lists all the available karaoke songs by title. "The rules are written on the cover of the songbook. They stipulate that if you haven't purchased more time after fifteen minutes, you have to leave immediately."

He shrugs. "I'm out of money."

I eye his Gucci loafers. "I highly doubt that."

"They're not mine."

I frown. "You stole them?"

He pauses, then says slowly, "You could say that."

Is he lying? Somehow I don't think so. I hadn't seen him come into the bar. How long has he been in this room? Alone. Who does that, unless they're hiding from something? And maybe it's because I just watched *Ajeossi*, but my mind jumps to one conclusion.

I step closer. He seems to mirror my movements, leaning away from the wall.

"Do you—" I drop my voice low. "Do you need help?" In crime dramas, the people my age aren't ever in the gang because they want to be.

He shrugs. "Right now, fifty dollars would be great."

I shake my head. "I'm asking if you're in trouble? Like . . . with a gang."

For a moment, he looks taken aback, his eyes widening slightly. Then my words seem to click into place and he drops his gaze. "Ah, so you've guessed it."

I nod fervently. "You must be sixteen, seventeen . . ." I press.

"There are laws to protect minors in the United States." Maybe they're holding something over him, like the safety of a sibling or a friend. "If you need help, you only have to ask."

There's a short pause, then he says softly, "If I asked you to save me, would you?"

My heart breaks a little. "I can try."

He lifts his eyes to mine, and my breath catches. It's almost unfair that someone could be so . . . beautiful. His skin is flawless. He has dark eyes and soft hair, and a full, cherry-red mouth.

He drops his head and his shoulders start to shake. Is he . . . crying? I move closer, only to see that he's . . .

Laughing. He even slaps his knee with his good hand.

What a jerk! I was *concerned* for him.

I stomp out the door.

In the foyer, Uncle Jay glances up from where he's adding hours to one of the rooms. He takes one look at my expression and sighs. "Kid's not leaving, huh? Don't worry, I'll take care of it."

He starts to come out from behind the bar, but I hold up a hand. "Wait." His words from earlier echo back to me. *Live a little.* "I've got this."

Two

The boy is still sitting in the corner when I enter the room. And maybe I should be ticked off that he clearly didn't listen to me, but it doesn't matter.

"Here's the deal," I say. "I added an extra twenty minutes to your room."

He arches a brow. "How generous."

"It's not a gift. I challenge you to a karaoke battle."

He stares at me blankly.

"Let me show you." I scoot into the seat opposite him, pick up the device that controls the karaoke machine, and press the Score button. "Now the machine will score our performance once the song is over," I explain. "If you win, I'll give you another hour in this room. No charge. If I win, you have to leave."

I'm a little surprised that I'm doing this. I would never in a million years think that I would challenge a stranger—a boy my own age who's probably the most attractive person I've ever seen in real life—to a karaoke battle. But after getting the feedback from the judges, I'm determined to do *something* about it.

Maybe Uncle Jay was right. Maybe getting out of my comfort zone and putting myself out there will make a difference.

I bite my lip and wait as the boy mulls over my offer. Honestly, it's a win-win situation for him. Without paying, he *would* have to leave eventually. So either he has to do what he was always going to do, or he gets a free hour in relatively safe comfort.

Finally he taps the songbook with his good hand. "All right. I'll play your game. But you're about to be disappointed. I'm actually decent at singing."

From the smirk on his face, I can tell he's already planning his hour of squatter-living. Little does he know that though I might not have the best voice, karaoke machines score on pitch, and mine is perfect.

He starts to push the songbook across the table.

"I won't be needing that." I pick up the controller and look up the artist by name, plugging in my selection. The instrumentals for Gloria Gaynor's "I Will Survive" begin to play.

I stand, microphone in hand, then proceed to belt out the song. I mostly chose this one because of the fast pace. I have no time to think or doubt myself when I'm trying to breathe. It doesn't hurt that it also has lyrics like "Walk out the door" and "You're not welcome anymore."

When it's over, I collapse onto the couch. My score appears on the screen: 95.

The boy taps his good hand on the table in a slow clap. "That was . . . something else."

I'm breathless; my cheeks are flushed. "We only have eight minutes on the clock. Hurry, pick a song."

I look up to find his eyes on me. "You choose for me."

"Are you sure?" I pick up the book and turn to the back where all the recent songs have been added. "You're going to regret this." There aren't many choices for American songs, but the Korean songs fill up two pages. I read the artist names aloud.

"XOXO? What kind of name is that?" I laugh.

He scowls. "Seven minutes."

There are so many possibilities. I'm almost gleeful with power. "Do you prefer a song in English or Korean?"

"It doesn't matter."

"I mean, we're at a noraebang, you might as well sing a Korean song. I just don't know many."

"Really? Not even, like, the anthem?"

I'm about to answer with a snarky comeback, when I hesitate, remembering. "I know one . . ."

"What's it called?"

"I don't know the title." I hum the melody by memory, but it's been so long since I last heard it. "Sorry." I shake my head, feeling silly for having brought it up.

"Gohae."

I blink, startled. "What?"

"'Confession.' That's the title of the song. It's famous."

I stare at him. I can't believe he *knows* it, and just from a few bars of melody. "It was one of my dad's favorites."

"It was mine too," he says.

I frown. "It was your favorite song?"

"My father's."

There's a beat of silence between us as we both recognize we're speaking of our fathers as if they're no longer here.

Reaching out, he takes the controller, and with one hand, switches the language from English to Hangeul and plugs in the numbers, his fingers quick and sure.

When the instrumentals begin to play, I feel everything inside me go still. *This is the song.* I recognize the melody and the distinctive sound of a keyboard, then the boy starts to sing, and I forget to breathe.

I never paid attention to the lyrics before, but now they wrap around me like silk.

He sings about daring to love someone though the world would stand against them.

His voice is far from perfect, rough and not always on pitch, and yet there's a rawness and vulnerability to every phrase, every word.

A memory washes over me, from five years ago, sitting cross-legged at the foot of my father's hospital bed. We were playing cards on the blanket, and this song was playing in the background. And we were laughing. So hard that there were tears in our eyes, and I remembered thinking, *I'm so happy. I never want this feeling to end. I want it to last forever.*

But nothing ever does.

On the screen, a score appears: 86.

The time runs out on the machine. The boy gets to his feet, adjusting his cast. I instinctively stand to face him.

"Thank you," he says, hesitantly. He then bows, and I bow back, which should be weird but for some reason isn't.

I want to tell him that he should have won, that any judge would have scored his singing above mine. After all, a true musician doesn't just perform a song but makes you feel something. And it's clear with how my heart aches from the memory and the music, he has the spark. I want to ask him where it comes from, and how can I find it for myself.

But I say nothing and he quietly leaves the room, the door clicking shut behind him.

Three

In the foyer, I find Bomi pulling a UCLA sweatshirt over her head. "Hey, Jenny," she says, catching sight of me. "Are you going home?" She stuffs her sweatshirt and the rest of her belongings behind the bar. "Avoid Olympic and Normandie on your way out. There's some sort of Korean festival going on and the streets are blocked."

Uncle Jay sweeps back the curtain to the kitchens, holding a tray with a plate of kimchi fried rice topped with an egg.

Bomi doesn't look up from where she's exchanging her bag for mine. "Boss . . ." she begins, handing me mine across the counter, "can I get off early on Sunday? I have to study for an Econ final."

"Sure, sure. I am nothing if not accommodating." He glances at me. "Don't forget to take your leftovers from the fridge."

"It's banchan, not leftovers," I correct.

"Man," Bomi laments, "I wish someone would give *me* side dishes. Instead I'm stuck with making ramen out of a rice cooker."

Uncle Jay and I both stare at her. "Why don't you use a stove?" I ask.

Bomi shrugs. "I'd rather not leave my room if I can help it."

Uncle Jay hands her the tray. "So glad you could honor us with coming to work."

I shake my head with a smile and lean down to retrieve Mrs. Kim's banchan from the fridge. Standing, I hold the plastic bag of Tupperware to my chest. This is probably the best time to make my exit, but I linger behind the bar. Bomi switches the monitor to an indie rock playlist—her favorite genre of K-pop—before heading off down the hall to deliver the kimchi fried rice. At one of the tables in the foyer, four college-aged students hit their shot glasses together, celebrating the weekend.

I feel a tightness in my chest. Maybe Uncle Jay and Bomi need some help. I don't *have* to leave. I need to wake up early for my cello lesson tomorrow, but maybe I could stay.

"Jenny, you're still here?" Uncle Jay appears beside me, this time carrying a watermelon on a tray, halved and hollowed and filled with a mixture of watermelon, soju, and lime-soda. "You'll miss the bus if you don't head out soon." He walks from behind the counter, calling over his shoulder. "Text me when you get home!"

I've been dismissed. Sighing, I adjust the strap of my tote higher on my shoulder and head toward the front door, pushing it open. Cool air washes over my face.

It's almost ten o'clock and yet it's as bright as day with all the neon lights issuing from the signboards of most businesses on the block. Sookie's Hair Emporium is closed, but in the Boba Land 2, a pigtailed shopgirl chews bubblegum as she scrolls through the messages on her phone. On the corner, the Korean BBQ restaurant is hopping, groups of college students and business types chatting while they cook meat over charcoal grills.

I notice the bus parked at the curb, letting on passengers, and I hurry to the end of the line. After paying, I shuffle down the aisle, adjusting Mrs. Kim's banchan as I reach up to take the handrail. I brace myself as the bus jerks forward and my bag hits the person sitting in one of the single passenger seats.

"Sorry!" I wince. The guy looks up.

It's him. The boy from the karaoke bar.

"What are you doing here?" I blurt out. Though the answer is pretty obvious; he's riding a bus. "I mean, I thought you said you didn't have any money."

He holds up a single-ride bus ticket. "What about you? Did you get off work?" He pauses, and then a small smirk forms on his perfect lips. "Or did you follow me here?"

I sputter. "I didn't—"

"Are you going to take that seat?" A woman taps my shoulder, pointing to the seat behind him.

"Oh, no." I move back so she can sit down, and now I'm just hovering here awkwardly over both of them. Turning around, I move to the other side of the bus, cheeks flushed from embarrassment.

The bus slows as it nears West 8th Street, letting on a bunch of college students and an elderly Korean grandmother, easily identifiable with her short gray hair in a perm. The students must have just come from a bar because their voices are loud and they smell like chicken and beer. Without a place to sit, they block up most of the aisle, chatting in groups as they hang onto the railings. They're so preoccupied with one another, they don't notice the grandmother trying to squeeze past them.

The bus pulls away from the curb. A look of fear flits across the grandmother's face as she tries once more to get past the students. She looks up, but the handrail is too high for her to reach. The wheels hit a pothole and she stumbles.

"Watch out—" I lurch forward.

The boy from the karaoke bar catches her by the arm. "Halmeoni," he addresses her in Korean. Her lips tremble at the sight of him. "Are you all right?" She nods that she's okay. He leads her to the seat by the window, the one he'd previously occupied. "Please sit," he says, indicating for her to take it. As she settles, she pats his arm, praising him in Korean.

I tear my gaze away. My heart is racing. She could have fallen. If he hadn't noticed her and already made the choice to give her his seat, if he hadn't had the quick reflexes to catch her, she would have.

The handrail to my right creaks as someone grabs hold of it.

I stare forward out the window as the bus takes a detour around a coned-off street lined with market stalls.

Beside me, the boy from the karaoke room leans forward, peering out the window. "What's going on?"

I'm feeling generous toward him after that whole saving the

halmeoni thing. "LA's annual Korean festival. Apparently they blocked off some of the roads." A crease forms between his brows and I realize that if he's not from around here, he might not know the streets. "Where are you trying to go?"

"I'm not sure."

I frown. "What do you mean?"

"I'm in the middle of running away."

I wait for him to crack a smile, but his face is serious and a little sad.

"From gangsters?" I deadpan.

I feel a sense of satisfaction when he smiles.

"From . . ." His smile fades marginally. "Chaegim-kam. What's the word in English?"

"Responsibility." A word that could mean so many things, at least in the Korean community, from taking out the trash to behaving in a way that won't bring shame to your family. Studying his reflection in the window, I wonder what responsibility he's referring to.

I think back to earlier tonight, when I first entered the room in the karaoke bar. At that point, he'd been alone in there for an hour, maybe two. And now he's on a bus without a destination in mind. A part of me—a large part—is curious about what he's running away from, about why he felt like had to. But the other part remembers what it's like, when the only way to escape the enormous feelings inside you is . . . to run.

"For what it's worth," I say, "I think it's important to take time for yourself, even with responsibilities. You can't be there for other people if you're not first there for yourself."

It feels weird giving advice to someone my age, but these are words I need to hear too. Luckily he doesn't seem put off, mulling them over; his mouth has a contemplative edge to it. His eyes search mine and there's an intensity to his gaze that does strange things to my heart.

"It's not easy for me to believe something like that," he says. Standing this close to each other I can see the color of his eyes, a rich, warm brown. "But I want to."

Someone bumps into him from behind and he winces, letting out a soft curse. Moving slightly closer to me, he adjusts his cast. The guy who bumped into him—one of the university students—is joking around with his friends.

"Hey," I say, annoyed at both this incident and earlier with the grandmother, "Can't you see his arm is broken? Give him more space."

Outside, the bus approaches the Olympic stop. The doors open behind us and a few passengers exit. The university student, clearly inebriated, looks confused why I've spoken to him. Then he sneers. "It's a free country."

"That's right," I shoot back. "You're free to be a considerate human being or you're free to be an asshole."

Shocked silence follows this statement. The university student's face starts to turn a peculiar shade of red. Oh, shit.

The boy and I make eye contact. He reaches for my hand. I don't have to think twice. I grab it, and together we jump through the closing doors.

Four

We've landed in the middle of the festival. A banner hanging above the street reads LA Korean Festival, and in smaller print across the bottom: Celebrating the Cultural Diversity of Los Angeles for over Fifty Years. Lining the sides of the street are food carts serving traditional Korean food, tteok-bokki simmering in vats of gochujang and eomuk skewered and collected in hot anchovy broth, and more fusion-style food, scallops grilled with mozzarella and cheddar and hot dogs coated in batter, then deep fried.

I look down to find the boy from the karaoke bar and I are still holding hands so I quickly let go.

"Sorry," I say, turning away from him to hide my flushed cheeks. "About getting us kicked off the bus." Well, technically we jumped off. But the results are the same.

I feel bad, though. He might not have had a destination in mind, but I'm sure it wasn't here, a few blocks from Jay's Karaoke.

"This place seems as good as any to wind up," he says glancing up at the banner.

"Do you . . . want to take a look around?" I gesture vaguely at the festival. "We're already here."

His eyes return to me, and again I feel that odd feeling in my chest.

"I'd like that."

We start to walk down the street lined with food carts. It doesn't escape me that I could just go home. Earlier in the karaoke bar, with the competition results churning in my pocket, I'd felt this urge to do *something*, and I sort of acted on impulse. But challenging him to a karaoke battle wasn't exactly practical experience. Realistically, I should go home and practice tonight to prepare for my lesson tomorrow morning.

The only thing is . . . I don't *want* to go home.

I'm having more fun than I've had in a long time, and it can't hurt to indulge these feelings, at least for one night.

"My name's Jenny, by the way."

"Mine is . . ." He hesitates. "Jaewoo."

I'm about to tease him for having apparently forgotten his name when I catch sight of someone I vaguely recognize down the street, but then she enters a tent, disappearing from view.

"Is Jenny also your Korean name?" Jaewoo asks.

"My Korean name is Jooyoung."

"Jooyoung." He pronounces the syllables slowly. "Joo. Young. Jooyoung-ah."

"Okay, but no one ever calls me that." I'm feeling a little

24

warm, so I accept a plastic fan someone's handing out and start fanning myself.

This festival seems to be comprised of booths advertising different kinds of businesses; that and a ton of food carts. We pass one selling dakkochi. A man wearing giant gloves flips skewers over a grill with one hand while alternatively coating the chicken with a thick sauce using a basting brush. He then blowtorches them to get the charred crispiness. I watch as two girls approach the stand.

In an impressive display of ambidexterity, the man takes a twenty-dollar bill from one of the girls and gives her change with one hand, while transferring a skewer onto a plate and passing it over to her friend with the other.

"I feel like I'm back in Seoul," Jaewoo says deadpan.

I laugh, then add thoughtfully, "I've actually never been to Korea."

"Really?" He glances at me. "You don't have family there?"

"My grandmother on my mom's side, but I've never met her. She and my mom have a strained relationship." Honestly, I never really thought about their relationship or that I don't have one with her. My grandparents on my dad's side are like super grandparents, always sending me presents on holidays, money at New Year's. One of the reasons my mom thinks I should apply to schools in New York City is to be closer to where they live in New Jersey.

If Jaewoo thinks it odd that I've never met my grandmother in Korea, he doesn't say anything.

"So you live in Korea?" I ask.

"Yeah, I'm originally from Busan, but I go to school in Seoul." He pauses. "A performing arts school."

"I knew it!" I shout, and he grins. "*Decent* at singing. Please."

As we've been walking I've noticed that Jaewoo keeps eyeing the food carts. Catching his attention, I point to a small tented area where an older woman is serving traditional Korean street food to a few customers seated on low stools. "How does second dinner sound to you?"

His eyes light up and dimples appear in his cheeks. "Like you've read my mind."

We head over and he holds back the tarp of the tent so that I can step inside.

"Eoseo oseyo!" The tent cart owner welcomes us in a loud voice, gesturing for us to take stools side by side across the counter from her. "What would you like?"

Jaewoo looks at me, seeing as I'm the one with the money. "Get whatever you want," I tell him. "I like everything."

As he places the order, I unknot Mrs. Kim's plastic bag of side dishes. Inside are five small plastic containers. I put them on the counter between us and take the cover off each one.

"You've got quite the haul," Jaewoo says, studying my movements.

I finish taking off the last lid to reveal garlic chives kimchi. "Never underestimate a friendly neighborhood ajumma."

"Ah, I can relate. My mom's a single mom, so while I was growing up, the neighborhood women were always pestering her and giving her unsolicited advice, but that didn't stop them from dropping off food almost every day."

I laugh. "Koreans truly are the same everywhere."

And he and I are the same, at least in that we were both raised by single mothers. It's not so uncommon, but it makes me feel closer to him for some reason.

I reach for the wooden chopsticks in a cupholder filled with them. I snap a pair apart and hand it over to Jaewoo. "You're lucky you broke your left arm and not your right. If you *are* right-handed, that is."

"I am. Though I'm not sure if I'd call myself lucky."

Ugh, yeah, that was insensitive of me. "Sorry—" I start to apologize.

"If I'd broken my right arm, you'd have to feed me." He reaches out with his chopsticks to pick up a slice of braised beef from the container of jangjorim.

I eye him. Did he just *say* that? I glance around at the other tent cart patrons, but the only one paying us any attention is a girl sitting with a friend to the left of him, out of his line of sight. She's been watching him since we entered the tent, presumably because of how good-looking he is.

"Your food is here!" The tent cart owner hands three dishes over the counter. Jaewoo's ordered a few classic pojang staples: tteok-bokki, eomuk, and kimchi pajeon—kimchi pancakes with green onions. With all the plates and containers of banchan, there's zero space on the table. We have to play Tetris with the dishes in order to make things fit.

As we eat, our chopsticks reach for food and crisscross one another. At one point, the owner offers Jaewoo a small cup of broth and he reaches across me to accept it. As he stands, his shoulder bumps mine.

"Sorry," he says.

"It's fine," I say, though I feel a tingling sensation where he touched me. Like before, I look around at the other patrons, noticing that the majority of the people at the other tables are couples, flirting over food and drinks.

Jaewoo pushes the plate of tteok-bokki toward me, and I see that he's left me the last piece. Anyone observing us might think *we* were on a date.

Behind Jaewoo, the girl who was staring earlier approaches, along with her friend.

I glance at Jaewoo, wondering if I should warn him. He probably gets hit on by people on a regular basis. Though I wonder who these girls think *I* am? What if this were an actual date? Are they really about to flirt with him in front of me? For some reason, I have this sudden urge to scowl.

"Hey," the first girl says, "you look so familiar. Have I seen you somewhere?"

The cup Jaewoo is holding stops midway to his mouth.

For a moment, no one speaks. Then I look up and realize the girl's eyes are on me.

"You were at the All-State competition last weekend, weren't you?" she says. "I saw your performance. It was incredible."

I stare at her. I don't know what to say. I've been praised

before, usually following performances, but no one has ever approached me out of the blue, as if I were a celebrity. Jaewoo slowly puts down his chopsticks. Propping his good elbow on the counter, he rests his cheek against his hand as he watches for my reaction.

I wave off her compliment. "Thank you."

"Seriously, my mother, who was a cellist for the Los Angeles Philharmonic, said you're very talented."

"I don't know what to say—" I start, then cut off when I meet the eyes of the second girl. "Eunice."

Eunice Kim, Sookie's daughter. She glances at the counter and I have this wild premonition that she'll yell at me for sharing her mom's cooking with a boy.

"Hey, Jenny. I'm surprised to see you out on a Friday night." She smiles, and it's subtle, but she looks a bit hurt. "You're always so busy. I didn't think you had time to hang out."

"Oh," I say, "yeah, it just turned out that way." Could I *be* more awkward? It's just that we haven't really spoken much in the past five years, and before that, we were practically inseparable.

"Anyway, we gotta go," Eunice's friend tugs at her arm. "Enjoy your meal!"

Eunice throws me one last glance. "Bye, Jenny." They leave the tent.

In the awkward silence that follows, I say hurriedly, "We used to be friends when we were younger. But then I started to become more serious about cello and . . ."

I don't know why I'm telling him this. It's like whiplash, one girl telling me how great I am in front of him, only for another to reveal I'm actually a terrible friend.

Jaewoo leans back from the table. "Something similar happened with me. When I moved to Seoul from Busan, some of my friends back home thought I was a sellout."

"Wow." I don't really know much about cities outside Seoul, but I guess the equivalent would be someone moving from their hometown to New York City.

"So you're a cellist," he says.

"Yeah."

"Was that always your dream? To be a cellist."

"Sort of. My dad played the cello. He wasn't a professional or anything, but when it came time to choose an instrument, a rite of passage for all Asian American kids—"

Jaewoo laughs.

"My dad's cello was there and, yeah, I ended up really loving it. It's also been nice having that connection to him."

This is the most I've opened up about my dad to anyone. I wait for that sense of sadness, that familiar pain, but all I feel is comfort. Five years isn't a long or short time, but it is *time*.

I look at Jaewoo. What is it about him that makes me want to open up to him? Is it because I know I won't see him again after tonight or for another reason entirely; that with him, I can be myself?

"That's really cool," Jaewoo says. When he smiles, I feel my heart melt a little.

"What about you?" I ask, hoping the dim lighting beneath the tent will mask my blush. "Do you have any dreams?"

An indecipherable expression flits across his face, gone in a second. "I don't sleep enough for dreaming."

"Wow," I drawl, "what an answer."

He winks.

On the other side of the tent, a group of people enter. I glance at my phone to see that it's a quarter to midnight already. Jaewoo hands over our empty plates to the tent cart owner as I start to cover and pack the leftover side dishes. As we stand, I lift my head and make eye contact with a guy directly across from me.

It's the rude guy from the bus. He's surrounded by his college friends, most of whom are jostling for a seat at the counter.

"What are the odds he recognizes us?" I say to Jaewoo, who's noticed the direction of my gaze.

At that moment the college guy points at us, like we're in some sort of action movie and Jaewoo and I are criminals.

"I'd say very likely."

Five

I don't know who moves first or why we both jump to the same conclusion, but we make a run for it.

Neither of us looks back as we sprint back the way we came, past the food carts, making a sharp right into an office building and down a flight of stairs.

Here we stop to catch our breaths. The basement level appears to be a shopping center. Most of the businesses are closed—a nail salon, several retail stores, and a lunch box shop—but a few are still open, including a twenty-four-hour spa and an arcade.

"There!" I point to a freestanding photo booth, one of those sticker booths where for a couple dollars you can take photos with cute backgrounds that are then printed on the spot.

Jaewoo pulls me inside and I close the curtain behind us. In the darkness, our faces illuminated by the neon fluorescent light given off by the touch screen, we stare at each other.

"Why did we run?" he asks.

"I—I don't know."

He blinks. I blink. Then we both start to laugh. Why *did* we run? There really was no reason to. It's not as if those college kids would have actually beaten us up—we were in a public space, with adults. Still, it was exciting. My heart is still racing from the adrenaline. Or maybe because, shoved into this small space, I'm practically in his lap.

Were photo booths always this tiny? He's pressed all the way up against the far wall, on the bench with his long legs diagonal across the entirety of the booth. One of my legs is propped beneath me, the other draped over his. I have one hand gripping the edge of the seat and the other pressed flat against the back wall.

"How tall are you?" I blurt out.

"One hundred eighty-two centimeters."

Right. I forgot nearly all other countries besides the US use the metric system.

His brow furrows. "I think that's five foot eleven?"

"You just calculated that in your head?"

He shrugs. "How tall are you?"

"Five six. I don't know what that is in centimeters."

He nods slightly. On the touchscreen, the ad for the photo booth plays on repeat, showing smiling faces of groups of people in twos and threes, and a few alone.

He adjusts the sling of his cast, tightening the strap.

"How did you break your arm?" I ask.

"An accident."

"Had you ever broken a bone before?"

"Once, when I was a kid." He stops fiddling with his sling and looks up. "Have you?"

"No." It doesn't escape me that, as a cellist, a broken arm would have felt like the end of the world. "Does it hurt?"

"Not as much as the first time."

I have to bite my lip to keep from asking more questions. He hasn't been exactly forthcoming about the details of his life. Still, I want to know—why? Why does it hurt less this time than the time before? Because it's a different bone? Because he knew what to expect as he'd been hurt before?

I want to know more. What kind of accident was he in? Is that the reason he was running away?

Unlike in the karaoke room and at the festival, we're close enough that I can see the details of his face. His skin that's almost too flawless—is he wearing makeup?—his beautifully shaped eyes accentuated by dark shadow, his red, red lips.

Either that's lip tint or he kissed someone who was wearing it, and I don't know which I'd prefer.

That's a lie, I don't want him to have kissed anyone else.

I move closer, my fingers gripping his shoulder. He shifts to accommodate me, his good hand sliding against my back. His face is so close to mine, his breath on my lips.

There's a loud bang as someone knocks on the outside of the photo booth.

"Hello-o! Are you done in there? We want to take a photo."

I practically leap across the booth, which isn't that impressive of a feat, considering it's so tiny.

"Middle schoolers," I say, breathless. Their voices are too

high to belong to the college students. I reach for the curtain.

"Wait . . ."

I turn back.

Jaewoo's looking at the touchscreen. "Should we take a photo?"

I slowly sit back down. "Sure." I can't really think clearly so I click on a few buttons and soon four snapshots go off in quick succession. For the first two I must look like a deer in the headlights, but I manage a smile for the last two. Afterward, there are options to add borders and designs to the photos, but I just click print.

Outside the booth, we're met with the judgmental stares of a posse of sixth graders.

"You broke the machine," one informs me, and when I check the printer, I see that she's not wrong. Printing Error appears on the little readout display. It did print at least one of the two copies though.

The middle schoolers head toward the arcade and I bring my prize over to Jaewoo. "It only printed one."

"I'll take a photo of it," he says, reaching into his jacket and pulling out a phone.

As it turns on it immediately starts to ping and vibrate with messages.

He looks troubled, his lips thinning slightly. Then he flips his phone over and the front-facing camera is smashed. "I forgot about this. It must have happened earlier, when I broke my arm."

"Why don't I take a photo of it and send it to you?" I offer.

"Yeah, maybe that's better." He pockets his phone and accepts mine from my hand, plugging in his number.

When I take it back, I see that he's added +82 for the country calling code to South Korea.

We head up the escalator and out onto the main street.

He pats the pocket of his jacket where his phone is still vibrating. "They'll be here soon, now that they can track my phone. They're probably circling the area, waiting for me."

That sounds . . . ominous. "Can't you turn your phone off again?"

"I think it's time I go back."

"Are you really okay?" I ask.

He smiles, a sweet smile. "I am now."

My heart stutters.

"What about you?" He peers down the street. It's mostly deserted, the festival having ended. "It's past midnight."

"My uncle just texted," I lie. "He's coming to pick me up." I can walk the few blocks back to the karaoke bar, which doesn't close until three, or I can call a rideshare.

Down the street, a van with blackout windows approaches. Gripping my wrist gently, Jaewoo leads me to a shadowed area beneath the awning of a building. "Wait here. I don't want them to see you."

"Jaewoo, I'm worried."

My voice catches and he looks at me. "It's not what you're thinking. I'll text you as soon as I can." Then he adds, with a smile I don't think I'll ever forget, "Thanks, Jenny. I had a great time with you tonight."

Pivoting, he walks from beneath the shadows. The van, which had been slowly driving down the street speeds up, stopping right by the curb. The back door slides open, and I get a glimpse of another boy inside before it slams shut behind Jaewoo.

As the van pulls away from the curb, I step from the shadows. I watch until I can no longer make out the shape of it on the road, swallowed up by the lights of the city.

Six

The sticker picture is a series of four small photographs printed vertically in the order they were taken. In the top picture, I'm frowning at the camera while Jaewoo, his back against the corner of the booth, has his eyes closed, in the middle of a blink. In the second picture, they're open and he has a small smile on his face. I'm still frowning.

The third picture came out well. We're both smiling and looking at the camera. I remember how I'd held my expression in place, determined to keep my smile from wavering and my eyes open. I'm relieved to find I managed to do both—I look normal. Pretty, even.

As for Jaewoo, he's no longer leaning against the back of the wall, but sitting slightly forward. His head is tilted, and his eyes aren't on the camera anymore. He's looking at me, his expression caught between a smile and a laugh.

I feel my heart give a literal flutter in my chest.

Pulling out my phone, I snap a photo of the photo, then take it again when it appears washed out against my kitchen table.

When I'm satisfied, I open up the number Jaewoo saved in my phone.

Here's the photograph from tonight. I text. Btw, this is Jenny. I hit send.

There. That's straightforward. Casual.

Immediately my texts are marked "read" and three dots appear. He's typing! Was he waiting for my text? Also why does he have his read receipts on?

A message appears. Jumping on a plane. Text you when I land.

He's flying out *tonight*? I knew he was from Seoul, but I didn't think he was leaving so soon.

Okay. Have a safe flight!

My message is marked "read," then . . .

Thanks 😊.

Oh my god, he sent an emoji. How cute!

Footsteps approach the front door of the apartment, keys jingling for the lock. I quickly pocket the photo as my mom walks through the door.

She glances at me sitting at the kitchen table before sliding off her shoes, "You're still awake?" She hangs her coat in the closet, slipping on a pair of house slippers—mine, in fact. It's an easy mistake; we're the same size. Same shoe size, same height, same oval-shaped face. People always comment on how much we look alike.

"I thought you were working on a case tonight," I say. Usually on the weekends she takes extra cases and sleeps overnight at the office. As an immigration lawyer in LA, she's busy a lot.

"Change of plans." She starts across the kitchen, then stops, doing a double take. I realize I'm still in the clothes I wore to school this morning. "Did you just get home?"

For a moment I blank, unsure whether or not to tell her how I spent my night.

"Bomi had a project due," I say finally, "so I stayed late to help out Uncle Jay. He gave me a ride home." The last part is true, if not the first.

I feel a bit guilty. I hardly ever lie to my mother; there's no reason to. We literally have the same goal: for me to go to music school in New York City. And for the past five years, it's just been us, and Uncle Jay.

But if I tell her, I know she'll worry that I'm not focused enough or that I'll be distracted; we haven't had the "dating" talk, but it's heavily implied that I should wait until college.

She heads over to the rice cooker and pops it open, sighing when she finds it empty.

"You didn't eat at the office?" I ask.

"No time."

I point to the counter where I left the H Mart grocery bag. "Mrs. Kim gave us some banchan, if you want to eat that. There's jangjorim." It's her favorite.

Mom clicks her tongue. "Mrs. Kim should mind her own business. She can be so nosy."

"Well, I think it's nice of her."

"Don't tell me she didn't slide in a snide comment about my parenting."

40

I try to think back to what she said, but honestly can't remember. "There's also japchae."

"Fine. Can you make rice? I'm going to take a shower. And, actually, since you're awake, there's something I want to talk to you about."

When someone announces they want to talk to me, I always get nervous. Like, just say it. I don't like the anticipation of thinking it could be something bad. But Mom knows not to spring anything serious on me, not after Dad.

"Sure," I say, and she heads off in the direction of her bedroom. Our rooms are at opposite ends of the apartment, which is to say, they're almost right next to each other.

I pour two cups of rice into a bowl and wash out the grains in water, then dump the whole thing into the cooker.

Afterward, I grab a melon bar from the fridge and sit at the table, googling how long it takes to fly from LAX to Seoul.

Fourteen hours.

Then I google what the time difference is between Korea and California.

Korea is sixteen hours ahead.

Mom walks into the kitchen in a bathrobe twenty minutes later, her hair wrapped neatly in a towel.

When the rice cooker pings, she scoops up rice into a bowl and sits across from me at the table.

She doesn't comment on the low levels of banchan in the containers, so I refrain from enlightening her.

"I got a call from Seoul this morning," she begins, "about . . . my mother."

I sit up in my seat. "She's okay, isn't she?" Just tonight I mentioned my grandmother in Korea to Jaewoo. I might have never met her, but she's still family and I don't want anything bad to happen to her.

"She's fine," Mom assures me. "As fine as someone with colon cancer can be. It was her doctor who called. He thinks she might be healthy enough to get surgery in a few months, but she's refusing. It won't be for a while yet, and she still needs careful monitoring, but I thought I could go to Seoul for a few months, spend time with her and convince her to get the surgery."

A hundred thoughts pass through my mind. My grandmother has cancer, a different kind than my father, but she's sick. And my mom is going to Seoul to take care of her. Without me.

"I already called Jay," Mom continues, "and he said you could stay with him for the rest of the school year. I should be back by July."

"You're going to leave me until *July*?" I can hear my voice rising. "It's November now."

"No," she says calmly. "I wouldn't fly out until after the new year. Likely end of February. There's still some work things I need to take care of."

I'm still trying to process what's happening. My mother's leaving me *in the middle of my junior year.* "What about the end of the year performance. It's in May."

"There will be more performances. Jenny, my mother needs me."

I need you. I almost say it, aloud, but I don't. If I tell her I need her she'll only ask me why, and I can't explain it beyond the simple fact that I'll miss her.

"I wouldn't have decided on this if I didn't believe you would be all right."

"But, Mom—"

"If something happens to her and I'm not there, I'll never forgive myself."

Game. Set. Match. Because I can't argue with that. I would feel the same; I have felt the same.

"So you'll be in Korea," I say, and I sound exhausted even to my own ears, "That's a sixteen hour time difference."

"I—wait, how do you know that?"

"It doesn't matter." I stand up. I have some more choice words I could say to my mother, but as I study her, the anger inside me deflates. She looks as tired as I feel, dark circles beneath her eyes, and she's not even eating anymore, which is the greatest indicator that she's not her usual self.

I offer an olive branch. "Well, at least you'll be here through the holidays. And then, wow, Seoul, huh? You haven't been there for, what, six years?" And even then, only the one time since she first came to the US on a student visa. She stayed after marrying my dad.

"Seven," Mom sighs. She must feel a little better because she reaches for a slice of mung bean pancake. "I've been putting it off for long enough. It's about time I go back."

* * *

I'm almost late for my nine o'clock cello lesson the next morning, having not gone to bed until well after two. When I get there, I fumble over so many notes that Eunbi, my teacher, stops me in the middle of my solo piece for school.

"I can tell something's bothering you," she says. "Is it the results from the competition?"

It's wild to think that less than twenty-four hours ago, the answer would have been yes. I'm still upset about what the judges said, but also the judges aren't my mother, and they're not abandoning me for months on end.

"Here, let me get you some tea, then we'll talk." I leave the piano bench to sit on one of the wingback chairs in her living room. We don't do this often, but sometimes we'll skip a lesson to catch up on things outside cello. The first time, she sat me down, pointed to my head, my heart, and my hands, and said, "They're all connected." I don't think I quite understood then—I was eleven—but I think I do now. No practice and talent can overcome a troubled mind and heart.

She returns and hands me a mug of barley tea, taking the seat opposite. "I'm all ears."

I tell her everything, starting with my mom's call with the doctor and her decision to leave me behind.

Eunbi listens carefully, as she does when I play for her, with her whole attention. And maybe it's because of that, but I sort of dump all my feelings onto her.

"She just told me what her plans are. She didn't even ask me what I thought about it. She's literally abandoning me in the middle of my junior year."

Eunbi takes a sip of her tea. "Did you ask if you could go with her?"

I blink, taken aback. "I didn't think it was an option. I have school . . . and she's going to be there for five months."

"There are performing arts schools in Seoul," she says, not unreasonably, and I'm reminded that she went to one herself before graduating from Ewha Womans University with a degree in classical cello. "It's only a matter of forwarding your materials to one that takes international students."

I'm still trying to process the possibility of this. It hadn't even occurred to me, that I might *go with* my mother, that I might finish my junior year *in another country*.

I've never been outside California, let alone traveled to South Korea. I don't even know anyone who lives there, besides my grandmother.

Well, that's not true.

I know one other person.

"A friend of mine is the director of a music school in Seoul," Eunbi says. "If you send over your audition materials, I can email her a recommendation. The academic year in Korea starts in March, so you wouldn't be arriving in the middle of their school year."

"I should ask my mom, shouldn't I?" By now, she would have left the apartment for work.

"Maybe bring it up to her after you've done a little more research? For now, you can get the ball rolling. You'll need a passport, if you haven't one already."

I do, in fact. Last year, I was supposed to travel to Paris with my French class but had to cancel when I got the flu.

"You look overwhelmed." Eunbi takes back the mug of tea, which I've barely touched. "Why don't you sight-read Mozart, then we'll call it a day. You've a lot to think about."

That's an understatement. But also—*do* I have more to think about?

My heart is racing. My palms are sweating.

If anyone were to ask me now: *Do you want to go with your mom to Korea? Do you want to see the grandmother you've never met? Do you want to spend a season in Seoul, a city you've never been to, where both sides of your family originally immigrated from, with endless possibilities for new adventures and experiences?*

The answer would be a resounding *yes.*

All morning I've been googling things about Korea, and Seoul specifically. Apparently it has a population of almost ten million people, which is more than New York City.

When I look up my grandmother's address, I find out she lives in the Jongno District of Seoul, where a lot of historical sites are located, like Gyeongbokgung Palace and Bukchon Hanok Village. She also lives right around the block from a Paris Baguette. I'm exploring the area through satellite imaging when Eunbi texts me a link. I click on it and the website for Seoul Arts Academy pops up on my computer.

The campus is absolutely breathtaking, with state-of-the-art facilities, practice rooms, a two-story library, and dormitories across from a newly renovated student center, plus a world-renowned concert hall.

After an hour of browsing I doze off, only to be woken up by my alarm. I set it this morning when I calculated that a fourteen-hour flight would arrive at around three p.m. my time. Which means it's around eight a.m. in Seoul.

I open up the chat with Jaewoo and type. Did you arrive safely? When the message isn't marked "read," I assume either I miscalculated the arrival time or he doesn't have service for some reason.

"Jenny?" The front door shuts with a bang in the hall. "I'm home."

I drop my phone on the bed and follow my mom from the hall to the kitchen.

Surprisingly, she doesn't immediately reject the idea of my tagging along with her on her trip to Seoul.

"There are dorms at the school. I can stay there during the week and visit you and Halmeoni on the weekends."

"What about tuition?" She's asking logical questions. This is a good sign.

"Waived, if I can get a scholarship, and Eunbi says I have a good chance as a classical cellist."

She sighs. "You've really worked this all out, haven't you?"

"I don't see why I have to stay if I'll get as strong an education there as I do here. Maybe even stronger. It *is* Asia." I laugh and she shakes her head. *And I'll be with you.* This last thought I don't say aloud. My mother was never the lovey-dovey parent.

I say instead, "I want to see Halmeoni."

Mom doesn't speak for a whole minute, but then she nods, "She'll want to see you too."

I can't believe that within twenty-four hours, my life has changed so drastically. I'm going to live in Seoul for *five months*.

Back in my room, I check my phone. The text is now marked "read" but there's no response.

This is why I don't like read receipts. It's like psychological warfare. He *knows* I know that he read my message and *chose* not to respond.

Of course, maybe I'm just reading too much into it. He could be texting back someone more important than me, like his mom.

Don't tell me you were stopped at customs due to gang-related activity. I quickly type, then send, and immediately regret it. This is why people think before they act! That's not even a good joke!

The message goes from "sent" to "read."

I stare at my phone. A minute passes. Then another. I feel a strange sinking in my stomach.

I think of all the possible reasons that might keep him from responding. He has a bad connection (highly unlikely as South Korea has the fastest internet on the planet, according to Google). He *is* going through customs (but then why didn't he just send a text? It only takes a few seconds). Or there's another reason that I can't think of, but what could it possibly be?

I google why a boy might read your texts but not respond. All of the articles say the same thing: *He's just not that into you.*

Wow, thanks internet.

Even so, it's not like one text is a commitment. I throw my

phone across the bed and head over to my cello to practice. If I can't get a boy to answer me back, at least I can get a school to.

The following Monday, I talk to my guidance counselor about transferring for half the year and he gives me a list of required classes I need for graduation, most of which Seoul Arts Academy fulfills. The few that I won't be able to take at the school I can take online from LACHSA. It's almost as if I'll be attending two schools at the same time, taking classes like AP Lit and AP History through Los Angeles County High School for the Arts, and my performing arts classes through Seoul Arts Academy.

Of course, I first have to get in, but I think, for once, nepotism will pull through for me. And I have the grades and awards to prove myself a strong candidate.

Luckily, my premonition turns out true because by December, I'm not only accepted into Seoul Arts Academy, but given full room and board. They also offer me a scholarship that covers half my tuition.

The only disappointment throughout this whole thing is that Jaewoo never responded to my texts. I feel like I spend more time wondering about the reasons why than planning my trip to Seoul.

I just need to accept what the internet was kind enough to tell me, he just wasn't feeling it.

It's true that I was the one who approached him in the karaoke bar. I was the one who got us into the scuffle that forced us to jump off the bus.

Still, it would have been nice to have a friend.

I don't even know what school he goes to.

I decide to text him one last time, the day that I leave. Hey, so, I'm actually going to be in Korea for a couple of months to visit my grandmother. If you're around, I'd love to see you. There. Straightforward. The truth is, I don't like playing games. Life is too short. It's better to speak your mind, otherwise you'll only feel regret later.

He doesn't respond, and honestly, I don't expect him to.

Uncle Jay drives my mom and me to the airport. He'll be looking after our apartment while we're away.

Outside security, he hugs my mom and then turns to me, ruffling my hair. "Have fun, kiddo."

"Thanks, Uncle Jay."

Just a few months ago he said that I needed to try new things, live a little.

Well, I'm taking your advice, Uncle Jay. I'm about to live my very best life.

Seven

My mom and I arrive at Incheon International Airport at 4:55 a.m. After passing through customs, we pick up our luggage from baggage claim and head over to the money exchange kiosk to swap a few bills before leaving the terminal. In need of caffeine, we join a short line outside one of the few businesses open at five in the morning—Dunkin' Donuts. But it's different than in the States. Besides the fact that everything is written in Korean, the interior is brighter and the menu has more food options. Also the donuts are somehow . . . cuter.

"I think the cab driver is here," Mom says.

I look over to where an older well-dressed gentleman in white gloves holds a signboard with the names Susie and Jenny written upon it in English.

After making our purchases—Mom gets an extra drink for the driver—we follow him outside to a taxi where he expertly fits our four bags of luggage in the trunk. I'm glad for my thick puffer jacket, which I zip up all the way before getting into the car. Though it's almost March, it's about thirty degrees cooler here than in LA.

Mom makes conversation with the driver while I stare out the window at the foggy morning freeway.

According to the taxi driver's GPS, it'll take an hour and a half to drive from the airport—which is located in Incheon, a city right outside Seoul—to my grandmother's house. At one point, we cross over a long bridge and the driver tells us that the body of water beneath us is the Yellow Sea.

I fall asleep halfway through the ride, startling awake when the driver honks at a scooter that cuts in front of the cab.

At some point, we must have crossed into Seoul. There are more cars on the road, and the streets we're driving down are lined with tall buildings and signboards in Korean, with a few in English. We pass an entrance to a subway station. People dressed in business clothing enter and exit by escalators or by stairs, moving in a quick but orderly fashion. We left on a Wednesday in LA, but it's a Friday morning in Seoul. At an intersection, I count at least six cafés, four beauty shops, and three cell phone stores.

After five hundred meters, according to the GPS, the driver turns off from the main road into a series of narrower streets of residential apartments, mostly walk-ups. The cab pulls up in front of an older building with a small convenience store on the first floor, across from a flower shop and a tiny café. Mom pays the driver and we leave most of our luggage on the street, bringing up only my cello and our carry-ons.

Mom is quiet, which is odd, as she was positively talkative with the driver. After ringing the buzzer, she grips her elbows with her hands, a sure sign that she's nervous. This is the first time she's seen her mother since she went to Seoul for a wedding almost seven years ago. And she'd been with Dad then.

The door opens.

I don't know what I expect from meeting my grandmother in real life. My grandparents on my dad's side of the family are a lot like my dad, sweet and funny, with a fondness for hard liquor.

I knew my mom had a strained relationship with her mother but I thought that was just because of physical distance, and my mom's, well, personality. She doesn't waste emotions on things that aren't strictly beneficial to her, or me. Only my dad could bring out a different side of her.

If someone were to ask what I thought my grandmother would be like, I'd say she was probably similar to Mom—powerful, intimidating, and no-nonsense.

"Soojung-ah!" Halmeoni cries, calling my mother by her Korean name.

Mom stands stiffly as her mother throws her arms around her. She's so tiny, she has to tiptoe in her house slippers.

She looks like the sweetest grandmother in the world.

"Come in! Come in!" She ushers us into her home, pushing aside the shoes that are laid neatly in rows by the entranceway. "And this must be Jenny." She grabs my hands; hers are warm and soft. "So beautiful," she says, and I feel a rush of warmth inside because no one has ever called me that before, and she sounds so sincere. "How old are you?"

"I'm seventeen years old."

"Eomma," Mom says. "We still have luggage outside."

"I will call my landlord. He lives downstairs. He'll bring it up." She adds to me. "He always helps me with my groceries."

She looks young for a grandmother, but that makes sense because my mom was young when she had me. She has short permed hair, shot with streaks of gray and a warm, sunny disposition. When she smiles, her eyes crinkle at the corners, and it's the most adorable thing.

This whole time we've been conversing in Korean and I'm thankful that Mom forced me to stick with Korean class instead of quitting like I wanted to in second grade.

"It's fine, Eomma," Mom says. "Jenny's strong."

Mom nods at me and I race out the door to bring up the luggage while she unpacks in the only other bedroom in the apartment. It takes me four trips, but I manage to bring them all up. By the time I'm finished, Halmeoni has laid out breakfast on the small table in the kitchen. Toast slathered with butter, sunny-side-up eggs, and grilled spam. The bread for the toast must be from a bakery because it's thick and fluffy, the eggs are cooked to perfection, and the spam is salty and sweet. The last meal I had was on the plane, and I'm starving. I inhale the food while my grandmother peels an apple next to me, nodding encouragingly.

After Mom finishes unpacking, she heads over to the small table, and I stand so she can sit on one of the two chairs.

"Can I go out and explore the neighborhood?" I ask my mom in English.

Halmeoni looks up where she's begun peeling another apple. "Doesn't she want to unpack?" she asks my mom.

"Jenny's not staying," Mom explains. "The school she's attending has dormitories. She's moving in the day after tomorrow."

"Ah." Halmeoni nods knowingly, "Chelliseuteu." *Cellist.* Still holding the apple and knife, she raises two thumbs. "Meosisseo." *Very cool.*

Reaching behind her, she grabs a piece of paper and writes down 1103*—the code to the keypad of the apartment—slipping it into my hands along with several man-won, roughly the equivalent of ten-dollar bills.

While I search my suitcase for my ankle boots, my grandma expresses concern about me going out into the city alone. *She's never been to Seoul. She doesn't know the area. What if she gets lost?*

"Don't worry, Eomma," Mom reassures her, "Jenny is very smart, and she can read and converse in Korean. She also has her cell phone."

"Are you sure?" She sounds relieved. "She must be independent, like you."

My mother doesn't answer for a few seconds. "Yes, Eomeoni," she says, finally. "Jenny's had to grow up fast, like me."

A look passes between them, and I edge toward the door. Whatever they need to work through, it's better if I'm not around.

My first stop is the café across the street to load up on some caffeine. A chime twinkles when I open the door. When no one comes out to greet me, I leisurely move around the small space, which is about half the size of the foyer in Jay's Karaoke. Natural light comes through the eastern-facing window, gilding the plethora of fresh flowers on the sill, presumably from the flower shop next door. Small personal touches make the café seem homely and pleasant. Jazz plays from a speaker in the corner.

"Sorry, I didn't know anyone came in." A young athletic-looking guy in an apron steps through the curtain.

Then I notice what he's wearing. "You go to the Manhattan School of Music?" I ask in English.

He looks down at his sweatshirt, then back up at me. "Yeah," he answers, also in English. "I'm a sophomore, studying saxophone. Why?"

"I want to go there. It's my top choice." That and the Berklee College of Music in Boston. Except that Mom prefers I live in New York City, closer to my dad's side of the family.

The guy gives me an appraising look, and I instinctively stand up straighter. "Oh yeah? For . . . dance?"

I blush. "Cello."

"Right. So what brings you to Seoul?"

"I'm visiting my grandmother for a few months. I actually arrived here a few hours ago. From LA."

"That makes sense. You look like an LA girl."

I wasn't exactly sure about the dancer comment, but there's

something about this one that gives me pause.

I think he's flirting with me. This is the second time in so many months that a guy has flirted with me.

While not as absurdly handsome as Jaewoo, café boy *is* cute. And older.

The door opens behind me and a guy wearing a delivery outfit calls out, "I have a big order today, Ian-ssi."

"My name," the café boy says to me. "Ian."

"I'm Jenny."

"Wait one sec."

When he returns, he hands me a to-go cup. "My number's written on the side. I took a semester off from school to pay some bills, so I'll be in Seoul. If you have any questions about MSM or just wanna hang out, give me a call."

"I—I will, thank you."

"See you around, Jenny."

He starts readying the large order for the guy and I make my way to the door, glancing down at the side of the cup where he's written in neat marker: *Ian Nam, guide to all things MSM,* plus his phone number.

I control my facial expression until I'm out the door, then sort of fast-walk down the street, my heart racing. Within only a few short hours of landing in Seoul, a cute Korean boy who works at a café and goes to my *dream school,* gave me his number and may or may not have asked me out on a date.

Maybe this is a sign of how I should spend these next few months in Seoul, going on dates, spending my time on activities other than cello practice or lessons.

I stumble a bit, as a memory rises up, of Jaewoo across the table from me in the small tent stall in LA, listening attentively as I opened up to him about my father. I feel a tightness in my chest, remembering how happy and hopeful I felt that night, which makes it all the worse that he never texted me back. But it's my fault. I let my guard down. If I had just allowed that night to be what it was always meant to be—a distraction—then I would have never felt so disappointed.

Five months in Seoul, five months to have new experiences and make the most of each moment, and then I'll return home, hopefully armed with the fiery determination to go after the future I've always wanted.

Bolstered by this resolve, I spend the next hour walking around the neighborhood—there's a subway entrance only a few blocks from my grandmother's house and a restaurant that specializes in juk, or Korean porridge, tucked into a quiet corner—before returning to the apartment.

The rest of the day is spent with my halmeoni. She and my mom must have at least come to a truce because my mom is cordial and Halmeoni is positively chipper. We take a taxi to the clinic where Halmeoni will spend most weekends after her treatments. This is actually where I'll come to visit her, since when she's at the apartment during the week I'll be at the dorms.

Afterward, we grab lunch and walk around the area. Mom wants to avoid jet lag, so we attempt a little sightseeing but by six, I'm asleep on my feet. I manage to stay awake for another two hours but doze off on the cab ride back, waking only to stumble up the stairs to the apartment, where I hit the pillow and sleep for twelve hours straight.

Eight

The next morning Halmeoni takes Mom and me to the juk restaurant down the street. It's a chilly morning and the porridge, made of boiled rice, warms me right up. Afterward, we walk over to the area around Gyeongbokgung Palace. It's walled off and requires an entrance fee so we don't go inside, but Halmeoni and I have a fun time walking around arm-in-arm and exclaiming over the tourists and locals dressed in brightly colored hanbok, presumably rented from the traditional Korean clothing stores located on every street. Mom spends the majority of the time on her phone, already getting calls from her work back home, though I don't mind; it gives me more one-on-one time with Halmeoni before school starts.

Around noon, Halmeoni is showing signs of fatigue so we head back to her apartment. Then at four I go back out again, this time on my own. Since I'm moving into my dorm at Seoul Arts Academy tomorrow, I have to pick up my school uniform at a store in Sinsa-dong.

Mapping out a route on my phone, I head over to the subway, where I'm surprised to find it connects to a huge underground shopping mall.

I'm immediately overwhelmed by a hundred sights, sounds, and smells. Different aisles branch off in seemingly endless directions, filled with shops selling everything from Korean brand clothing to cell phone accessories to cosmetics to adorable socks for ₩1000 a piece, which equals to less than a dollar. There are dozens of food and drink stands, restaurants, bakeries, and cafés. I spot a few familiar chains, like Dunkin' Donuts and 7-Eleven, and a few unique to Korea and Asia, like Hollys Coffee and A Twosome Place.

I could spend hours down here and still not see everything. A group of schoolgirls pass in front of me, heading toward a shop selling corn dogs topped with cheese mustard and sweet chili sauce. I'm tempted to stop for a pre-dinner snack, but a glance at my phone reminds me that I don't have long before the uniform store closes.

Down on the platform, the train is preparing to leave, so I sprint to the doors, managing to slip through before they close.

A few passengers look up at my abrupt arrival, but then go back to peering at their respective devices. I take a seat next to two small boys playing video games on their handheld consoles. They don't seem to be accompanied by an adult, but I'm realizing now that's probably just how it is in Seoul, safe enough that kids can travel about freely.

Honestly, I'm a bit envious. My mom wouldn't let me take public transit on my own up until six months ago. And compared to LA's system, this subway car seems like it's from the future with a pleasant automated voice overhead explaining what station we're leaving, and air so well-circulated I feel like I'm in a department store. There's even a split-screen monitor attached to the ceiling. On one side is a depiction of the subway car as it leaves the station, moving onto the next stop on the line. The other screen shows the end of a music video. Four boys walk away from the camera, fire and destruction in their wake. On the bottom right side Joah Entertainment appears on the screen, as well as the artists' name, XOXO, and the song, "Don't Look Back."

The music video shifts to a commercial for an instant coffee brand.

I get off the subway at the right stop and follow my mapping app to the address the school had provided for the uniform shop.

I almost miss the building because of the crowd gathered outside it.

Girls, mostly middle schoolers in thick coats, huddle next to a black van parked near the entrance.

I shuffle my way through the crowd. At the front, a harried looking man in his thirties blocks the door.

"You can't enter," he says to me.

"I'm here to pick up my uniform." I pull up the email from my contact at Seoul Arts Academy and show him the screen.

The email is in English, but that doesn't seem to be an issue because he sighs, pushing the door open behind him. "Don't take any pictures."

I nod, though it's a weird policy to have. What if I want to show my mom my uniform? As I walk through, a few of the girls *scream*, and I stumble over the threshold. *What the hell?*

The door shuts, cutting off all noise.

With all the commotion on the street, I expect it to be chaos inside, but it's quiet. Other than myself, there aren't any customers. Uniforms hang on racks throughout the store. One of the two assistants behind the checkout desk approaches me. Like with the man outside, I show her the email. She quickly gets to work, taking down items in a few sizes for me to try—button-down shirts, skirts, pants, a sweater, and a blazer. She also adds PE clothing to the pile and a few accessories—a tie and a headband.

"Do you need assistance?" she asks after showing me the way to the changing rooms.

"No, I should be okay."

She hands me the clothing. "If you need help, ring the call button inside the changing room."

"Thank you," I say and she bows before walking back to the desk. I almost ask her why there's a crowd of girls outside the store. Is there a sale on the uniforms? That would actually be great.

I step through a drawn curtain that separates the main area of the store from the changing rooms. On the other side, there's a small room with a large three-sided mirror.

A guy stands against the wall, looking down at his phone. I'm momentarily surprised, only because I hadn't thought there was anyone else in the store.

He's around my age, lean but strong-looking, and wearing all black. I must have been staring because he glances up. I quickly look away and enter one of the three changing rooms.

I've never worn a uniform, but I quickly figure out the logistics of it, tucking the white shirt into the waistband of the skirt—I don't know how to tie a tie, so I leave that—and slipping the sweater over my head. I put the blazer over the whole thing, sticking my cell phone in the pocket. I turn to the mirror inside the dressing room, but it's pretty small, which explains why there's a full-body trifold in the main room.

I hesitate, remembering the guy on his phone. Am I really going to check myself out with him standing right there?

Oh, whatever. This is what I'm here for. I press back the curtain and walk out, careful not to look at the guy. Instead I approach the mirror and step up onto the little platform, offering me several angles to view how the uniform fits.

I must admit, I look good. The skirt hits an inch above my knees, which I'm not sure is standard, but makes my legs look great. I have wide shoulders, which I'm a bit self-conscious about, but they fill out the blazer nicely. Slipping my hands into my pockets, I do several poses to see how it looks from different angles.

A loud jingle starts to play. I reach into the pocket of my blazer and pull out my phone.

"Did you make it to the store all right?" Mom asks when I pick up. After hearing Korean all day, it's a relief to switch to English.

"Yeah," I say. "I'm just trying on my uniform now."

"Will you be home in time for dinner? Your halmeoni wants to treat you before you move into your dorm tomorrow."

"Yeah, I should be home in an hour."

"Okay, see you then."

I hang up.

"You go to Seoul Arts Academy?"

The guy from earlier has moved away from the wall and is now standing to the side of the mirrors. It takes me a moment to realize he's speaking to me. In English. Without an accent.

"Yeah," I say, "I'm transferring there, from Los Angeles."

"Los Angeles . . ." There's a strange expression on his face, like there's something about me that he can't make out. Maybe it's that I'm ethnically Korean, but I'm speaking in English. But I could say the same about him. "You live there?" he asks.

"Yeah. Why?" Staring directly at him like this, I can't help but notice how attractive he is. He has deep dimples, even unsmiling, and soft hair that hooks rakishly over his eyes.

He shrugs. "Nothing. You just look familiar. I'm from the US too. New York." That explains his English-speaking skills. And why he's talking to me.

"How did you end up in Seoul?" I ask.

He stares at me, and I wonder if I've somehow asked an insensitive question. "So you don't know who I am."

It's a statement, but it seems like a question.

"Should I?"

"Not particularly."

O-kay then. I feel like I'm missing a piece of this conversation.

He, however, seems to get more comfortable, leaning against the mirror. "An opportunity came up and I moved here. My family lives in Flushing."

"Wow," I deadpan, "you can't get more Korean American than that."

He laughs.

"Hyeong, are you speaking English?" A boy barrels out of the leftmost dressing room. If I had to guess, he's probably around fifteen, his most noticeable feature a shock of bright-blue hair. "What are you saying?"

Before answering, the guy in black asks me in Korean, "How are your conversation skills?"

"They're all right," I respond, also in Korean. "I can't discuss *politics* or anything." I don't know the word for politics in Korean so I just say it in English.

"Honestly, me neither." He turns to the blue-haired boy and pats him on the head. "Sorry, Youngmin-ah. When foreigners meet abroad, we can't help ourselves."

Youngmin glances at me, his eyes lighting up. "You go to Seoul Arts Academy?" I realize he's wearing the same uniform as me, though with pants instead of a skirt. "We go there too. I'm Choi Youngmin, a first year. Nathaniel-hyeong is in Year Three."

66

"Nice to meet you both. I'm Jenny, I'm in . . ."—the academic years in Korea are different than the States, with high school structured in three years—"my junior year back at home, but I guess Year Three, here?"

"Jenny's from LA," Nathaniel explains, looking down at his nails.

"Really?" Youngmin shouts. "We've been there!"

"Oh, yeah?" I smile. "What for?" Also, are they actual brothers? Youngmin had been calling Nathaniel "hyeong," which means "older brother" in Korean, but they look nothing alike.

Youngmin glances at Nathaniel before speaking, "To shoot our music video for 'Don't Look Back.'"

Music video? Something clicks into place. The schoolgirls waiting outside. The man standing at the door. Even Youngmin's hair, the bright color reminding me of the ads I've seen everywhere since touching down in Seoul.

"Are you . . ." Do K-pop stars call themselves K-pop stars? It's not like Ariana Grande calls herself an American pop star.

"Idols," Youngmin fills in. "We're two of the members of the group XOXO. I'm the maknae, the youngest in the group, and also the rapper. Nathaniel's a vocalist and main dancer. We also have our leader who's a rapper like me, as well as our main vocalist."

They must be pretty famous, if they already have fans following them around. I feel like a bad Korean for *not* knowing who they are . . .

"Wait, I've seen your music video!" I say. "In the subway on the way here."

Youngmin grins. "Maybe you'll become a fan?"

I wink at him. "Oh, for sure."

Nathaniel looks at me oddly. "You watched the whole thing?"

I guess it would be strange if I had seen the music video and not recognized them. "No, just the ending."

"It came out a week ago," Youngmin explains. "It's the main track off our first full-length album."

"Congratulations," I say and Youngmin beams. "So you filmed the music video in Los Angeles? Did you like the city?"

"I loved it! We had such a great time. Well . . ." His face falls. "Until the last day. There was an accident . . ."

"Youngmin! Nathaniel." The man who was standing outside the door pokes his head into the dressing area. "Oh," he says, when he catches sight of me. He looks suspicious for a second, like he thinks I might have snuck in here to accost Youngmin and Nathaniel, but then he notices that I'm wearing the uniform for Seoul Arts Academy. He turns back to the boys. "More fans are gathering outside the store. Are you finished?"

"Yeah! This one fits." Youngmin rushes back into the dressing room. The man, who must be their manager, doesn't leave, engaging Nathaniel in small talk, probably so that he doesn't speak to me.

I'm heading back to my dressing room when Youngmin dashes out, dressed head-to-toe in Nike and wearing a huge puffer jacket that almost hits the floor.

He waves at me and runs off, hooking arms with the manager. Nathaniel is slower to leave, glancing at me. "See you when school starts."

After they're gone, I quickly change and pay for my clothing so that I can get back to Mom and Halmeoni. Although the crowd outside the store has dispersed there are more people on the streets. I join the tide heading toward the subway, in a bit of a daze from this afternoon's events.

I just met two K-pop stars. Celebrities. Students at Seoul Arts Academy. I know a few kids back at school who would kill to be in my position.

Then again, it's not like I'll interact with them much. I'm sure they have their own friends, and fans. Though it would have been nice, to walk into school that first day and already have someone I know.

An image of Jaewoo flashes through my mind.

The last text message I sent him is still marked "unread." I'd checked it this morning, as I have every morning.

Stepping onto the escalator that leads down into the subway, I take out my phone and pull up Jaewoo's contact. I press the edit button and scroll down. I should delete his number once and for all. Maybe then I'll stop thinking about him.

A bright light shines up ahead as the escalator approaches the bottom. A massive poster takes up a huge portion of the subway wall, from floor to ceiling.

I stare in shock because it's *them*. XOXO.

There are four of them, just as Youngmin had said. On the far right, I recognize him. He has the same bright hair and smile. The boy on the far left must be the eldest member, the other rapper. Beside him is Nathaniel, looking absurdly sexy as he smolders at the camera. Not my type, but he must drive girls wild. And beside *him* is . . .

No.

No way.

Oh.

My.

God.

With shaking hands, I look down at my phone. I close out the edit screen and scroll up in the messages. To the photo taken in the sticker booth. I stare at the boy beside me in the photo, and then at the poster on the wall, where the main vocalist of XOXO is air-brushed, but just as gorgeous.

They're the same person.

He's the same person.

Jaewoo.

Nine

I google "Jaewoo XOXO" on the subway ride back to my grandmother's apartment and discover his age, seventeen years old, and birthday, September 1. And that he's 182 centimeters. He wasn't lying about that.

He was born in Busan, South Korea, and moved to the US when he was in elementary school, which explains his English-speaking skills, before moving back to Busan in middle school where he was "discovered" because of his good looks. He trained for five years, then debuted with XOXO last year.

They were already popular as a rookie group, but their recent release of "Don't Look Back" broke records on all the music charts.

No wonder Nathaniel was surprised I hadn't recognized him or Youngmin. I'm sure everyone in Seoul knows who they are.

Their fan club is called the Kiss and Hug Club, and this summer the band is going on a world tour, with a stop in New York City.

I put in my earbuds and open up YouTube, searching "XOXO." The music video for "Don't Look Back" is the first to come up. I click on it.

I watch the video in a stunned daze, trying to absorb both the gorgeous visuals and the lyrics to the song. The raps are too fast for me to understand, but the chorus goes something like: "Even if I'm crying, even if I'm on the floor and dying, don't look back, don't look back." Which is super dramatic, but, wow, I have chills. The video seems to be this reverse Orpheus and Eurydice concept where each of the boys is going through harrowing trials in a noir-underworld aesthetic, while in the background a girl, her back to the camera, is shown walking away.

Interspersed through it all are clips of them dancing in a warehouse, their movements synchronized and complex, and Jaewoo is *wearing the outfit that he wore at the karaoke bar the night that I met him*. He must have broken his arm during the music video shoot and then somehow ended up at Jay's after going to the hospital.

It's clear why Nathaniel is considered the "main dancer" of the group. He's incredible; it's difficult to look away from him when he's at the front of the formation, and yet . . . Jaewoo is the one who completely captures my attention. His movements aren't as electrifying as Nathaniel's, but they're clean and smooth, and his voice . . . He sings parts of the verses and harmonizes with the others for the chorus, but the bridge is completely his, the beat stripped out to accentuate his beautiful tone. At one point, he does a run, going from low to high, and my whole body shivers.

The video ends and YouTube recommends a performance video and a dance practice video. I watch both, and then another with XOXO on some sort of variety show where they play a very complex game of tag.

I'm so immersed in the videos I almost miss the friendly female voice over the subway intercom announcing that we've reached my station. I look up from my phone only to meet the gaze of a girl around my age seated next to me, who apparently was watching the screen of my phone over my shoulder.

She nods at me knowingly.

Back at my grandmother's apartment, Halmeoni's not feeling up to going out, so we order jjajangmyeon from a restaurant down the street, which delivers the black bean noodle in a record fifteen minutes.

After dinner, I collapse onto my bed—which is just blankets on the floor because my grandmother only has one guest bed—and continue my internet sleuthing.

The oldest member, Sun, is cold and handsome, famous for his long hair and slender eyes that make him look like a hot supervillain in a video game. Nathaniel *is* from New York, and intriguingly, the first article that comes up when his name is searched is about a scandal he had a few months back with an unnamed trainee—someone who hadn't yet debuted in a group or as a solo artist—from Joah, their entertainment company. Apparently he dated this girl in secret for months before

Bulletin, a major tabloid magazine, released photos of the two of them together, though the photos were blurred online. The trainee's identity was never released, but netizens have theories. Youngmin is not only the youngest in the group, but the youngest of five siblings. As for Jaewoo, there's very little about his personal life, besides the fact that he's originally from Busan. He hasn't had any scandals, and a recent poll claims that of the four members, he's the most likely to never disappoint his parents, whatever that means. His nickname is also "Prince" among idols because of his charming manners and stellar reputation.

"Shouldn't you go to sleep?" Mom says when she comes into the room around midnight. "What are you doing anyway? I've never known you to be attached to your phone."

"Nothing." I close out the browser and slip the phone under my pillow.

"Your halmeoni and I weren't able to go to the clinic like we planned today," Mom says, "so I want to take her tomorrow. I know I said I'd help you move into your dorm . . ."

"It's fine," I quickly reassure her, "I'll take a cab."

She turns off the lights and I settle onto my back on the blankets, though when I close my eyes, I can't seem to fall asleep.

I think it's finally dawning on me that the boy I met at the karaoke bar—Jaewoo—is an *idol*, famous enough that his face is plastered onto walls and his music video plays between ads on the subway.

Thinking back to that night in LA, I cringe to remember

some of things I said to him. I accused him of being a *gangster*, though now I know he was only dressed that way because of the music video. Was he laughing at me the whole time? I scowl at the thought, but I also feel a bit hurt. Though, even if he was laughing at my expense in the beginning, as the night went on, I feel like something did change between us, as we shared more about ourselves.

I have a sudden thought. If Nathaniel and Youngmin attend SAA, then it's likely Jaewoo does too.

Of course it's entirely possible that he doesn't go to my school. Yet, somehow I know that's not the case.

My heart beats thickly knowing that I might see him again, and soon.

What will he say to me? What will I say to him?

I take a calm, steadying breath.

There's no use worrying about that now. Or at least, that's what I tell myself, as for the next few hours, I toss and turn until finally succumbing to a sleep full of fitful dreams of the boys of XOXO as they were in the music video, except the girl walking away is me.

Ten

According to the dorm supervisor, I'm the only student moving in this morning; the majority of the students in Year Three are either returning students, who keep their same room, or live off-campus with their families. I could have opted to live with Halmeoni and my mom, but it would have been a forty-five-minute commute, there and back. And on campus, there are practice rooms where I won't annoy any sound-sensitive neighbors. Plus, with how many hours my mom works, I'm used to living more or less on my own.

"Though you requested a single room," the supervisor explains as we take the elevator up to the top floor, "we unfortunately didn't have any available."

"That's not a problem," I say.

The elevator opens to a clean hall with ambient light filtering through the high windows. I push forward the small cart that holds my suitcases and cello.

Halfway down the hall, the supervisor stops at a door with a keypad lock. "Did you receive an email from housing?"

"Yes." I pull out my phone, scrolling down in the email for the code to the keypad. I press the buttons and it makes a whirring sound as it unlocks.

"I have to sign in some deliveries," the woman says, distracted. "Will you be okay moving in by yourself?"

"Oh, yes, go on ahead."

She heads back in the direction of the elevator and I open the door to the room. I'm surprised to find it's more spacious than I expected, about twice the size of the guest room in Halmeoni's house. Propping open the door with my luggage cart, I slip off my shoes in the small entranceway. I open the cabinet to my left out of curiosity and gape at the amount of shoes already stockpiled inside. I spot Doc Martens, three pairs of sneakers, knee-high boots, flats, and a pair of stilettos. My roommate, whoever she is, has some serious footwear.

The room is split in half by a bookshelf divider with the area nearest the doorway clearly occupied. Besides the shoes, my stylish roommate has a standing rack with coats and dresses, presumably overflow from her already packed closet. Everything else about her side of the room is neat, her desk bare but for a computer and a few landscape photographs pinned to a corkboard.

I wonder if she's always this clean or if she tidied up in preparation for my arrival.

I drop my backpack beside the unmade bed on my side of the room and prop my cello against the wall.

I'm tempted to collapse onto the bed, but I know that if I do, I won't get up for another hour. I start to bring my luggage into the room, beginning with the one that has my bed sheets. I make a note to go down to the housing office to pick up a comforter and pillows.

I'm on my way out for the last suitcase when I bump into my roommate's desk. One of her pictures dislodges and floats to the floor. I quickly lean down and pick it up. It's not a photograph, but a postcard. From Los Angeles. I flip over the card to see a long message written in Korean. I'm glad my Hangeul is severely lacking, otherwise I'd be tempted to read it. I'm putting it back when a few words in English and a signature at the bottom catches my attention.

Chin up, Songbird.
You will always have my heart.
XOXO

"What are you doing?"

A girl stands in the doorway. Walking over, she snatches the postcard out of my hand.

"Oh my God, I'm so sorry," I say. As far as first impressions go, this is the worst. I feel awful. I shouldn't have looked at her things, even if it was by mistake. "I knocked into your desk and it fell."

She opens a drawer and drops the postcard inside, shutting it with a loud bang.

I wince. "I'm your new roommate, Jenny."

"I know," she says. She doesn't offer her name, though I'd seen it on the small placard outside our door.

Min Sori.

Her name is as beautiful as she is. She has cat-like eyes, a long, elegant nose, and gorgeous pouty lips. I thought I was tall for a Korean girl, but we're the same height, though she appears taller due to her ballerina-like posture.

"I wouldn't have been able to the read the postcard, even if I wanted to," I explain further. "I'm from the States. My Korean reading skills are the equivalent of a grade schooler's."

"Could you move?" she says. "I need to study."

I don't care much about honorifics, but it feels pointed that she isn't using any with me. Instead of familiar and friendly, her banmal sounds rude.

I step away from her desk and she sits down, opening up her computer and putting in her earbuds.

Well, these next few months are going to be awkward. I'm not usually intimidated by people, but she could freeze fire.

I spend the rest of the morning unpacking, careful not to disturb her, though she doesn't glance up once from her computer. At noon, she gets up and changes into workout clothes. I'm tempted to ask if she wants a running partner, but her earbuds are still in.

When she leaves the room, I let out a huge sigh. Damn. I've heard of tense roommate situations from Bomi who's already on her second year at UCLA, but this seems a little extreme.

Since Halmeoni didn't have a dryer at her apartment, I held off doing laundry. I decide to do a quick load now, grabbing my hamper and taking the elevator down to the dorm's laundry room. After starting the rinse cycle, I set a timer for thirty minutes on my phone and head outside in search of food.

Luckily, there's a convenience store across the quad in the student center. I purchase a few triangle gimbap—rice wrapped in dried seaweed and shaped like a triangle—and eat heartily, washing them down with bottled water. Then, because I still have fifteen minutes before my laundry is finished, I head over to where a couple of students have gathered around a series of monitors. They're all broadcasting the same program, *Music Net LIVE*, which I'd seen a re-run of when staying at Halmeoni's. It's a show that features popular and new artists who perform live on a stage in front of a studio audience.

On the screen, two MCs introduce the next performers. "Making their Music Net comeback with 'Don't Look Back,' XOXO!"

The camera angles an establishing shot of Sun, Jaewoo, Nathaniel, and Youngmin in formation on the stage, surrounded by backup dancers.

"Is this happening right now?" I ask one of the students.

"Yeah," the student—a boy—responds. "Every Sunday on EBC."

The camera zooms in on each individual member when it's their turn to stand at the front of the formation, whether to sing or rap their lines.

Jaewoo begins his verse, his voice clear and strong, even while dancing.

"They go to our school, you know," the boy says.

"All of them?" I don't know if I sound hopeful or full of dread.

The boy apparently doesn't either because he raises an eyebrow. "Three of them do." Jaewoo finishes his lines, and the oldest member of the group begins to rap. The boy nods at the screen. "Sun graduated last year."

So I will see Jaewoo. Tomorrow, since apparently he's performing live on a nationwide television program today.

I wrap my arms around my body, feeling the nerves I felt last night. I just don't know what to expect, having never *been* this situation before, meeting again the boy who basically rejected me over text. Oh, and he's a K-pop idol.

"A lot of trainees go here," the boy continues, oblivious to my inner turmoil. "From Joah and the other entertainment companies."

"I'm a trainee at Neptune Entertainment," a girl pipes up. "My label enrolled me at SAA since I'm still underage." She's a few inches shorter than me, with rosy cheeks and a sweet demeanor. "My name's Angela Kwang. I'm from Taiwan. I moved to Seoul about three months ago."

"Nice to meet you," I say. "My name's Jenny Go. I'm . . . American."

The boy nods at both of us. "Hong Gi Taek. I'm not a trainee, but I'm planning to audition for Joah soon. I'd say half the student body here is either a trainee or trying to become one."

"Joah is XOXO's label, right?" Angela asks. "I can't believe I'll actually be able to go to school with them, though I'm sure they never come to classes. They're probably so busy."

"They're here more than you would think. Joah Entertainment is practically down the street, and the CEO of the company is on the board of directors for the school."

Oh, wow. I knew SAA was a performing arts school, but I didn't know it had such a significant tie to the entertainment industry. But it makes sense why idols and trainees attend this academy. If it's anything like LACHSA, the school is probably flexible when it comes to excused absences and regular core classes, prioritizing the performing arts.

"What about you, Jenny?" Angela asks.

For a second, I think she's asking me if I'm excited to see XOXO, then I realize she means what am I studying at SAA.

"I'm a cello major."

"That's so cool!" Angela exclaims. "I've always wanted to play an instrument. But I just never had any talent. I mean, not that I have any talent in singing and dancing either." She giggles, and I smile, appreciating that she can laugh at herself. "But it's my dream to debut."

"Debut?" I ask. In my deep dive into XOXO's timeline, I'd learned they "debuted" only a year ago, though I wasn't exactly sure what that meant.

Gi Taek sighs, clearly disappointed that I'm lacking the basic knowledge of idol culture.

"Ooh," Angela says, eager to share hers. "It's pretty simple. After undergoing training with your company, which for me means learning choreography, taking voice lessons and language classes in Korean, Japanese, and English, as well as public speaking classes, a company will form a group based on a whole slew of factors—like branding and specific talents and voices. Then, they release the members' profiles and photos online in order to build up excitement for the group. Finally, they'll put out a single or an album. Once the group holds a showcase and starts promoting, they've officially debuted!"

I gape at her. If that's simple, what's complicated?

"Of course there's more to it than that," Gi Taek says, "but that's the gist of it. And even if it is your dream to debut, it's not a given."

I compare their experiences to mine. "That sounds a lot like what I'm trying to do with my cello playing," I say, thoughtfully. "Except I want to get into a music school instead of an entertainment company. And I want to join an orchestra instead of an idol group."

"That's exactly like it!" Angela says, beaming.

Gi Taek nods, giving me an appraising smile.

My phone buzzes in my pocket and I check it to see my timer has gone off for my laundry. "I gotta run," I say, then hesitate. It's been awhile since I've actively made friends and I'm not exactly sure how to go about it.

And though I don't necessarily *need* friends, seeing as I'm leaving at the end of the semester. Having them would make my time here at SAA that much more enjoyable.

Angela smiles. "I hope we have some classes together, Jenny."

"Me too," I say, then give a little wave. Before I turn toward the quad, I glance at the monitors. XOXO has finished their performance and a new group stands on stage, singing about youth and running toward your dreams with all your heart.

Eleven

Go Jenny, Year 3, Schedule: Monday to Thursday

8–8:10 Homeroom/Class Attendance

8:10–9:35 Period 1 or 4

9:40–11:05 Period 2 or 5

11:10–12:35 Period 3 or 6

12:40–13:15 Lunch

13:20–16:00 Arts

16:05–18:00 Study Hall

On Fridays, the schedule changes

9–9:10 Homeroom/Class Attendance

9:10–10:25 Arts

10:30–12:35 Study Hall

12:40–13:15 Lunch

13:20–16:00 Arts

Sunday night I go over my schedule for the one hundredth time. I have my own separate study hall when my classmates are taking Korean, English, science, and history. But I'll sit with them in classes like computer, math, and PE, and of course all the music classes, which includes orchestra and solo performance.

I'm also enrolled in dance, an elective that I was sorted into last-minute due to my late transfer. I'm fine with it for now, but I need to talk to my counselor to see if I can switch it to a study hall. As a musician, I don't lack rhythm, but my body doesn't know that.

When my alarm goes off the next morning, Sori is already gone. I take my time getting ready, just now realizing the biggest pro of a uniform—I don't have to decide what to wear in the morning.

In the hall, I'm immediately glad I showered the night before because there's already a line forming outside the communal bathroom. I find an open space in front of the mirror to apply eyeliner and a sweep of gloss to my lips. I actually don't know what the dress code is for makeup, but with so many cosmetic cases lined up in front of the glass, it can't be that strict.

Since it's the first day, an all-school assembly is being held in the world-renowned concert hall. As I make my way toward the building, I look around for the boy and girl I'd met in the student center last night, Gi Taek and Angela. I'm feeling jittery and anxious, my gaze darting across the quad, heart stopping every time my eyes land on a particularly tall boy. I try to tell myself it's first-day-of-school nerves, *first-day-of-school-in-a-new-country nerves*. And while that's a part of it, I know I'm also nervous about seeing Jaewoo. I just want to get this second meeting over with so that I can get on with my life in Seoul.

Inside the auditorium, students are already finding their seats.

"Jenny!" My heart stops, but it's Gi Taek, heading over with Angela in tow.

"You'll need to fix your tie," he says, in place of good morning. "You'll get demerits if one of the teachers notice."

"I love your hair!" Angela says, gesturing to my side pigtails, which I mostly braided out of stress.

"Let's take our seats before it gets too crowded," Gi Taek says.

We enter through the double doors and I have to stop for a moment to take in my surroundings. The performance hall is huge with a high domed ceiling to maximize sound and acoustics. The stage is a gorgeous rosewood-mahogany color, the seats fanned out from the center for optimal viewing.

"I see three seats together!" Angela points to the back row. "Let's take them before someone else does."

I look for my roommate as we make our way over and spot her a few rows down to the left. She's sitting apart from the rest of the students, with the two seats on either side of her—*and in back and front of her*—empty. Yet her isolation seems like a choice she made rather than for any other reason. She sits with her arms crossed, gaze straight ahead, giving off talk-to-me-and-you'll-die vibes.

I'm immediately distracted when someone shouts, "Yah! Choi Youngmin!"

I whip my head in the direction of the doors where Youngmin has just waltzed through. The noise in the auditorium rises as kids start whispering to each other in excitement.

Youngmin skips to the front, joining a group of first year boys who give him high-fives.

Then Nathaniel steps through the doors, and it's truly as if a celebrity has arrived, his hair artfully messed and his tie askew. It's strange to see him in real life, when I spent all weekend watching him in videos. I wonder if it's just as weird for the students at SAA who've gone to school with him and the rest of the members of XOXO, to see their peers, maybe even their friends, achieve the dream they've wanted for so long.

Nathaniel takes the closest available seat to him in the section for Year Three and is immediately swarmed by girls.

I manage to tear my gaze away long enough to notice that Sori's attention has shifted to the door. As if realizing this herself, she quickly looks ahead.

At 8:09 another student slips into the auditorium, but it's not Jaewoo. Then another, and another. At 8:10 exactly, a teacher appears and shuts the doors.

Is he late? No, he would have come with his bandmates, if he was going to come at all. Maybe he's decided to finish his diploma online. Or he's doing some sort of promotional work overseas. K-pop idols do stuff like that all the time, right?

I'm so caught up in my own thoughts, I almost fail to notice the woman who walks onto the stage, taking her place behind a podium.

She introduces herself as the principal of Seoul Arts Academy, an institution that was established fifty years ago and has taught many prestigious alumnae, including a few names that get "oohs" and "aahs" from the students. She goes on to talk about the expectations the academy has of its students, which includes upholding the reputation of the school in conduct and character, as well as dedication to the arts above all things. She also mentions something called the "Senior Showcase," which creates a stir of interest among the students.

"All seniors are required to participate," Principal Lee informs us, "whether as a part of an ensemble, collaborators, or soloists. This is the best opportunity to showcase your talent. Representatives from all the major universities will be in attendance, as well as a few from overseas, Berklee College, Tokyo University of the Arts, and the Manhattan School of Music."

She goes on to say that recruiting officers from the major entertainment labels will also be in attendance, but I've stopped listening. A representative from MSM will be in the audience on the night of the showcase. If I can get a solo and put on a great performance, then I might be a shoo-in. I can feel my heart start to race. Everything is falling into place, the stars aligning.

"And now we'll have our welcome address from this year's senior class president."

Until now, the students had been sitting politely through the principal's address, but now they start to whisper excitedly to one another.

My heart, which had stuttered to a halt, picks up again.

A familiar figures steps from the wings. Jaewoo, Karaoke Boy, K-pop idol, and the senior class president of my high school.

Twelve

At one point during Jaewoo's address to the student body, he looks directly into the crowd and I instinctively lower into my seat, which is unnecessary. He can't see me, sitting as I am in the back row, farthest from the stage.

Unlike with the principal, I listen attentively to his speech. His low, smooth voice, accentuated by the mic at the podium, fills the hall. He's not even saying anything that interesting—his words sound rehearsed—and yet everyone is enraptured, giving him their full and complete attention.

"Class president, lead singer of XOXO, handsome, and kind. What can Jaewoo *not* do?" Angela says dreamily.

Answer texts, I think to myself, though I don't say it aloud.

"Did you know he writes all the lyrics for XOXO's songs?" Gi Taek says.

That surprises me. Though I don't know why it should.

"Sometimes another writer or another member works with him," Gi Taek continues, "but he's credited on all their songs."

"No wonder he's the most popular in XOXO," Angela says. This time I'm not surprised. Of course he would be.

Jaewoo finishes his speech to deafening applause, bowing before walking to the wings. The principal then comes back out to introduce the assembly's guest, a pianist from Ewha Womans University, an SAA alumna a few years back, who performs a medley of piano arrangements from popular Korean dramas. Afterward, we're dismissed to our homerooms.

Mine is in A Building, which is beside the student center, and attached to the cafeteria. Neither Gi Taek nor Angela are in my homeroom, but we do share a few other classes. We agree to meet for lunch before heading in opposite directions.

The hall outside my homeroom is already crowded, students calling out to each other and catching up after a long winter break. I spot Sori up ahead, noticeably alone again, and hurry in her direction.

"Jenny-nuna!" Youngmin barrels toward me, stopping short of collision. "How's your first day of school going? If you ever need someone to point you in the right direction, just ask me!"

I blink at him, surprised that he's talking to me. Though I don't know why I should be, he was so friendly in the uniform store. I glance around and a few people are looking at me curiously, but most are grinning at Youngmin.

"Nice hair, Youngmin-ah," someone says, and I notice that his hair color's changed since I last saw him, now a midnight blue when before it had been cerulean.

"It's going great," I say, once his attention has shifted back to me. "And I'll definitely take you up on that."

"If it isn't Jenny," a low voice says in English. Nathaniel.

I shift to face him. I'm about to answer in kind when I notice Sori down the hall. At the same time, she meets my gaze. Quickly she turns away and enters a classroom.

"Is something the matter?" Nathaniel asks.

"No . . ." For a moment—before she looked away—there was an expression on her face that I hadn't expected to see. Misery. "It's nothing. What's your homeroom?"

"Classroom B."

"Mine too." I sigh in relief. It'll be nice to have one friendly face in homeroom.

"Ai—shh," a voice groans from behind me. "It's only the first day back and I'm already worn out."

I freeze in place.

In front of me, Youngmin's eyes light up. "Jaewoo-hyeong! We missed you this morning."

"Ah, yeah, I meant to take the van with you, but Sun wanted me to listen to a track in the studio."

"Your speech was inspiring," Nathaniel says, deadpan.

"I wrote it for you," Jaewoo replies, not missing a beat.

"Have you met Jenny?" Youngmin says.

"Jenny?"

I knew this moment would happen eventually, but I thought it would be somewhere less public, or at least come as a surprise so that I wouldn't have time to freak out, like I am now.

I take a deep breath and turn around.

Our eyes meet. His widen slightly, and it's like I can see a million thoughts flit across his face in the space of a second. Then his expression shutters. "Ah," he says. "Nice to meet you."

My heart sinks. I didn't think he'd be *happy* to see me, not after the way he ignored my texts, but I didn't think he'd pretend we'd never met.

"We ran into Jenny at the uniform store the other day," Youngmin informs Jaewoo, who nods absently. "She's from LA."

"Is that right?" He turns to Nathaniel. "I have to go pick up something from the office." He adds, as an afterthought, "Fix your tie. You'll get demerits on the first day back."

I think he's talking to me, but then Nathaniel says, "It's not like they'll kick me out."

"One can hope."

And then he's gone, walking down the hall without a backward glance.

"I'm going to be late to class!" Youngmin says. "Bye, Jenny, Nathaniel-hyeong!" He gallivants off in the opposite direction to Jaewoo.

"That's our classroom," Nathaniel points a few doors down. "Shall we?"

I follow him, though I'm not really paying attention to where I'm going. What just happened? In all the scenarios I'd imagined for our second meeting, I never thought Jaewoo would dismiss me. It's like in this new setting, he's a completely different person.

"Jenny?" Nathaniel's waiting for me, sliding back the door to the classroom. "You coming?"

"Yeah." I hurry forward.

Inside, the classroom is laid out with rows of desks facing a whiteboard. The teacher hasn't yet arrived, so I check the seating chart on the podium at the front of the room. I'm seated a row from the back, next to the windows. As I approach my desk, I notice that all the seats are paired in twos, and my seatmate is none other than Sori. She appears as thrilled as I am at this turn of events.

"Good morning," I say. At least I can attempt a new start.

She turns her head to look out the window.

I sigh, pulling out my seat. On the opposite side of the classroom, Nathaniel is seated by a tall, lanky boy who is engaging him in animated conversation.

Everyone seems to be talking to their seatmates, except for Sori and me. I wonder if we could have been friends if I hadn't bumped into her desk and read the message on that postcard.

A message that had been signed: XOXO. Which could either be a well-used sign off or . . . a secret hidden in plain sight.

I go through the possible candidates. Youngmin's too young, I can't see it. Sun maybe, but he wasn't in the hallway just now, when I caught sight of Sori's expression. Also, the end of the postcard was written in English, not Korean. Which leaves Jaewoo and Nathaniel. I look over at Nathaniel, who's currently laughing and joking with his seat partner, the complete opposite of my roommate. Sori and Jaewoo share at least one thing in common: At any given moment, I have no idea what either of them are thinking.

My phone chirps in my pocket. I slip it out to see a text from my mom.

I paid the school your tuition. My scholarship only accounted for half. Let me know if there are any issues.

I text back, Okay. Thanks, Mom.

No, "hope you're having a good first day of school," but that's not a surprise.

I'm about to put my phone away, when I hesitate. I open up my messages and scroll back to a few days ago, to when I sent the text message to Jaewoo that I was coming to Seoul.

Hey, so, I'm actually going to be in Korea for a couple of months to visit my grandmother. If you're around, I'd love to see you.

The message is now marked "read."

I blink a few times. But when did he read it? A few days ago or just now when he saw me in the hall?

Sori bumps me hard in the shoulder and I look up to see a girl standing in front of my desk, tapping her shoe against the floor.

"You have to wear the uniform correctly," she says, pointing to my sloppy tie, "otherwise the whole classroom will be penalized."

Is she serious? I look over at Sori, but she's gone back to staring out the window.

"Hurry," the girl says, "you still have a few minutes."

I scramble up from my seat.

Outside in the empty hall, I pick a direction at random, hoping to stumble upon a bathroom. I curse my past self who hadn't carefully read the rule book. I'm going to be late for my first day of class.

"Student!" A teacher approaches down the hall, and I sigh in relief. He can help me— "You need to be in your classroom right now!"

I stare at him, confused why he's so angry. "I was told I needed to fix my tie—" I begin.

"Your classroom, now!" He's literally yelling at me, spittle flying.

"You don't understand. I'm a new—"

"GET TO YOUR CLASSROOM!"

And now I'm on the verge of tears. Why is he shouting at me? "But—"

"Seonsaengnim." Jaewoo appears from out of nowhere, addressing the teacher by his title. "She's a new student. I was showing her to her classroom."

Suddenly the teacher is all smiles. "Ah, Jaewoo-ssi. Of course."

Jaewoo gives him a close-lipped smile, bowing as the teacher walks away. He then presses his hand lightly against my back, leading me to a door that he pushes open.

We're in a stairwell, light filtering in through a skylight above us. I step forward, taking deep breaths. When I've composed myself, I turn to face Jaewoo who's now leaning against the door.

"Are you all right?" he asks in English.

"Yeah," I say. "Thanks for . . ." I wave in the direction of the hallway in a gesture that's meant to encompass everything.

"He shouldn't have yelled at you," he says gently.

I stare at him, wary. He's acting like he did back in LA, a complete one-eighty from pretending like we'd never met.

"Why weren't you in your homeroom?" he asks.

"A girl told me if my uniform broke regulations the whole class would be penalized."

Jaewoo offers a sympathetic smile. "She was just messing with you."

That's so mean! I'm a new student! Why didn't Sori say anything?

"Still," Jaewoo says, "uniform violations will get you points off your next test, that or you'll be made to run around the track field a few times."

"Really?"

"Really."

Wow, Korean schools are pretty strict.

"The truth is . . ." I kick my feet against the floor. This is embarrassing. "I don't know how to tie a tie."

"Really?"

"Really."

He shakes his head. "What kind of education were you getting in the States?"

"A public school education."

He steps away from the door, his hands reaching for my

collar. Slowly, he loosens the sloppy knot I'd managed this morning. A small crease forms between his brows as he concentrates. Undoing the knot, he evens out the sides of the tie. Sliding one side down, his knuckles brush my shirt. I suck in a sharp breath.

"Sorry," he says, hands going still for a moment. He bites his lip, then continues, Adam's apple bobbing.

He makes a new knot by slipping the tie through a hole and pulling gently.

I observe him as he works. Unlike when I met him in LA, he's not wearing makeup. He looks younger without it, but just as handsome. His left arm is also clearly not broken anymore, as he uses his left hand to hold the tie in place, tightening the knot. The tattoos on his wrist are gone too.

"What are you doing here, Jenny?" he asks softly.

"I swear I didn't follow you," I say.

He pauses in his movements. He blinks once, twice, then laughs. "I'm not as self-absorbed as that. Not yet, at least. I meant, what are you doing here in Korea, at this school?"

I frown. "Didn't you get my text?"

"What text?"

"The one I sent you, you know, where I told you I was going to be in Seoul for a few months."

He sighs, does one more pull on my tie, then drops his hands. "My phone was confiscated. After that night in LA, my manager took it away. I was given a company phone a week later, with approved contacts. What did you say?"

"Guess you'll never know."

Now it's his turn to frown.

I didn't say anything that revealing, but I'll let him stew in curiosity for once. Above us, the school bell rings.

"We better go," I say.

"I'll walk you to class."

We exit the stairwell and head back down a now empty hall.

"I'm sorry," Jaewoo says after taking a few steps, "for not texting you. I . . . wanted to."

I study him out of the corner of my eye. His lips are pressed together, his expression conflicted.

"Why did you pretend like you didn't know me earlier?" I ask.

"I didn't want people to know we've met before. I trust my classmates, but rumors have started from less. If it was just me to consider . . ."

We reach the door to my classroom. Inside, I can see the figure of an adult at the podium. "Jenny," Jaewoo stops me. "The thing is"—he watches me carefully, gauging my reaction—"*we* don't have to pretend we don't know each other."

"What do you mean?"

"When it's just . . . you and me."

"Like secret friends?"

He rubs the back of his neck. "I mean, when you put it that way, it sounds bad."

I wonder if I should be offended. I mean normally I would be, but I'm sure he probably has more things in his life to consider than a friendship with some random girl from LA—his reputation as an idol, for one.

"I get it," I say. "Things aren't exactly normal for you."

"Yeah," he says, a tentative smile on his lips.

Still, *I* don't have to agree to a secret friendship, not when I have people in my corner willing to be my friend, like Angela and Gi Taek. Even Nathaniel and Youngmin have been friendly, and in public too. What makes Jaewoo and my relationship so different? Is it because he's the class president, the most popular member in the group, a "prince" in nickname and reputation?

Maybe it's my hurt pride, but I have enough on my plate right now—adjusting to a new school, *getting* into a top music school of my choice. I don't know if I want to put in the energy into figuring him out.

"As for being friends . . ." I step closer, and he leans in, almost instinctively. "I'll think about it."

His smile drops.

Reaching for the door of the classroom, I slide it back.

Thirteen

As expected, everyone turns when I enter the classroom five minutes after the bell rings. The teacher looks at a loss for words, probably unable to comprehend how a student would be late on the first day of school.

"She's a transfer student," Jaewoo says, entering the class behind me. "She was lost." I look at him, surprised that he's come inside with me.

"And you found her," the teacher says warmly. "We wouldn't expect anything less from our class president."

Jaewoo approaches the podium, passing by me. Reaching into his school bag, he pulls out a folder and hands it to the teacher. "These are the papers you asked me to pick up from the office."

He bows, and instead of walking back out the door, heads down the aisle of seats, taking one in the back row, farthest to the right.

It's the seat directly behind mine.

Which means *he's in my class.* He doesn't look at me, resting his chin on his hand as he looks out the window. Even from the front of the classroom, I can see the smirk on his face.

"Jenny," the teacher says, "why don't you introduce yourself to the class?"

Oh my God, forced public speaking is the absolute worst.

I take a deep breath. "My name is Jenny Go," I begin. "I'm seventeen years old . . ." A few of the students in the front row frown, and I remember that in Korea, you're considered one year old the day you're born, and depending on your birthday, could be one to two years older than your American age. I'm not quick enough to figure out my Korean age so I say the year I was born instead. Everyone nods in understanding. "I'm originally from Los Angeles, California. And I'm a cellist."

Finished, I look at the teacher, who seems to be waiting for something. I bow.

"Perfect!" The teacher says, "Baksu!" She claps her hands and the rest of the students half-heartedly join her. "You can take your seat now."

Well, I guess after that introduction everyone now knows that I'm an international transfer student, and they'll be more forgiving of any cultural faux pas on my part.

Or not. I remember that girl who'd lied about the uniform violation. She was sitting in the front row during my introduction, and the whole time she and her seatmate had been looking me up and down and rolling their eyes.

As I take my seat, I glance at Jaewoo, but he's still looking out the window.

In front of him, Sori mimics his pose exactly, not acknowledging me as I pull the seat out beside her.

The rest of homeroom is spent going over class expectations for the year and assigning chores. Apparently the students take turns cleaning the classroom. The teacher also mentions the senior showcase, which happens in June. Each program head will share further details when we meet with our respective departments after lunch. I make a point to ask mine the steps to audition for a cello solo.

A little after an hour, the bell rings, signaling the end of Period 1. Most of the students remain seated; the next class is apparently advanced Korean, a literature class. Me and a few other students pack up our things to move rooms.

"Jaewoo-yah." Sori shifts her legs so that they're facing the window.

They *do* know each other, and not just know each other. If she's using his name in that familiar way, then they're close.

He glances up from where he was reading his schedule. "Min Sori."

"Why didn't you text me back?" Why is *she* on his list of approved numbers?

"Sorry, I left my phone at the studio," Jaewoo says. "What's up?"

"I congratulated you on your performance last night." I glance in her direction, but her face is turned away. It's subtle, but there's a hitched quality to her voice. "On *Music Net*."

"Oh, thanks."

"You'll find your phone, won't you?"

"Yeah."

"Don't ignore my texts," she says softly.

I quickly finish my packing and practically flee from my seat. Nathaniel catches my arm as I'm walking out the door.

I almost forgot about him, which is wild. How could anyone forget about Nathaniel?

"What's your next class?" he asks.

"I have study hall, but I guess English." Since Korean literature is too advanced for me and English language is too easy, LACHSA is letting me do an online version of their English literature course.

"And after that?" He shakes his head. "You know what, why don't you text me your schedule." He hands me his phone.

I stare at it, still a little dazed from what I just witnessed. Also the settings on his phone are all in Korean.

"Oh, sorry, here." He opens up the new contact info page. "Just type in your number. I'll fill in the rest."

Afterward, he takes it back and types in English "Jenny Go" all on one line.

As I leave the classroom, I catch sight of Liar Girl and her friends—a boy and girl—glaring at me. Honestly, at this point, I couldn't care less.

I spend a few minutes of my study hall reading the syllabus my English teacher sends over, and the rest of it wondering if Jaewoo was the one who sent Sori the postcard. If so, then why did he hang out with me in LA? And what about earlier in the hall, when he asked to be secret friends? How would Sori feel about that? How do *I* feel about that?

Not great.

The last period before lunch is PE and I quickly rush back to the dorm to change before meeting my class on the field.

"Jenny!" Angela greets me, looking adorable in pigtails and a pink hoodie over her uniform sweats. It's freezing outside and most of the students are running in place or doing jumping jacks to warm themselves up. "I'm so glad we have this class together!"

"Me too," I say, especially when I catch sight of Liar Girl and her friends. And Sori, though she stands apart, which seems to be her general state of being.

"Who's that?" Angela asks, following my gaze. "She's so pretty."

"Min Sori," one of our classmates answers, a girl with purple-tinted hair. "She's a trainee at Joah Entertainment."

So that's how she knows Jaewoo. Also maybe why she's an approved contact in his phone.

"I envy her," Angela sighs.

"Oh, yeah?" The girl smirks. "Wait until you hear who her mother is." The girl pauses dramatically.

I don't give her the satisfaction of asking.

Angela—on the other hand—is not petty, like me. "Who?"

"Seo Min Hee, the CEO of Joah Entertainment."

Angela gasps. "Her life is so blessed. Though I'm sure she would have gotten into Joah even without that connection."

I aspire to be as sweet as Angela when I grow up. The girl, however, doesn't seem to share my feelings and heads over to join her friends.

Today we're running the Korean equivalent of "the mile," which is four laps around the track. I'm fine with the first lap, huffing and puffing after the second, breathing heavily after the third, and then almost dead by the fourth, collapsing on the lawn with the students who'd finished ahead of me. Angela's still running, so after a short break, I walk over to the water fountain at the edge of the field to wash up.

Liar Girl is already there with her friend. In order to avoid them, I go to the other side of the fountain, splashing cold water onto my face from the spigot that shoots the water into a shallow basin. Lifting my head, our eyes meet. This close, I can read the nametag on her uniform: Kim Jina.

While holding my gaze, she nudges her friend and says something in Korean.

I frown, not quite understanding. Yet with how loud she spoke, I was clearly meant to hear.

Her friend glances over at me, and then says something back, and then it clicks.

They're purposefully speaking in slang, so that I won't understand.

At my confused expression, they start to laugh. They then exchange a few more words and *these* I can recognize because curse words are some of the first words you learn in any language.

I walk away with my face dripping water, the girls' laughter trailing behind me.

I feel an odd sort of disconnect with my mind. My whole

body is shaking, hot with frustration and fury. And all I want to do is lash out, but what would I even say? I'm not fluent enough to curse someone out in Korean, which is what I *want* to do. And they wouldn't understand me if I did it in English. They'd just laugh more, and I'd feel like an even bigger loser.

And it sucks because usually I'm pretty good at defending myself when the rare occasion presents itself for a good put-down. My mom, an immigrant with an accent, knew the power of language, which to her was like a weapon to use against people who claimed she didn't belong. That's why she became a lawyer.

And now the weapon of language is being used against me, but in a different country.

"I'm soooo gross," Angela says, walking toward me, her pig-tails drooping, "and now we have to go to lunch." She frowns when she catches sight of my face. "Are you okay?"

I nod, refusing to let Jina and her friend ruin my day. "I'm fine. I *am* starving though."

"Me too," Angela says. "Let's head over before the lines get too long."

The cafeteria is located next to the student center, across from the dorms. Even though we arrive five minutes before lunch officially starts, there's already a line forming outside the cafeteria window. A menu on the monitor above the station shows the different meal set options to choose from: bulgogi patty set, grilled mackerel set, and braised tofu set, all of which come with banchan and whatever the soup of the day is. Today's soup is sigeumchi-guk, spinach boiled in an oyster soup base.

As students order and retrieve their trays, the long tables in the cafeteria begin to fill. People also arrive from the student center, where a walkway connects to the cafeteria, bringing with them food purchased at the snack bar and convenience store.

At one point Angela stops an Indian girl who's passing by and introduces her as Anushya, her roommate. She's British Indian and from Bristol. We chat a bit in English about moving to Seoul—she's been here for two years—and then a boy from a table nearby calls her away. Though SAA isn't an international school, I was surprised to find out from the website that there's a good amount of international students, maybe one-fifth of the student body.

After we retrieve our trays—I choose the bulgogi patty set, Angela the mackerel set—we search for Gi Taek among the chaos of students.

"I see him!" Angela says, holding her tray with one hand and pointing across the cafeteria to where Gi Taek sits alone at one of the long tables, watching a video on his phone. We hurry over and join him.

He pauses the video, which a quick glance shows to be one on choreography. "How's your first day of school?" he asks. "I see you both came from PE." Unlike Angela and I in our sweats, he's still wearing his uniform from the assembly.

"Great!" Angela says, taking the seat across from him. "I had homeroom with you and then math." She makes a face.

"Study hall for me," I say sitting to his right. "I'm taking classes through my school in the States."

"Well, I had English and Korean back-to-back," Gi Taek says. "My brain is fried."

I pick up a piece of acorn jelly with my chopsticks, plopping it into my mouth. "So, what happens after lunch?" I know how it works at LACHSA, but I'm curious if it's different here.

"We switch from academics to the arts," Gi Taek says. "You're a cellist, so you'll go to orchestra. I'm a dance major, so I'll head over to the performing arts studio, and you . . ." He points at Angela. "You go to the studio at Neptune, right?"

She nods, though she seems preoccupied, a frown on her face.

"Trainees who already have contracts with management labels get their arts credits from their companies," he explains to me.

"Aren't you going to eat?" Angela blurts out, and I notice that Gi Taek doesn't have lunch.

He shrugs. "I'm on a diet."

"But you shouldn't skip meals . . ." Angela says.

"Mind if I join you?" Nathaniel pulls out the chair across from me, dropping his tray on the table.

I'd think the wide-eyed expressions on Gi Taek's and Angela's faces comical if I probably didn't have a similar one on my face.

It's not his appearance that surprises me so much as to why he seems to keep seeking me out. A glimpse around at the other tables shows a few students taking notice. Does he just not care about his reputation, like Jaewoo does? Maybe having already had a scandal, he doesn't have much to lose.

When I turn my attention back to the table, I notice Gi Taek and Angela seem to be trying to communicate something to me with their minds.

"Nathaniel," I say, "do you know Angela and Gi Taek?"

"Yeah." He points at Gi Taek with his spoon. "Dancer, right?"

"Yes." Gi Taek nods vigorously. Nathaniel then turns to Angela and lifts his hand. "I don't know you, though. My name's Nathaniel. Nice to meet you." She takes the tip of his fingers between both her hands. After she drops them, he laughs, shakes his head, and returns to his food, which he eats with gusto.

Gi Taek looks between Nathaniel and me. "How do you two know each other?"

When Nathaniel doesn't look like he's going to answer—his mouth full of food—I explain, "We met at the uniform store when I went to go pick up mine."

Angela sits forward in her seat. "Did you know who he was?"

"Not then."

"But now you do," she prompts.

"I mean, sure. I watched your music video," I inform him.

"Oh yeah?" Nathaniel says. "What'd you think?" Now it's my turn to get the spoon pointed at me. "Couldn't take your eyes off me, could you?"

Angela giggles.

"Yeah . . ." I say, though it's not Nathaniel's part in the music video that replays in my head. That's replayed in my head since the first time I saw it.

There's a stir at the entrance of the cafeteria.

I look up to see Jaewoo walk into the cafeteria . . . with Sori.

I've never seen a more striking pair. They look like they stepped out of a catalogue.

"Is it weird if I take a picture?" Angela asks. "Like as a souvenir for myself. I've never seen such great visuals."

"I wouldn't," Gi Taek says, answering her seriously. "What if that picture got out somehow? It could create a scandal. I mean, do you remember—" He cuts off abruptly, looking stricken.

Nathaniel glances up from his tray. I stare at Gi Taek, whose face has gone completely white.

"What's wrong?" I ask.

"Nothing," Gi Taek says. "It's nothing."

Nathaniel puts down his spoon and sits back in his chair, an amused expression on his face.

I have a distinct impression that I'm missing something here.

"I guess you wouldn't know," Nathaniel sighs. "Min Sori and I dated for six months before her mother found out and forced us to break up."

"Oh my God," I say.

He shrugs. "Messed up, right?"

Nathaniel is the writer of the postcard. Relief washes over me, quickly followed by guilt. Several times today, I caught Sori looking over. I thought something was off about her expression and yet I was more jealous than sympathetic.

Even now, she can't keep her eyes off our table; the look on her face can only be described as miserable.

The postcard didn't even sound like Jaewoo, now that I know who wrote it. Remembering the words in English at the end of the postcard, I fill in his name at the end.

Chin up, Songbird.
You will always have my heart.
XOXO
Nathaniel

Fourteen

The rest of the day is a blur. After lunch, I attend orchestra ensemble and meet with my cello instructor for solo performance class. She has me play a few scales and my competition piece from last fall. I'm a little rusty from not practicing for over a week. Then she gives me a schedule to sign up for hours in the academy's practice rooms. When I bring up the showcase, she tells me we won't start preparing our pieces until late April.

After class, Gi Taek and I decide to grab a quick dinner down the street at Subway, since Angela's still at rehearsal.

Back in the dorms, I take a long, hot shower, then wrapped in only a towel, I sprint down to the hall to my room. I can tell Sori's back because the lights are on when I open the door. As per usual, she doesn't look up from a dance video she's watching on YouTube.

Putting on my pj's, I pick out a sheet mask from the set of ten Halmeoni bought me, slipping out the dewy mask from the package and placing it carefully onto my face. I then plop down onto the bed, phone in hand, laying a towel over the pillow to protect it from my wet hair. Honestly, there's nothing better than self-care after a long day.

Putting in my earbuds, I pick up my phone. The browser opens to the last thing I googled, right after lunch before I had to rush over to orchestra.

Nathaniel. XOXO. Scandal.

I glance through the bookshelf divider to where Sori's still watching videos. Is it weird that I'm googling my roommate? It's none of my business.

Except, it *is* kind of my business, since I live with her. Or at least, that's what I tell myself.

I click on the first link. Back in November—around the time XOXO was in LA shooting the music video for "Don't Look Back"—*Bulletin* had released photos of XOXO's Nathaniel with a "mysterious trainee" from Joah Entertainment. Photos of them walking down a dark street holding hands. Photos of them leaving Nathaniel's dorm, where he lives with the other XOXO members. Photos of them in Nathaniel's car. The face of the girl in the photo is blurred out, but now that I know her identity, it's clear the mysterious trainee is Sori—same body, same hair. Same clothes. I can see the pink bomber jacket in one photo hanging on the clothing rack in our room.

I wonder if Joah Entertainment paid *Bulletin* not to reveal Sori's identity. She *is* the daughter of the CEO. Either that or they weren't legally able to, Sori being a minor and, as a trainee, not yet a public figure.

"Jenny?"

I almost tumble out of bed in alarm. Sori stands by her desk, one hand on her now-closed laptop, as she looks over in my direction.

"Yes?" Thank God my voice sounds like I haven't just been stalking her on the internet.

"Never mind." She moves toward the doorway to turn off the light.

I almost call out for her to wait. Does she want to ask me about Nathaniel? I could ease her mind, that I'm not interested in him, that the person I *am* interested in is spending more time with her than me. Oh, and that he thinks I'm a shameful secret.

Instead, I say nothing as she shuts off the light and climbs into bed. I take off my sheet mask and place it on my nightstand to throw away in the morning.

She's not a snorer so it's silent in the room. I can't tell if she's asleep or if—like me—she's looking at the ceiling, dizzy with thoughts.

I want to ask Sori about herself. What's it like to be a trainee at Joah Entertainment? Did she always want to be a K-pop star or was it something she had to do, because of who her mother is?

Why is she always alone at school? I haven't seen her speak to anyone besides Jaewoo. Why did she even opt for having a roommate when she could have had a single? Was she hoping that *I*, said roommate, could have been a friend? An ally? A confidante?

Had I ruined that when I read that postcard? At this moment, I don't think I've regretted anything more in my life.

Most of all I want to ask her what it's like, to love someone whom you can never have. Not to say she was in love. . . .

Or that I am.

I wonder if she would have ever started, if she knew how it would all end. . . .

This is the last thought I have as I drift into oblivion.

Sori's alarm goes off at five the next morning. I lie in bed, listening to her get ready, changing into workout clothes and slipping out the door, duffel bag in hand.

Unlike yesterday, the cafeteria is open for breakfast and I join a bleary-eyed Gi Taek and Angela at our same table from yesterday. They're sharing a package of morning rolls from the convenience store. Gi Taek passes me one and I nibble on it as my eyes scan the room.

"The members of XOXO won't be here today," Gi Taek says, as if reading my mind. "They have rehearsals from nine to eleven, then a taping from two to four."

"How do you know that?" I ask. That information seemed very specific.

"It's on their fan café."

I don't even want to ask what that is.

Still, I can't help feeling disappointed that I won't see either Jaewoo or Nathaniel at school today. I can feel my shoulders drooping as I walk into class and spot their empty desks. Sori's already seated, so I head on over, glad that I'm neither late nor incorrectly dressed—Angela let me borrow her elastic tie—on the second day of school.

The first class is math, which is an "experience," as it's taught in Korean. Luckily, the unit is one I'd already covered at LACHSA and I manage to solve the problem when the teacher calls me to the board.

Afterward, I have study hall/history. As I'm packing up my things, Jina walks over, followed by a boy. They make a point of having a loud conversation in front of my desk.

They're speaking in slang again, but I recognize a few words, namely bitch and slut.

This girl is the literal worst. It's like she's never seen a movie or watched reality TV. Doesn't she know: the meaner you are, the uglier you get?

Sori abruptly stands up, her chair falling backward behind her. Gathering up her books, she flees from the classroom.

I realize, belatedly, that I wasn't the target of their torment this time around.

Hurrying out of the classroom, I catch sight of Sori already halfway down the hall. She's pushing open the door to the girls' bathroom.

I follow, stepping aside to let two girls exit. They glance over their shoulders, whispering to each other. Inside, the area between the stalls and the sink is empty. The sound of sniffles comes from the last stall, the only one with a closed door.

I approach and knock on the stall door. "Sori? Are you

okay?" The sniffles become muffled, as if she's holding a hand to her mouth. "I heard what Jina said. That wasn't nice, nor is it true."

The door opens and I step back. She must be wearing waterproof mascara because her makeup looks immaculate, though the corners of her eyes are red. "How do you know if it's not true?"

Damn. She doesn't make this easy. There's an answer I could give her, that's easier said in English. That words like "bitch" and "slut" have been used systemically to belittle women and entrench misogyny in all cultures around the world, that I wouldn't want people to judge me or boil all my decisions down to a single word, without nuance or context or compassion.

We're just . . . girls. No more, no less. But before I can figure out how to say any of this she says, "I don't need your pity." Sori shoulders past me and exits the bathroom with a slam of the door.

Fifteen

I'm already exhausted and the day's not even half over. I spend most of study hall in the library, alternating mulling over how I could have handled the situation with Sori better and my first class of dance. I'd been meaning to talk to my counselor about switching out of it, since it's not exactly an elective I'd have chosen for myself, but haven't yet had the opportunity.

Still, it's too late to back out of the first day so I head over to the performing arts building, which I've never been in, though I know this is where Angela and Gi Taek have most of their classes. Though I'm early, I'm not the first there.

Sori stands by the floor-to-ceiling windows that line the back of the room, on the opposite side of which are mirrors. She's wearing stylish activewear, a cropped tank and biker shorts, which I didn't know was an option, otherwise I'd have dressed in something besides my PE clothes.

Sori doesn't acknowledge me, so I drop my school bag in

the corner and sit on the floor to stretch.

A few minutes of silence pass, then the door opens again. I expect the teacher or another student, but Nathaniel steps into the room.

"Fancy seeing you here," he says in English, then his eyes trail over my shoulder and he seems to freeze in place.

Through the mirror I can see that Sori has turned from the window at his entrance. I have this weird out-of-body experience where I can see him in front of me by the door, and her behind me through the mirror, and the expressions on both of their faces is full of an inexplicable emotion, one that is way too intimate for me to witness. Then it's like they both close off at the same time.

Nathaniel grins, like he hasn't a care in the world.

"Min Sori. How have you been?"

She turns abruptly back to the window. "Don't speak to me. Don't look at me. Don't even breathe near me."

He shuts his mouth. Throwing his bag against the wall, he plops down next to me.

Like Sori, he's dressed in stylish workout clothes.

"I thought you had rehearsal," I say.

He raises a single eyebrow.

"Gi Taek told me," I explain.

"Ah, yes, Gi Taek." He stretches his legs out in front of him, arching his back as he looks up at the ceiling. "I did have rehearsal, but then we decided to head back to campus instead of waiting around in the van for an hour."

"We?" I say.

The door slides open again.

"Jaewoo!" Sori rushes from the window to grab onto Jaewoo's arm. This seems a little dramatic for her, seeing as how I've never heard her use a tone of voice that would include an exclamation point at the end.

Jaewoo looks down at Sori with a quizzical expression, then at Nathaniel, who shrugs. Then his eyes land on me.

As with every time he looks at me, my heart does a somersault in my chest.

"Jaewoo," Nathaniel says, "you remember Jenny, right? From LA? Plays the cello."

Jaewoo glances at Nathaniel, then at me. "Why are you taking dance if you're a cellist?" He starts to take off his large puffer jacket. Like Nathaniel, he's dressed in stylish sportswear, men's joggers and a hoodie.

I realize in this moment that I have a thing for guys and sportswear. Jaewoo's black sweatshirt clings loosely to his shoulders and chest, his sweatpants riding low at his hips.

"Why wouldn't Jenny take dance?" Nathaniel says, answering for me, and also reminding me of what was asked. "Not everything has to be done for a reason. Sometimes you just do things for the fun of it."

Jaewoo and Nathaniel exchange a look and I wonder if this is an old argument.

The door slides open for the third time and the rest of the students enter the room, followed by the teacher. She claps her hands. "Everyone move to the sides of the room," she says without preamble.

The students hesitate, and it's obvious they're waiting to see which side of the room Jaewoo and Nathaniel head toward. When they move in opposite directions, there's this moment where the students realize they'll have to choose, which is sort of like choosing your favorite member in XOXO.

The students each start heading toward one or the other side of the room, and it seems like an even split, until only Sori and I are left standing. She looks at me, tosses her hair, and moves toward Jaewoo's side of the room.

And now I'm just standing here alone, like the last person picked for a dodgeball team.

Except I'm the one doing the choosing. I glance over at Jaewoo, who's watching me with an unreadable expression on his face.

Then I glance at Nathaniel, who beckons me over.

I guess the choice is clear. I should go where I'm wanted. I walk over to Nathaniel who shifts to the side to make room for me.

"For those of you who don't know me," the teacher begins, "my name is Ms. Dan. This is an elective class for Year Three. If you are a dance major, you will not receive credit toward your major, understood?"

"Yes," all the students reply in unison.

"Perfect! Does anyone want to read the class expectations from the syllabus?"

A boy from Jaewoo's team—I mean, side of the room—volunteers. I listen carefully as he reads aloud from off Ms. Dan's tablet. For the most part, I'm fine with the lessons, which are broken down into genres of dance, like ballet and jazz. I'm not looking forward to the group project though, where groups of four or five of us will have to a pick a song and choreograph a dance to it.

Luckily, Ms. Dan informs us that choreography won't start until next week so we spend the rest of class stretching.

"Why are you hanging out with me?" I ask Nathaniel, who's pretty much only talked to me since the class started. On the other side of the room, Jaewoo is practically holding court like the prince he is, doling out his attention like favors.

Is Nathaniel *using* me to make Sori jealous? That seems mean-spirited, especially with how much I believe he still cares for her. The way he looked at her when he first entered the room said it all. There must be another reason.

"We're countrymen," he says, and I roll my eyes. "I like to practice my English?"

"I don't buy it."

"Damn, Jenny. Maybe I like to hang out with you 'cause you don't take my bullshit."

I laugh, but I wish he'd just tell me. It can't be just that I'm American. There are other kids from the US here. I'd *like* to think it's because he just likes me—as a friend—but I don't know, something about his attention seems pointed.

Yet if it's not to make Sori jealous then why does he keep singling me out?

"Jaewoo-yah! What are you staring at?"

I look over to see Jaewoo's head turn toward a girl who's approaching him. Though I listen carefully, I can't make out his response from across the room.

After class, everyone packs up and leaves quickly, presumably to get in the lunch line. When I look over, Jaewoo's moving as fast as the rest of them, though for a different reason. According to Gi Taek's recounting of XOXO's schedule, he has a recording session to get to.

"See you later, Jenny," Nathaniel calls as he rushes out.

I pack my things at a much slower pace. Honestly, I'm a little disappointed.

After separating to opposite sides of the room, Jaewoo and I spent the entire class apart. I know I said I'd "think" about being his friend, but seeing as he ignored me all class today, and I pretended to, what would that even mean?

It sucks watching him talk to other people when he won't talk to me. I know it can't be the same as it was in LA, but I miss how it felt that night, to have all his attention on me.

I resolve to talk to my counselor about switching out of dance class sooner rather than later.

Outside the studio, the hall is empty, all of the students having gone to lunch. As I make my way toward the elevator, a door to my left shifts slightly open.

"Psst," a voice calls out.

I approach the door slowly. "Jaewoo?" I ask in surprise. It's definitely him, though his hood is up and his face is in shadows. "What are you doing?"

"Is there anyone in the hall?" he asks.

I glance around. "No."

"Good." He grabs my hand and pulls me in.

Sixteen

"First a stairwell, now a broom closet."

"If you're thinking of small places we've been in," Jaewoo says, a hint of mischief in his voice, "the stairwell wasn't the first."

His reference to the picture booth, and that moment inside, makes my stomach do all kinds of twists and turns.

"I still have that sticker photo," I say.

"Oh, yeah?" He leans back, not quite touching the rack of cleaning supplies behind him. The closet is so small that if I were to spread my arms, I could touch the door and the back wall. "Do you have it with you? Right now?" His eyes drop, then slowly move upward. It's obvious that if I had that picture, it would be in my backpack, not on my person. Is this an excuse to check me out?

Normally I would be thrilled if it were, except that I'm wearing my decidedly uncute PE clothes.

Not like him. Dressed to impress, even in sweats. Speaking of which . . .

"Don't you have a recording to go to?" I ask.

He frowns, clearly confused, then says, "Oh, Nathaniel told you."

Sure.

"I have some time. Our performance isn't until the end of the show, so technically we don't have to be there until then."

"I see."

"Still, it's polite to get there early and stay the whole time."

Meaning, he really *should* be there, but chose to stay *here* longer, with me.

My heart swells in my chest, which is not exactly helpful when I'm trying to keep a level head. Concentrate, Jenny. Don't let the cute boy's words distract you from the times he's brushed you off in the past.

Outside in the hall, voices approach. We both listen carefully until the voices grow distant, disappearing altogether.

"I wanted to talk to you," Jaewoo says, "about Nathaniel."

I blink, surprised. "What about him?"

"Stay away from him."

I cross my arms. High-handed, much?

He hurries to explain. "Last fall, a tabloid released an article about Nathaniel, that he was dating someone . . ."

"I know," I say. "He told me about it."

"He did?" Jaewoo looks surprised. "Did he give any details?"

"Just that the other person involved was Sori."

Jaewoo sighs. "It came at a bad time. We were only six months out from our debut, preparing to release "Don't Look

Back." Then we got the news that *Bulletin* dropped that bomb. We had to cancel shows, interviews. Of course it was the worst for Nathaniel. Not only was he forced to break up with his girl-friend, but he stopped getting invited to do solo activities, and his SNS accounts were flooded with hate comments."

It's hard to imagine anyone getting upset enough at another person for dating and openly attacking them for it on their social media profiles. Especially Nathaniel, who's so friendly and easygoing.

"Honestly, I don't know how he does it," Jaewoo says. "He claims none of it matters, but it can't be easy."

"And Sori?" I ask. "What was the fallout like on her side."

"Luckily her mother *is* the CEO of Joah Entertainment, and she was able to force the tabloids to blur out Sori's face in the photographs. There were some rumors at school . . . but that's it."

Well, not exactly. Even if her character wasn't attacked by trolls on the internet, people like Jina, and I'm sure others, bully her at school. I've also only ever seen her alone.

"Okay," I say. "I'll try to stay away from Nathaniel. For *his* sake," I clarify. "Not because you told me to. I don't want to get him into trouble."

I can see now that Jaewoo, unlike Nathaniel, is very careful with his public image, talking to everyone equally and not sin-gling anyone out for special attention. Nathaniel is the complete opposite. He really doesn't care.

"It's not *just* out of concern for Nathaniel," Jaewoo says.

Even with only the dim light of the bulb above us, I can see the high color in his cheeks.

"I don't want you to be friends with him," he says. "Not in the way you're friends with me."

It takes me a moment to realize . . .

He's jealous.

"I meant everything I said." He looks down, unable to meet my eyes. "But my motives aren't entirely selfless."

In the distance, a bell rings, signaling that lunch has officially started.

"We should go," Jaewoo says, but neither of us moves.

I wonder if he sees the irony that in order to warn me away from a potential scandal with Nathaniel, he's pulling me into stairwells and closets. But of course I'm not going to point that out to him.

A lock of his hair has fallen forward and I reach up, my fingers sweeping slowly across his brow.

"Jenny . . ." His eyes are heavy-lidded, his lips parted. As he moves closer to me, I grab onto the front of his hoodie, clutching it. Just as my eyes flutter closed, the door swings open.

Seventeen

Youngmin stands outside the door, his eyes trailing from me to Jaewoo. "Why are you in the broom closet with Jenny-nuna?"

I'm frozen in place, wondering how I must appear with my face flushed. I quickly let go of Jaewoo's hoodie. Luckily Youngmin doesn't seem to notice the movement, his eyes on Jaewoo.

"Why do you think we're in here?" Jaewoo says.

Oh boy. He's stalling.

"Were you looking for something? I saw the light was on. Though . . ." He frowns. "That doesn't explain why the door was clo—"

"You dyed your hair!" I interrupt, pointing to Youngmin's head. His hair, which was blue yesterday, is now fire-truck red. "It looks good!"

My distraction seems to work because Youngmin beams. "Thank you! Our manager says I'm the only one in the band who can really pull it off. He sent me to get you, Jaewoo-hyeong.

We were supposed to have left for EBC fifteen minutes ago."

"Oh, right," Jaewoo says. "We shouldn't keep him waiting."

I wonder if Jaewoo and I will ever acknowledge what almost took place in the broom closet, or if, like before, we're going to pretend it never happened.

"Hyeong," Youngmin says, hesitating, "that ajeossi is outside again."

It's like these words flip a switch inside Jaewoo because his whole demeanor changes.

With jerky movements, he takes out his phone, quickly tapping against the screen, then holding it to his ear. Catching my eye, he explains, "I'm calling campus security. Hello?" Someone must have picked up on the other line. "There's a suspicious adult, male, mid-forties, hanging around the arts department." He holds his hand to the receiver. "Which side?" he asks Youngmin.

"East side," Youngmin tells him, and Jaewoo repeats it to the operator.

"Thank you." He hangs up. "Don't worry, Youngmin-ah. They'll get rid of him."

We start walking, Jaewoo at the front, flanked by Youngmin and me. Tension radiates from Jaewoo in waves. Something about the appearance of this man has really ticked him off.

"Who is he?" I ask Youngmin.

"A paparazzi ajeossi," Youngmin explains. "He's the one who sold the story of Nathaniel and Sori to *Bulletin*."

Jaewoo's anger suddenly makes a lot more sense. This is the man who hurt his group member, his label-mate and friend. With him, it's personal.

"Do you get followed by paparazzi a lot?" I ask.

Youngmin wrinkles his nose. "Not really. Though sometimes they wait for us outside the company . . ."

"That's different," Jaewoo says, and his usually even-toned voice has an edge to it. "At concerts, at fan events, even in places where there isn't a designated media zone like outside Joah's building or the broadcasting stations, media are expected, even invited. But at our school? Outside our dorm? At the homes of our families? That's not right.

"When our fans take photos of us it's because they want to feel close to us, they support us and have our best interests at heart. Paparazzi just want money; they want to expose our private lives for profit."

"People have even gotten hurt," Youngmin says. "There have been cases where idols have gotten into car crashes trying to get away from paparazzi."

"Wow, that's awful."

We reach a hallway that splits in two directions. Jaewoo finally stops and turns to me. "Youngmin and I will go out the east side. If you follow this hall it'll take you out the north exit. Follow the garden path to the cafeteria."

I feel like we're in a war film and he's drawing the fire. It's a similar feeling to how I felt that night in LA, when an unmarked van had pulled up to the curb to take him away.

"The paparazzi ajeossi should be gone by now," Jaewoo says, and I know he says it to reassure me.

They both wait for me to leave first. "Good luck on your live show," I say. "I'll be sure to watch."

Youngmin holds up his thumb and pointer finger, pressing the pads together and crossing them slightly until they form the shape of a tiny heart.

"If you see me making this sign to the camera, know that it's for you!"

Later that night, Angela, Gi Taek, and I watch XOXO's performance on *Top Ten Live* in a small restaurant right off campus that sells Korean food at cheap prices. We split a plate of tteok-bokki between us as we wait for our other dishes to arrive.

Gi Taek spears a cylinder of the spicy rice cake with a toothpick. "Don't let me eat more than three. I'm on a diet."

"How can you stop at three?" Angela exclaims. "I could eat a whole mountain of tteok-bokki." She's foregone the toothpicks in favor of chopsticks for easier access.

I rest my chin on my hand and watch the entirety of XOXO's performance, noticing details I hadn't picked out the first time around. Like how even the choreography tells a story. As the camera pans closer to the performers, Youngmin flashes the heart sign to the camera.

"That's not usually part of the routine," Angela says. "How cute!"

A jingle above the door signals the entrance of another

customer. I'm surprised to see though that it's Sori who steps through the door. Without so much as a glance in our direction, she walks over to the counter, places her order, and takes a seat at a table a little way down from us.

Angela leans across the table and whispers, "Should we invite her to join us?"

Gi Taek shakes his head. "She'd never say yes."

The restaurant owner calls out our order and Angela dashes from the table, coming back with a plate of kimchi fried rice. We dig in with our spoons.

"What are your plans for the weekend?" Gi Taek asks us. He's far surpassed three tteok-bokki by now.

"I'm going to visit my halmeoni on Sunday morning," I say.

"Where does your halmeoni live?" Gi Taek asks.

"She lives near Gyeongbokgung Palace, but I'm actually visiting her at the health clinic where she stays on the weekends. It's also around there, though a few stops away on line three."

"That's not far from Ikseon-dong," Gi Taek says. "My sister lives in the neighborhood. There are a lot of cool cafés nearby. We should hang out."

"I'm in!" Angela says.

"I'd love that," I say.

We make plans to meet on Sunday in the late afternoon after I visit my grandma.

The bells above the door chime again. This time Jina enters, accompanied by a few of her friends.

She glances over at our table, then says something to the boy behind her, who laughs.

"She's in your class, isn't she?" Gi Taek asks. "Kim Jina?"

"She is. She's also in our PE class," I say, nodding at Angela. "Do you know her?"

"I went to middle school with her. She doesn't exactly have a great reputation, like there were rumors of school bullying."

Angela and I exchange a look. Why am I not surprised?

After ordering at the counter, her group completely ignores our table; they have a more vulnerable target in mind.

They take seats at the table directly next to Sori's, talking loudly to one another. Their voices carry throughout the small restaurant:

"She's sitting alone."

"Doesn't she have any friends?"

"What a loser."

Sori, who'd ordered a hot noodle dish, bends slightly forward, her hair falling over her face.

The restaurant owner calls out that the last food items we ordered are ready. Gi Taek, Angela, and I all stand at once. There are three plates of food on trays and we each take one.

We form a line, with me in the front, and head through the restaurant, bypassing our table, where we'd already cleaned up the food on our dishes.

We set our trays down at Sori's table. I sit opposite her, while Gi Taek and Angela sit beside us.

And then we proceed to completely ignore her, continuing

our chat. At one point, I think Sori might get up and flee, her spoon hovering in the air. But then she resumes eating.

We stay—eating and gossiping and joking and laughing—until she's finished her meal.

Eighteen

I think I have a handle on my classes and schedule by the end of the week. After the ten minutes of homeroom, I have math or computer in the mornings, followed by study hall where I take my LACHSA courses online, then either PE or dance—which I've decided to stick with for now, since besides homeroom, it's the only class I have with Jaewoo. Then after lunch follows orchestra, individual practice, and more study hall.

Though I'm wondering if it was a mistake to stay in dance for that reason, when it's not like Jaewoo and I ever speak to each other, both of us adhering to the whole "secret friends" policy.

I just wish it was easy for me as it clearly is for him. Maybe having secret friendships is part of an idol's training, like that whole list Angela went over: dancing, singing, and learning how to ignore a specific girl all day long only to pull her into a broom closet and almost kiss her.

It seems effortless for him to pretend I don't exist while my eyes are pulled in his direction constantly. Even my thoughts won't give me a break. What did that moment in the closet mean, if it meant anything at all? I'm just so confused.

It's honestly a relief when the weekend finally comes around.

I spend Friday emailing back and forth with my world English teacher, who assigns me excerpts from the *Norton Anthology of World Masterpieces*, which I purchase online as an e-book. When I notice that there aren't any Korean authors or poets listed in the syllabus, I email to ask if I can supplement a few for extra credit, and he emails back with an enthusiastic "go for it." Riding that high, I text Eunbi about my portfolio for music schools.

Sunday morning, I grab my dad's ratty old Dodgers cap and my cello already packed in its travel case, then hop onto the subway, transferring once to the orange line and taking that all the way to my grandma's clinic located in the northern part of Seoul.

Outside the station, I breathe in the crisp mountain air. Ice from the night before still lingers on the streets, and I'm careful as I make my way past a small neighborhood market putting up its produce stand for the day and a bakery with freshly baked loaves of bread in the window. Backtracking, I purchase one. The friendly shopgirl wraps the loaf in brown paper, slipping a wildflower beneath the twine.

My grandmother's clinic is tucked right off the main road in a place called Camellia Health Village, which is comprised of several small health-care facilities with different specializations.

The village surrounds a beautiful private park full of gardens and walking paths. Before heading to Halmeoni's clinic, I stop and watch a young boy and his grandfather fly a kite on the lawn.

This place is so peaceful. The path to the clinic is lined with cherry trees that even now have small buds upon their branches. In less than a month's time they'll be in full bloom.

Up ahead, I notice a guy has stepped off the path, standing beneath one of the trees. He's tall, wearing a camo jacket and dark jeans. I'm instantly reminded of Jaewoo, which seems to be my subconscious's evil way of toying with me.

I sigh, passing by the tree.

"Jenny?"

I almost fall over.

Jaewoo jogs across the grass. "What are you doing here?"

He looks great. I mean, he always looks great. But this is the first time I've seen him in casual clothing that isn't workout clothes, and he's giving off extreme "boyfriend" vibes. When I realize I'm staring, I answer, "I'm here to visit my halmeoni. She's in the clinic. What about you? What are you doing here?"

His smile falters.

"You don't have to tell me," I say quickly. I don't want him to share anything he's not comfortable with, especially if it's about his health.

"No, it's okay. I was seeing my therapist."

"Oh," I say. "Cool." I went to a few sessions with a therapist when my dad passed away. It helped me a lot, and my mom too, though she hasn't gone in a few years.

I know mental health is stigmatized in Korea in a way that it's not in the US. It makes sense that Jaewoo has a therapist, with all the pressures and stress that comes with being an idol.

"Yeah," he watches me oddly. His gaze travels to my shoulder. "Is that your cello?" He nods to indicate my travel case. "It looks heavy."

I adjust the strap. "I'm used to it. I've been playing since I was eight."

"I'd say I was singing since I was four." He grins. "But probably so have you."

"Not as beautifully, believe me."

He raises a single eyebrow.

I wave my hand in the air, as if brushing off what I said. "You know you have a beautiful voice, come on."

He shakes his head, a small smile on his lips. "So did you bring your cello to play for your halmeoni?"

"Yeah, she's actually never heard me play. Is that weird?"

"My father has never heard me sing."

He says it without any inflection in his voice, as if he were discussing the weather. I recall from that night in LA that he was raised by a single mother.

"Is he completely out of the picture?" I ask softly.

"Since I was four. Now that I think about it, for as long as I could sing." He grins, clearly teasing me, and himself, and yet the subject is sad, no matter what. But I also know why someone might use humor to mask pain. I've done it myself.

"Are you heading out?" I ask, for a lighter change of subject.

"I was . . ." he says. "I have no other plans for the day . . ." He bites his lip, waiting expectantly.

"Do you . . ."—he concentrates on my mouth, as if willing the words from my lips—"want to visit my halmeoni with me?"

He grins widely. "Are you asking?"

I roll my eyes. "Come on."

We start to walk side-by-side down the tree-lined path.

I don't know what compelled me to invite him, especially with how uncertain I am of what we even are to each other. Secret friends. Secret friends who almost kiss. And if I'm okay with that. Then I realize it doesn't matter. I'm just happy he's here with me, and it's a beautiful day.

"Do you usually come here alone?" I ask. "When I met Nathaniel and Youngmin in the uniform shop, there was this guy with them . . ."

"You must mean Nam Ji Seok, our manager. He actually does come with me, when I have my weekly sessions, but today both Sun-hyeong and Youngmin had activities on their schedules that required more of his attention. Youngmin's shooting a commercial and Sun is filming a cooking-themed reality TV show."

It doesn't escape my notice that he hasn't mentioned Nathaniel. I hope that the reason he doesn't have a solo activity is because, like Jaewoo, he had a prior commitment, and not that he wasn't asked.

The path opens back up to a small lawn. In the distance, I

catch sight of the grandfather and boy with the kite.

Jaewoo offers to carry a few of my things. I won't give him my cello, but he insists on holding the loaf of bread.

When we reach the door to the clinic, Jaewoo holds it open for me. I head over to the desk to check myself in, writing down Jenny Go + 1 in the visitor logbook.

When I turn around, Jaewoo's gone. I'm still looking around the waiting area when he emerges from a small gift shop bearing a bouquet of pink carnations.

My heart does a little flip flop in my chest.

He's also wearing a face mask, one that covers his nose and mouth, presumably to hide his identity. This *is* a health clinic, where extra precautions are appreciated.

The receptionist buzzes us into the ward. We approach the nursing station and I introduce myself, while Jaewoo hands over the loaf from the bakery. The nurses behind the desk "eomeona" and "ah" over the baked goods, but mostly over Jaewoo, who even with his face covered, charms them easily. Then the head nurse leads us to my grandmother's room, which she shares with three other patients.

She's in the bed closest to the door, and when she catches sight of me, her whole face lights up. "Jenny-yah!"

I walk over and take her hands. Earlier, Mom called and said she wasn't coming until later today, but that I should go ahead and visit by myself. I've never been alone with my grandmother, and at first I think it'll be awkward, but her warm smile melts my worries away.

She leans in and says, not quietly, "Is he your boyfriend?"

"Halmeoni!" I gasp. "I've only been in Korea for a week."

She giggles. "When I was your age, boys were constantly bringing me presents and telling me they liked me."

Jaewoo laughs. "It's still happening, Halmeoni." He leans over to hand her the flowers.

"Eomeona!" she shouts. The other elderly patients, who've obviously been eavesdropping, all chuckle appreciatively.

Jaewoo and I pull up chairs beside Halmeoni's bed, and she asks us how the first week of school has gone—great!—and then asks me if I've made any friends. She pats Jaewoo's hand. "Besides Jaewoo-ssi, that is."

I tell her about Gi Taek and Angela. I almost tell her about Nathaniel, but it seems a little awkward with Jaewoo sitting right beside me. I *have* been putting distance between Nathaniel and me, but it's hard without telling him *why*, though I think he's starting to notice.

"What about your roommate?" she asks.

"She's . . ." I hesitate. "She's considerate of my space." I feel like that's a diplomatic way of saying we're not friends.

Halmeoni clicks her tongue. "You should try to be friends with her, if she'll let you. A good roommate can be a friend for life."

All the other grandmothers in their beds concur loudly.

After chatting, Halmeoni asks Jaewoo to turn on the TV. He obeys, picking up the remote and switching to the channel she requests. It's a taping of *Cooky's Cooking Show* with a few special guests, including Oh Sun from XOXO. The show plays a clip of "Don't Look Back" during Sun's introduction, but Halmeoni and her friends don't seem to make any connections between the boy in the room and the one on the screen, nor do they care. They're more interested in the veteran actress who's also a guest.

After the show, Halmeoni gives Jaewoo and me a tour of the clinic's facilities, including the cafeteria and exercise room. As we walk, she holds onto my arm for support, her small bird-like bones so weak and fragile. I feel such a rush of love for her. Which is odd, since I don't think we've spent more than twenty-four hours together in my whole life.

The final stop on the tour is the recreation room. I realize Halmeoni must have notified the staff of my intention to play for her because chairs have been set up facing a small platform against the far wall. Most of the seats are occupied by patients, including Halmeoni's three roommates.

"I'll get your cello from the room," Jaewoo says. By the time he returns, all the seats have been filled. Even some of the staff have decided to take a break from work to listen.

I feel *nervous*, which is out of character for me. I've played for much bigger crowds than this; I've played for much more *prestigious* crowds than this, for people whose judgment would determine if I would receive a ribbon or a medal.

But I've rarely played for anyone who *I* care about, whose opinion matters to *me*. "You'll do great," Jaewoo says confidently as he hands my cello over, and my heart warms in response. In the front row, Halmeoni is bragging loudly that

I'm her sonnyeo, her granddaughter, and I feel her pride in me wash away the last of my nerves.

I glance toward the door, imagining my mom walking through. I'd brought my cello today not only to play for Halmeoni, but because I thought she might be here too. I'm a little disappointed that she isn't, but that's a small thing compared to the excitement I feel to perform for Halmeoni and all her friends. And Jaewoo.

I remove my cello from its traveling case. Slowly, I go through my normal routine, placing my cello between my knees, stretching my hands and tuning the strings. I bow the G note, letting out its full sound, and a few of the halmeoni and harabeoji clap excitedly.

There's no music stand, which means I'll have to play something by memory. I take out my folder and flip through the sheet music, looking for inspiration. I'd play the piece I'm working on for my solo performance class, except I've only memorized the first movement. A few of the other pieces could work, but something about them doesn't feel *right*.

I don't want to play anything too long. A few patients in the back row are already falling asleep. And I also don't want to play anything that might bore them. Classical music isn't for everyone.

My fingers brush against the last piece in my folder. Slowly I pull it out. It's the sheet music for Saint-Saëns's "Le Cygne," or "The Swan," a beautiful piece composed as a cello solo. It was originally included in my portfolio for music schools, but I'd taken it out after the results from the competition in November.

While Jenny is a talented cellist, proficient in all the technical elements of music, she lacks the spark that would take her from perfectly trained to extraordinary.

It seems so long ago that I'd complained to Uncle Jay about my results and he'd told me to "live a little," the night I'd met Jaewoo. I look up across the sea of expectant faces to where he stands at the back of the room. I wonder if part of the reason I'm so drawn to him is because of the way he made me feel that night, like I was chasing the spark that lit between us.

It seems almost like a challenge, to the judges, and to myself, to play the piece *now*, for no other reason than because I want to.

I pick up the sheet music and read over it quickly. I haven't played "Le Cygne" since that day, but I have confidence that I'll remember the notes. It's a short piece, and I'd played it over and over again for months leading up to the competition. Just in case, I lay the pages out on the ground at my feet.

"Do you want me to hold it up for you?" a harabeoji asks, sitting in the front row.

"No, but thank you," I say politely.

I take a deep breath, centering myself. I try not to concentrate on the sounds in the audience, the creak of chairs as people get comfortable, a cough.

I look to my grandmother, whose hands are clasped together, and then at Jaewoo, who gives me a single nod.

I close my eyes and begin the song.

The music is beautiful, elegant, slow, and powerful. As I play, my breathing seems to follow the melody, rising and falling, and rising again. It's as if I replay the emotions of the week in the ebb and flow of the song, the excitement of being in Seoul, of making new friends, of getting to know my grandmother, the distance between my mother and me, the what-ifs about my future and music school, everything that Jaewoo makes me feel: anticipation, frustration, joy, and something else, something more.

I've never felt more connected to a song than in this moment.

When I finish, holding out the final note, the whole room is silent. Then it bursts into enthusiastic applause. A few of the patients give a standing ovation. I feel triumphant. That was undoubtedly my best performance of "Le Cygne," perhaps my best performance ever.

My grandmother is clapping in the front row, tears in her eyes. I bow, smiling widely at the crowd, and then my eyes eagerly search for Jaewoo at the back of the room.

When he's not in the spot where I last saw him, against the wall, I start looking for him in the audience. But none of the beaming, happy faces belong to him.

The joy inside me begins to dissipate, until I feel an awful tightening in my chest.

He's gone.

Nineteen

I should have dropped dance when I had the chance. At this rate, I'm going to fail a class, and it doesn't matter how amazing my portfolio is or how well my audition goes, I'll never get into a top music school with a failing grade.

"You weren't kidding about your lack of dance skills," Nathaniel says after the third time I've stepped on his foot in a half hour. At the start of class, Ms. Dan told us to all grab partners, and before I could ask someone else, Nathaniel had practically tackled me. "Honestly, I think you're doing the world a service by playing cello," Nathaniel muses. "At least you have to sit for it."

Outside, thunder rumbles in the distance, storm clouds rolling in from the west. We're due for a downpour. Hopefully tonight, when I'm back in the dorms.

"Jaewoo-seonbae!"

As if pulled by a string, my head snaps in the direction of the voice. On the other side of the studio, a classmate approaches Jaewoo.

We've been avoiding each other all week, ever since he left my grandmother's clinic without saying goodbye. There's no excuse for why he left, and I'm not about to listen to any, even if he should pull me into a ceiling vent.

"You'll get it eventually, I'm sure," Nathaniel says. "Either that or fail."

I glare at Nathaniel. All day he's been snappy. What's put him in a mood?

"Thanks for the boost of confidence."

We spend the rest of the class working on the group project, devoting the last fifteen minutes to a section of the choreography where Nathaniel has to spin me around in a circle.

"Bae Jaewoo!"

I trip over my feet.

Nathaniel follows the direction of my gaze. "What do you keep looking at?"

"Nothing!" I attempt a change of subject, "You're from New York."

"This is true."

"What's it like?"

My grandparents on my dad's side only recently moved to New Jersey to live closer to my aunt, and I haven't yet had the chance to visit them.

I never really thought about New York other than it being the city where the Manhattan School of Music was located. But now that I'm in Seoul, where the city is so much a part of everyday life and culture, I'm curious what it's like.

"Think of Seoul," Nathaniel says. "Picture it in your head." I close my eyes, seeing the city in my mind, the constant movement, the cars, taxis, buses, and motorbikes in the streets, the huge buildings with bright signs in Hangeul and English, the hundreds of restaurants, cafés, shops, markets, the museums and palaces. It's like a symphony in my head.

"Are you picturing it?"

"Yes," I breathe.

"Now picture a thick layer of dirt over it all. That's New York."

I scowl.

After class, I quickly pack my bag and leave, wanting to avoid both boys in XOXO. I don't make it far.

"Jenny!" Nathaniel says, catching me in the stairwell. A few students cast us curious glances.

"What's up with you?" he asks, pressing his shoulder to the wall. "You've been ignoring me all week."

This conversation was bound to happen, and I owe Nathaniel an explanation.

"Yeah, I know." I sigh. "I'm sorry. It's just, you're . . ." I gesture at him, a movement meant to encompass the entirety of his being. "An idol."

"Yeah, I know," he repeats. "We've established that."

I lower my voice as a group of underclassmen pass us on the stairs, their eyes flitting from Nathaniel to me. "I just don't want any rumors to start."

"Who cares what people think?" he says.

"I care," I hiss. "I don't want you to get into trouble because of me."

Nathaniel just stares at me, as if I've grown a second head. "What?" I say, now feeling self-conscious.

"Is this really coming from you?" His eyes narrow. "Jaewoo said something, didn't he?" When I don't immediately answer, he curses. "I knew it! God, he thinks he knows what's best for everyone."

"He's just concerned for you," I say, though I don't know why I'm defending him. I'm just as annoyed with Jaewoo as him, if not more so.

An odd look appears in Nathaniel's eyes. "Jaewoo should worry about himself."

Like *that* doesn't sound foreboding.

"You hungry?" Nathaniel asks abruptly, dropping the subject. "I'm starved. Let's go get lunch."

The storm that had been brewing all morning has finally arrived, and Nathaniel and I have to sprint across the quad to avoid getting soaked. We still end up having to wring water out of our uniforms before entering the cafeteria. Gi Taek and Angela are speaking with their program directors today—they'd told me about it when I'd met them after visiting Halmeoni on Sunday—so it's just Nathaniel and me. The main dish on today's lunch set is spicy stir-fried pork, one of my favorites. After claiming our trays, we head for our usual table, only to find it occupied.

"Let's go to the student center," I say. Because of the storm, the cafeteria is more crowded than usual.

"No, wait. I see two empty seats." Nathaniel wades into the sea of students. I follow at a close distance, trying to keep my tray from knocking into anyone.

Reaching his destination, Nathaniel plops his tray onto the table next to . . .

Jaewoo.

Sori's seated across from him.

"Sit down, Jenny," Nathaniel says, either oblivious of the awkwardness or pointedly ignoring it, maybe even enjoying it. Most likely the latter. "I think it's about time we all sit down for a chat."

Sori makes to leave. "I should go."

"Don't run for my sake," Nathaniel says.

She remains seated.

I feel as if I've stepped into a scene from a K-drama. The main characters are Jaewoo, the stalwart class president, and Sori, the chaebol daughter of a huge entertainment company, which I guess would make Nathaniel and I the disreputable American secondary characters, there to disturb the otherwise idyllic life of the leads.

"Jenny?" All three of them are looking at me expectantly.

"Oh, sorry." I take the seat next to Sori.

"You two are roommates, aren't you?" Nathaniel asks.

I glance at Sori but she doesn't look like she's going to answer, shuffling the food around on her plate with her chopsticks. "Yes," I say.

"Well, that's surprising."

When he doesn't elaborate, I sigh. "Why is that surprising?"

"Oh, that Sori's parents allowed her to have a roommate, seeing as how they have complete control over her life."

Damn, Nathaniel! I give him a wide-eyed look. *Stop!*

He gives me a shrug. *What?*

Out of the corner of my eye, I see Jaewoo watching us.

"I just mean," Nathaniel acquiesces, flicking his gaze at Sori, "they're so protective of you. As they should be. You're their precious daughter."

"What about you two?" I say, trying to take the heat off Sori. "You live together, right?"

Nathaniel switches his gaze from Sori to me. "Yeah, we live in a dorm down the street from Joah. But we're moving soon to a bigger place. When we're all settled, you should come over."

I wave him off. "I'm sure you'd have to ask your other roommates."

"Oh, Youngmin won't mind. And Sun is hardly there. I don't know about Jaewoo though." He turns to his bandmate, all innocence. "How about it, Jaewoo? You want Jenny to come over?"

Something is definitely going on here. Nathaniel must know *something* about Jaewoo and me. But how? I doubt Jaewoo told him, not when he kept it from Youngmin.

"We're not allowed to have girls at the dorm," Jaewoo says coolly, though his eyes narrow a margin.

"Bae Jaewoo . . ." Nathaniel laughs without humor. "Always a rule-follower."

Jaewoo grits his teeth. "I follow rules so that others don't get hurt."

"Even when it's the rules that hurt the people you care about the most?"

Beside me, Sori's stopped even pretending to eat; her hand that holds her chopsticks is trembling.

"Sori," I say, "what you said before was a good idea. We should go."

She ignores me. "Jaewoo's right, Nathaniel. Rules are made for a reason, not just to protect our company, but also to protect our dreams, what we've been striving for our whole lives! You wouldn't understand. You're not like us."

"Why? Because I entered the game late? Because I wasn't brainwashed at a young age to believe that I had to give up everything for my family? Or is it because I'm Korean American? I just don't get it because I'm different, because I have—I don't know—a mind of my own?"

The cafeteria has gone silent. Everyone is watching, listening.

"Sori . . ." I tug at her sleeve. "Seriously, we should go."

"And *you*," she turns to me, and the venom in her voice actually makes me wince. "You think you're so great, waltzing in here, making friends, showing them off to me. When you were the one who intruded into *my* life, nosing into *my* business, reading *my mail*. Are you even here for music? You can't dance. I doubt you can sing. You don't belong here. You're nothing."

My heart feels as if it's dropped into my stomach. This is

what she's thought of me this whole time. I can hardly hear what's going on around me, a ringing in my ears.

"You're wrong, Sori-yah."

Everything within me goes still. Sori, wide-eyed, lifts her head. I turn slowly.

"You shouldn't say those things about Jenny," Jaewoo continues. "She's an incredible musician. She's also a devoted daughter and granddaughter. And a loyal friend. You would know all of this about her, if you gave her a chance."

I feel a wave of emotions sweep through me: shock, adrenaline, gratitude, and confusion. Why is he saying this *now*, after abandoning me the other day, after ignoring me all week?

How am I even supposed to react to this . . . defense of my character? We're not even supposed to *know* each other.

Sori stands up abruptly, the chair clanging to the floor behind her. Tears are streaming down her face. Without another word, she rushes from the cafeteria.

I hurry to follow, leaving behind a stunned crowd.

Twenty

"Sori!"

She hasn't gone far because of the storm. Standing outside the cafeteria doors beneath the overhang she looks out at the rain pouring down in long sheets that cascade diagonally across the quad. On the opposite side is the dorm, the lights twinkling blurrily through the rain. She seems like she's thinking of making a run for it.

"Sori!" I call out, pressing open the door. "I didn't know you felt that way. I'm sorry about the postcard, you don't know how sorry."

Wrapping her arms around her body, she turns to face me. The makeup around her eyes is smudged, possibly in an attempt to wipe away her tears.

"Why are you apologizing to me? I just said terrible things about you."

It's a valid question. It's not like I'd apologize to Jina. But I never thought Sori was cruel. Sure, she's been haughty and cold, but anything she's ever said about me, she's said straight to my face, which I can appreciate. Plus, I live with her; I know that when she's not studying or working out, she's watching K-dramas or reading smutty romance manhwa. Besides having a closet to die for, I know that her favorite genre of music is R&B and she has a plant by her bedside that she waters every night from her We Bare Bears water cup. It's endearing, how nerdy she is.

Why did she sign up for a room with a double if she could have had a single? I'd asked myself that question before, and I'm more confident than ever of the answer: she hoped for a friend.

"I'm apologizing to you because I did read your postcard that morning and that was shitty of me." Even if it was an accident, I should have put it back without looking at it. "But I won't apologize for the other stuff you accused me of. I respect that you feel that way, but I can't in good faith apologize for it . . ." I pause. "Except maybe the dancing. Nobody should have to suffer through that."

She holds my gaze for a few seconds longer, then looks away, shaking her head. "You're weird."

I scoff. "Please. I'm not the one who rolls her face with a rock every night to get a V-line jaw."

She gasps, placing a hand dramatically to her chin. "Way to judge me." But there's a small smile on her face, and I know we've crossed a bridge.

"Sori!" The door to the lunchroom bangs open and Nathaniel rushes out.

The smile on Sori's face drops and I shoot Nathaniel a look of resentment.

He doesn't notice, his entire being focused on Sori. "That went too far. Forgive me."

She takes a step backward, the rain pouring onto her shoulder.

"Wait," he says. "You'll catch a cold." He takes a step back. "I promise I won't chase you. Just don't . . . run."

"Stop it!" She places her hands to her ears, as if to block him out. "Just stop it!"

"Sori-yah."

"Stop taking care of me! Stop making me miss you. It hurts. It hurts so much, Nathaniel."

"It wasn't my decision to break up," he says quietly. "You know that."

"I—I can't do this."

She turns, disappearing into the rain.

Nathaniel kicks the door. "Dammit."

As promised, he doesn't chase her.

I wonder what it says about me that between the two of them, I'm more upset with Nathaniel than Sori even though Nathaniel and I have been friends for longer.

"I know you're having a moment," I tell him, "but you totally interrupted *my* moment with Sori."

He sweeps a hand through his hair. "I feel like I have whiplash. That was rough in there."

"Um," I say. "No thanks to *you*. Why were you acting like that, anyway? Like, besides negging Sori, what was up with you and Jaewoo? Aren't you two friends?"

Nathaniel grimaces. "Promise not to get angry."

Which is a sure sign that I will get angry. "No."

He sighs. "I was in the van in LA."

I frown, unsure what he's talking about. "Like . . . back in November?"

He nods slowly.

"So . . . what," I ask, "you . . . saw me that night?" If he saw me, then he's known who I was this *entire* time. Which means . . . "Did you recognize me in the uniform store?"

"I did."

Some of his odd behavior falls into place: how he was curious about whether I've always lived in LA, if I'd seen the entirety of the music video for "Don't Look Back," because if I'd seen it from the beginning, then I should have recognized Jaewoo.

"Was Youngmin in the van?" I ask.

He shakes his head. "No, I was alone in the back. Our manager was driving. He didn't see you. I only got a glimpse of your profile, and even then, I wouldn't have recognized you if it wasn't for the picture."

The picture of Jaewoo and me. The one we took in the photo booth.

"He showed it to you?" I ask, incredulous.

"I saw it over his shoulder at the airport."

I take slow, deep breaths. This is a lot to take in.

"Why?"

I feel like that single word encapsulates all the questions I

160

have. Why didn't you say anything? Why did you pretend like you didn't know who I was? Was any of our friendship even real?

Nathaniel sighs. "In order to answer that, I have to start from the beginning. I've known Jaewoo since I joined the company almost four years ago. In all that time, he's never broken a rule. He always shows up on time. He does everything the company asks of him. I don't know if you know this, but he became an idol because of his family, in order to support them financially. Everything he does is for them. And for us. When XOXO became a group, we became a part of his family."

Nathaniel's story mirrors what Jaewoo said the night we met about being overwhelmed by a feeling of responsibility.

"That day in LA," Nathaniel says, "he broke his arm at the music video shoot. And then he just . . . disappeared. We drove around the city for hours. We were so worried. I thought maybe he reached his limit. . . . But then, around midnight, his phone came back on. We were already in K-town, so it was only a matter of minutes before we tracked him to that street."

"I remember," I say. "You showed up so quickly."

He nods. "I was curious about who you were. At the airport, I asked him about you, but he refused to say anything. And honestly"—Nathaniel shakes his head—"I was hurt. I thought he trusted me. Then all that stuff happened with Sori and I forgot about it. I was in a bad place. He was there for me through it all; they all were."

I'm glad that even though Nathaniel and Jaewoo face

difficulties as idols, they have each other, and the rest of the members of XOXO.

"So, yeah, I did approach you in the uniform store because of Jaewoo but I stuck around because of you. And I *am* sorry. For not telling you sooner."

"It's fine—"

"It just frustrates me to no end that Jaewoo has something that he wants and he won't *do* anything about it."

My heart hitches at the implication that Nathaniel thinks Jaewoo wants *me*. "Is that why you went off on him just now?" I ask.

"That and because I was pissed off that he told you to stay away from me. Like I get that he has more at stake . . . but don't take it out on me, you know?"

He has more at stake. Not just with his image and the group's success, but his family's well-being as well. It must be overwhelming, that kind of responsibility—enough that he'd tried to run away from it back in LA.

I'd always known our lives were different, but it hadn't really hit me until now to what extent.

The rain, which had been pouring not a few minutes ago, is now a shimmer in the air.

"I should go back in there," Nathaniel says with a sigh. "Help Jaewoo clean up the mess I made."

I follow the direction of his gaze. "What do you think he's saying?"

"I'm not sure, but he'll think up something. He's good at

getting people to see things his way."

I wonder if this statement applies to me. Maybe it does, because I agreed to keep our friendship a secret. But also maybe it doesn't, because I don't think I can do it much longer.

We part ways: him to help Jaewoo, me to find Sori. Halfway across the quad, I close my eyes and lift my face to the rain.

Twenty-one

I find Sori laid out on her bed in our dorm room, uniform still on. Her hair is covering her face, which I'm starting to suspect is her anxiety coping mechanism. Except with the rain, her hair's a little wet and she looks like an Asian water ghost. I'm proud of myself for not pointing this out to her.

"Do you . . . want to talk about what just happened?" I ask, slipping off my shoes.

"Not really," she mumbles.

I wonder if we're going to go back to the way we were before. Strangers living together.

Then she abruptly sits up. She whips her hair back, and it's like she's instantly transformed from a ghost to a mermaid, her smeared mascara only enhancing the beautiful shape of her eyes. "I'm sorry," she says.

"For . . . ?"

"You apologized, but I never did. I'm sorry for what I said about you, especially for what I said about your musical ability.

As a musician myself, that was uncalled for." Reaching out, she grabs her We Bare Bears cup from her nightstand and takes a sip.

"Is that cup for kids?"

"What do you mean?" She still has the cup to her mouth as she speaks.

"Like, was it made for little kids to use?"

"No. It's for all ages."

"Oh, sorry. I got distracted. I mean, it's fine."

"No, it's not fine. We're roommates and I have no idea, like, what you *do* even."

"I could show you," I say.

The dorms discourage playing instruments in our rooms since the walls aren't soundproof, so I grab my phone.

Sori pats her bed, indicating for me to sit next to her. I scurry over and plop down.

"Oh my God, is this Egyptian cotton?"

"Focus, Jenny."

I open up the last video saved on my phone, one my grandmother sent me. Apparently one of the nurses in the clinic recorded my performance of "Le Cygne"

I hold my breath as Sori watches, her expression giving nothing of her thoughts away. I didn't think I could be so nervous watching her watch a video of me.

When it ends, she hands me back my phone. "Jaewoo was right. You're incredible."

I'm *blushing*.

"I've heard that piece before," she says. "There's a famous ballet choreographed to the music."

"You know ballet?"

"I study it along with other dance forms, like contemporary and hip-hop."

"So you want to be a dancer?"

She slides me *a look*, like I've said something foolish. "I want to be an idol. For that, I need to know how to dance, sing, and have a personality."

"You definitely have two out of three." She narrows her eyes, and I say, "Kidding, kidding."

"Is this what I've been missing out on all this time?" But she says it with a curve to her lips, so that I know she's okay with my teasing. "But let's talk about *your* dancing. I don't think you're going to pass the class, at the rate you're going."

"I *know*," I groan. "I'm a cellist. We're a sedentary breed."

"You just need a little practice." She bites her lip, watching me. Then says, "Later tonight, do you want to get out of here?"

I frown. "Won't the facilities be closed?"

"You're talking to the daughter of the CEO of Joah Entertainment. My mother owns thirty percent of the shares for this school."

"What are you saying? I'm just a peon. You need to speak my language."

"I have a key."

* * *

It's less that she has a key and more that she knows the code to the electronic lock on the door. Entering the dance studio, we drop our bags to the floor. Before leaving the dorms around ten, we changed into workout clothes and packed two tote bags full of snacks because, as Sori ominously predicts, "we're going to need fuel."

She switches on only one of the lights. Luckily this studio faces the back of the school, not the quad, making it less likely a security guard might notice our presence.

"Is this where you go in the mornings?" I ask, taking a seat on the floor and spreading my legs out to stretch.

"Yeah, I practice here for an hour, then go to the gym before washing up before class."

That all sounds awful to me, but impressive.

After stretching, she brings her phone over to the wall, hooking it up to the sound system. "Let's go through the whole choreography."

Sori's clearly a skilled dancer because I only have to do the whole thing once for her to figure out the steps. She then proceeds to demonstrate how it's supposed to be done, and it's a wonder to watch her, especially during the more powerful parts, like when she's krumping.

"Concentrate!" she yells, catching me gaping at her in the mirror.

After an hour, I'm sweating from all my pores and ready to pull every single strand of hair off my head. "I suck at this."

"Stop being so hard on yourself," she says, raising her water bottle to her mouth. "Your body has to memorize the steps before it will actually look good to others. You're trying too hard to learn it all at once. Isolate the movements. Don't tell me you were a master at cello when you first started."

"I wasn't awful," I mumble to myself.

"No one is judging you here," she says, ignoring me. "Just remember that I heard you play the cello. I acknowledge you're amazing at it. But this is my specialty, and I'm trying to help you."

I stare at her. Like really look at her. "You're good at this."

Now it's her turn to blush. "I like . . . helping people. I had this dream, when I first started high school. . . . I wanted to be called 'seonbae.'" She must see that I don't know the term because she explains, "'Seonbae' is what underclassmen use to address upperclassmen. I wanted one of the younger students to call out to me Sori-seonbae and ask for my help." She curls her hair around her finger. "Embarrassing, right?"

I have this sudden urge to hug her. She's *adorable*. Of course Nathaniel couldn't help falling for her.

"That's so . . . pure," I gush.

She laughs, and then says, seriously, "From the top?"

By the time midnight rolls around, I'm actually kind of getting the hang of the choreography. It's like my body has gone through the movements so many times that I don't have to think about what comes next. After I finally nail a tricky bit of footwork, Sori calls for another break and we bust out the snacks. Vitamin water and crunchy rice bars for Sori, shrimp crackers and Gatorade for me.

After eating, we lay down on our backs in the middle of the studio, look up at the ceiling, and just talk. I tell her about my life growing up in LA with my mom and dad, about how they both worked food service jobs while my mom went through law school. Then how a few years after the karaoke bar opened, he got the diagnosis. I skip over the hard years, when he was in the hospital, and fast forward to my plans for the future—college in New York City, complete independence.

Sori tells me about her life growing up in the affluential neighborhood of Apgujeong, how she's an only child too. That besides her mother being the CEO of Joah, her father is a politician, which meant that a lot of her friends were either children of chaebol families or kids from school whose parents forced them to befriend her.

How a couple of years back her father had had a highly publicized affair, which resulted in her so-called friends turning their backs on her. It was an awful, exhausting time, and the person who was there for her, who was her rock through it all, was Nathaniel.

She smiles as she recounts her impression of him at their first meeting, both thirteen years old. She thought he was a punk and a troublemaker. For years they teased and tried to one-up each other.

"You know," she says, "how sometimes in middle school a boy will be mean to the person he likes?"

"Wow, Nathaniel," I drawl. "Totally not cool."

"I know, right?" She laughs though her voice has a sad quality to it.

"Do you *want* to get back together again?"

She's quiet for a long time, I'm not sure if she'll answer. Finally, she says, "I want to be an idol. It's my *dream*, Jenny."

"O-kay, but you can still be an idol and date Nathaniel, can't you? Or is it your mom?"

"It's not *just* my mother or the company. It's more than that."

"What reasons are there besides that?"

She turns on her side to look at me. "You really don't know?"

"No," I say, "but I want to."

For her. For Nathaniel. For Gi Taek and Angela, who share the same dream.

For Jaewoo.

"It's a great honor to be an idol. You've achieved a dream that so many people want as well. But that's only the beginning. You have to work hard to release good music, maintain your image and brand, perform well, win awards, top charts, hold fan signings, go on variety shows, support your group members' solo activities, have your own solo activities . . ." She stops, catching her breath. "When you add another person into the mix, some people think it takes away from all of that. Like you have a person who is more important than all those other things, a part of your life you're not sharing, when, as an idol, you agreed to share your whole life with your fans, so that they can love you without fear that you'll disappoint or hurt them."

She sighs. "At least, that's how I've always thought of it, and it's the reason I can most understand. I want to make people smile. I want to warm their hearts. And if dating makes people worry or feel like I'm not trying hard enough, then I . . . won't."

I try to understand what she's saying; it's so out of the realm of anything I've ever had to worry about. "I don't think being in a relationship takes away from all your hard work. You can't aim to please everyone, you can only aim to please yourself."

She offers me a bemused smile. "That's very American of you to think that way. Nathaniel's like that too. Screw everyone else. Live your best life."

"I mean . . . not exactly *that*. More like, you need to be strong for yourself first, be healthy and happy for yourself first, before you can be strong and give happiness to others. The healthier and happier you are, the more you can give to your fans, right? They should want that for you."

She rests her head on her hands, nodding slowly.

"Plus, come on, don't you think after falling in love, you'll just have that many more love songs to write?"

She laughs. "We're jumping ahead of ourselves. I don't *have* any fans, Jenny!"

"That's not true. You have me."

"I know we just recently went from roommates to friends," she says shyly, "but can I hug you?

"Um, yes!" I reach out and take her into an Uncle Jay–like hug, slightly suffocating.

"You're sweaty!" She giggles.

"You are too!" I push her away and she laughs, placing her hands over her face.

It's one o'clock in the morning. We sprawl on our backs again. Neither of us speaks for a while, and I think Sori's half asleep when she rolls to her side and murmurs, "If cellists have fan clubs, Jenny, I want to join yours."

Twenty-two

On Sunday, I visit Halmeoni in the clinic and we watch a weekend drama with her roommates on the TV in the room. It's already on episode seventy-eight of what my halmeoni tells me is a one-hundred-episode drama.

From what I gather from the other halmeoni and the drama itself, the story follows a young woman who, as a child, was lost at sea during a boating accident, only to be adopted by a fisherman. Turns out, she's the actual daughter of a billionaire and heiress of a huge conglomerate in Seoul. But her identity was stolen by a woman who witnessed the accident and instated her own daughter in the young woman's place, so *she* grew up the heiress. Meanwhile, the young woman is torn between the love of two men, a boy from her village who raised himself from nothing to become a fishing tycoon and the son of another chaebol family who was betrothed to her from birth. Also possibly her mother was murdered, and she might have a terminal illness?

After the episode is over, I pull out the food I'd bought from the bakery, a loaf of sourdough bread, thick, creamy butter, and blackberry jam.

"You're so lucky, Eonni," Halmeoni's neighbor in the bed to her right says, "to have such a caring granddaughter."

Her neighbor in the bed across the room shakes her head, clicking her tongue disapprovingly. "If only your daughter showed you as much affection."

"No bad words about my Soojung," Halmeoni chides her friend. "I'm proud of her and how hard she works."

Mom was supposed to join Halmeoni and me today, but she's been busy with a new case that her colleague back in the States forwarded to her, an immigration dispute concerning North Korea. Mom couldn't resist, and I can't exactly be upset she's not here. She's doing important work and I'm proud of her.

But it does suck not spending more time with her, like I thought I would. Still, she'll come to the showcase at the end of the semester, where, hopefully, I'll have a solo.

"You remind me so much of Soojung," Halmeoni says. "She was always so independent. So sure of what she wanted in life. She knew as the daughter of a fish stall worker, the odds were stacked against her success, so she studied hard, worked part-time to earn money to pay for English classes, and finally got a scholarship to attend college in America, where she met your father and had you." Halmeoni smiles, but there's a sadness to her eyes. She's always so cheerful that it catches me by surprise.

"I know she's always been resentful that I sent her away . . ."

This must be the reason for Halmeoni and Mom's strained relationship. But I think Halmeoni's being too hard on herself. It's Mom's fault if she can't see that *her* mother was only trying to give her the best life, by not holding her back.

"She's like that heroine in the drama," I say to make Halmeoni laugh. "At least the fish part."

When she does laugh, I feel warm and fuzzy inside. I spend several more hours with her, though after seeing that flash of sadness, I can't unsee it.

I *know* she loves me and is happy to spend time with me. But I can tell with her longing glances at the door, that she wishes her daughter were here.

And the thing is, I don't blame her, because I do too.

It's late afternoon by the time I leave, feeling emotionally exhausted. Out in the quad, I stand in the middle of the lawn, lifting my face to the sun as if I can absorb its energy.

As I turn around I see a man wearing a bucket hat and sunglasses is loitering beneath the trees. I wouldn't normally take notice except that he's carrying a large camera bag.

After the broom closet incident, when Youngmin came to find Jaewoo because there was a man who was stalking him, I'd looked up the photographer credited on the photos of Nathaniel and Sori. I'm not positive this is the man who took the pictures, but just in case, I need to warn Jaewoo. It's later than the time I ran into him last week when he was here for therapy, but I want to make certain.

I watch the man out of the corner of my eye until he passes, then whirl around. I quickly pull up a map of the Camellia Health Village on my phone, finding a building nearby that sounds promising: Camellia Counseling. I make my way over, keeping a brisk but even walk. Should the man look over and catch sight of me, there's no reason for him to take notice. I'm not wearing my Seoul Arts uniform, just my favorite faux leather jacket and my Dodgers cap.

I reach the building of Camellia Counseling and the doors slide open soundlessly at my approach.

Inside, the setup for the building mirrors my grandmother's clinic, with a waiting area and a receptionist desk. The interior walls are painted in calm, light-blue colors, and there's a small indoor waterfall.

The woman at the desk smiles serenely at me, which is at odds with the adrenaline coursing through my body. What do I even say to her? *Is Bae Jaewoo a patient here?* She'll think I'm a stalker and have me booted from the premises, which will only draw unnecessary attention.

"Jenny?"

"Jaewoo!" I grab his arm and drag him behind a wall, away from the windows.

I'm momentarily distracted because he's wearing a black sweater cut low around his neckline, showing his collarbones.

"What are you doing here?" he asks.

Focus, Jenny. I look up at his face. "I'm here to warn you."

He raises a single eyebrow.

"Okay, that was a little dramatic. But in my defense, I just spent the morning watching this wild makjang K-drama with my grandma." I take a deep breath. "There's a man with a camera outside. I think he's that paparazzi ajeossi you were telling me about before."

A scowl descends across his handsome features. "Wait here." Pressing his back to the wall, he glances around the corner. He only looks for a brief second before he returns, grabbing my hand. "It's him, all right," he says. "We'll avoid him by going out the emergency exit."

Jaewoo's grip on my hand is tight as he leads me down one hall, then another. Technically there's no reason for me to go with him—the paparazzi ajeossi isn't after me—but Jaewoo doesn't let go. And after the day I had, I don't want to let go either.

A black van is waiting across the street from the back exit, idling by the curb. Jaewoo releases my hand only to slide the van door open, gesturing for me to climb in first. I take the seat by the far window and Jaewoo jumps in after, sliding the door closed. He hits the roof of the car. "Let's go, Hyeong."

That's when I notice that XOXO's manager is in the driver's seat. I recognize him from the uniform store. He doesn't question Jaewoo—a quick getaway must be a common enough occurrence—switching the gear shift and accelerating from zero to sixty kilometers in a matter of seconds.

He slows down after driving a couple of blocks, checking his side mirrors to ensure no one is following us. He then looks up, studying me through the rearview mirror. "Who . . . ?"

"She's a classmate of Nathaniel's and mine," Jaewoo explains. "We were being trailed by that reporter who works for *Bulletin*."

He must not have seen Jaewoo holding my hand because he doesn't comment on it. Either that or he's used to keeping the boys of XOXO's secrets.

"Where are you going, Jenny?" Jaewoo asks me. "Can we drop you off somewhere?"

"We're running late as it is," XOXO's manager says.

"It's fine," I say. "I can take a cab from wherever you're going."

Jaewoo doesn't press the issue.

XOXO's manager, Nam Ji Seok, whose name I remember now from when Jaewoo told me, flicks on the turn signal, maneuvering the van onto a ramp that'll take us over a bridge across the Han River. I know from Gi Taek that a good manager is someone who fulfills many roles in an idol's life besides organizing their activities—bodyguard, driver, confidante, friend.

I wonder if Jaewoo has even told him about *us*. Though, what is there to tell?

Last time I saw him, he defended my character in front of Sori and Nathaniel and an entire lunchroom. But before that, he'd walked out on me as I gave one of the best performances of my life, without an explanation.

I *want* to be his friend. Ever since that night in LA, there's been a connection between us. A spark. But I feel like my heart is constantly being pushed and pulled. I'm only here in Korea for five months—four now—do I really want to wait for him to make up his mind about me?

I'm tired of waiting.

"Jenny?" I must have been staring into space because when I focus on Jaewoo, he's studying me. "Is everything all right?"

"Yeah, I was just . . . making my mind up about something." He frowns.

The navigation on the GPS pings and a woman politely tell us in Korean that we'll be arriving at our destination shortly.

XOXO's manager turns from a main road. Up ahead is a large building, the letters EBC, for Entertainment Broadcasting Center, in blue at the top.

As we approach, Nam Ji Seok slows the car. Outside the station, a huge crowd of people is gathered, even more than were in front of the uniform store. Most of the people are young, middle- and high-school students, wearing masks over their mouths, presumably to conceal their faces in case they're caught on television skipping cram school to follow idols around.

"We'll have to go around back," Jaewoo says.

"There's not enough time," Ji Seok responds.

A van pulls ahead of us, parking in front of the building, and the crowd immediately swarms it.

"This is our chance!" XOXO's manager jerks the van forward. "You'll have to come inside with us," he tells me. "I can't risk leaving you alone in the van. Here, wear this." He throws me a cloth face mask. I put it on, hooking the straps around my ears. I'm already wearing my Dodgers cap, so I lower it over my eyes. "You can pass for a backup dancer or a stylist. Just keep your head down. Ready?"

Everything happens so fast. He pulls up in front of the building, behind the other van. The doors must have an automatic open feature because they open on both sides. Jaewoo hops out of one side, Ji Seok and I hop out of the other.

"Jaewoo-oppa!" someone screams.

The ground beneath our feet begins to rumble. I look over to see a rush of people coming at us, like an oncoming tidal wave.

Then Ji Seok grabs my arm and we sprint past the crowd and through the doors of the broadcasting station, the security guards quickly closing them behind us.

I put my hands on my knees to catch my breath, then take a look at my surroundings.

It's markedly quiet after the tumult of the crowd.

The group that entered before us lingers, talking among themselves. They must be another boy group, like XOXO. Unlike Jaewoo, they're already dressed in their stage outfits, lots of red and black leather and tight pants.

"Hurry up," Ji Seok says, calling us over to an unmarked door in the lobby.

"I should go," I say when Jaewoo starts to follow. At my voice, he turns to look at me. "I can just slip out the back."

"There are too many people outside," Jaewoo says, a frown edging his lips.

"It's fine," I say. "I'm used to disappearing into crowds." Wow, that sounds dramatic. "I mean, I'm used to crowds. Like in general." I take a step back. "I'll just . . . see myself out."

As I turn, Jaewoo grabs my wrist.

Across the lobby, the boys in the other group have all quieted, staring.

"What are you *doing*?" I hiss.

"I'll worry if you go out there," he says.

I gape at him. There's a reckless, stubborn look in his eye.

"Jenny, Jaewoo!" Ji Seok barks and I jump, eyes wide. He points a finger at me. "You can leave once the show starts and the crowd's dispersed. Now, come on!"

We hurry forward, Jaewoo dropping my wrist.

Past the unmarked door is a hallway crowded with idols, backup dancers, stylists, makeup artists, managers, production assistants, and a ton of other people whose purpose I'm unclear on, but who look stressed out enough to belong here. As we pass by different idol groups, they either bow to Jaewoo or vice versa. I know from Gi Taek's K-pop lesson 101 that there's a hierarchy between idols depending on who debuted first, and I follow Jaewoo's lead, bowing like I'm part of his entourage.

Ji Seok leads us to a dressing room with a sign on the door that reads: XOXO. He opens the door without knocking. Inside, Youngmin swivels on a chair in front of a mounted wall TV, while Nathaniel is playing with a baseball, throwing it in the air and catching it, and Sun is reading a book. All three look up at our entrance.

"Jenny-nuna!" Youngmin says, jumping out of his chair. "What are you doing here? Have you come to watch us perform?"

Nathaniel grins, standing. "Oh, who's this? Have you brought us a new backup dancer?"

"Har, har, very funny," I say.

Sun closes his book with a snap.

"Why are none of you dressed?" Ji Seok groans, exacerbated. "Or at least in makeup?"

"We were waiting for—" Nathaniel begins. Behind us the door bursts open and men and women carrying piles of clothing, accessories, and makeup kits rush in. Suddenly it's chaos, Youngmin getting cornered by a stylist, a makeup artist chasing Nathaniel down, and Sun consulting calmly with a hairstylist. As for Jaewoo . . . our gazes meet. He makes a move toward me, but suddenly Ji Seok's between us, pushing me out of the room.

"The boys need to get ready," he tells me. "You can wait over here." He starts shuffling me down the hall to a door that opens backstage. Loud music fills my ears, the floor seeming to thrum with it. "You can watch the performance from the wings. It's the best seat in the house." His phone then lights up and he scurries away, leaving me alone backstage during the middle of a full-blown K-pop show.

I watch through a monitor as an idol girl group dances in perfect synchronization, their voices smooth and dulcet. The camera pans to the audience. Someone must have let in the crowd that was waiting outside because the studio is packed. Dozens of boys, mostly, shout-sing along with the lyrics, holding up signs and soaking in the excitement of the performance.

After the girl group's performance ends, the show goes to a commercial break. Several security guards rush into the crowd, ushering out the people standing in the front and letting in new people. As I observe, I realize what's happening. Though the main audience seated in the stadium remains the same, the people standing in front of the stage changes depending on the idol group they support. The group entering the roped off area now have with them a banner with the words Kiss and Hug Club written across. All of them are gripping lightsticks shaped like either an X or an O, and a few hold signs with the members' names written on the front. Jaewoo. Sun. Youngmin. And Jihyuk, which I know is Nathaniel's Korean name.

There's a shift in the noise backstage and I look over to see the members of XOXO, Sun leading, and then Nathaniel and Youngmin.

They look incredible. Their stage outfits can only be described as post-apocalyptic chic, artfully ripped designer wear, their hair seemingly wind-tossed—well, not Sun. Sun's long hair is impeccably straight.

And then I see Jaewoo.

Somehow, in the span of a few minutes, he's transformed from a handsome high-school boy to an alarmingly attractive K-pop star.

He's in all black, a silky, ripped top and tight-fitting pants. His hairstylist has managed to give his dark tresses a sort of wet appearance, as if he's stepped in from the rain. His eyes, as they meet mine, seem darker than usual—or is it the makeup?

Sun walks by without acknowledging me, but Youngmin grins and waves, doing the heart sign with his fingers.

Nathaniel pauses to say, "Wish me luck."

And I answer, "Break a leg."

Then Jaewoo's in front of me.

"Will you stay?" he asks. "Until after the performance. There's something I want to talk to you about."

Before I can answer, he's being called onstage. I watch as he moves to the front of the formation.

Then the stage lights go on and the music begins.

Twenty-three

At the beginning of the song, the fans chant each member of XOXO's names. Oh Sun. Lee Jihyuk. Bae Jaewoo. Choi Youngmin. It sets the mood and the boys give a spectacular performance.

Afterward, the rest of the idols who performed earlier make their way to the stage. It's getting crowded where I am, so I go in search of a quiet area to view the show's awards ceremony. I wind up in XOXO's dressing room, after remembering the TV there. Sitting on Sun's couch, I pick up the baseball Nathaniel had been playing catch with earlier and click on the monitor. Two MCs with a bouquet of flowers and a crystal award walk over from where they'd been hosting the show from a separate area of the studio. They approach XOXO and the rest of the idols.

"Wow, what a great performance by XOXO!" the boy announcer says.

"Right, Seojun-ssi?" the girl concurs. "Maybe they'll have their first win this week!"

"We'll find out soon! It's time to tally up the votes."

On the monitor, a graphic appears showing the three idol groups in contention to win the award.

"Who will take first place this week?" the boy announcer says.

I stand up, holding the ball tight.

The numbers tallying up the votes begin to spin upward, presumably measuring how well the single performed on digital charts and social media, as well as album sales and real-time voting.

"And the winner is . . ." the girl says.

The numbers suddenly stop, with the highest number belonging to . . .

"XOXO!" The two MCs shout together and I scream, accidentally releasing the ball, which goes flying across the room and behind a rack of clothes.

As confetti cannons explode onto the stage, I head over to the rack, getting down on my hands and knees.

Still, I'm beaming. I'm so happy for them! What did the female MC say before? *This is their first win.* I can hear Sun accepting the award on behalf of XOXO, thanking their fans and families for supporting them.

The door to the dressing room opens. Voices flood in, drowning out Sun's on the television. I'm about to pop out from behind the rack like a ghoul when one of the voices says, "Did you see that girl with Jaewoo?"

"Nathaniel says she's a classmate of his," another voice answers. "From his high school."

I press my back against the wall and peek around the rack. Two of XOXO's stylists are in the room, cleaning up their stations.

"Tonight was the boys' first win. This is probably the most important time in their career. If they can keep the momentum going, they could be huge global stars. They can't afford another scandal. They almost didn't come back from that last one."

There's a brief silence, then the other murmurs in agreement.

"She could ruin everything."

Once the stylists pack up their things and leave, I'm quick to follow. Outside the station, the crowd from the audience is making their way to the subway. I join them, blending in. Reaching into my jacket pocket, I wrap my hand around the ball, which I totally stole from Nathaniel. I *will* give it back. Eventually. I just need something to hold onto right now.

I think I understand now why Jaewoo left that day after my cello performance. Because he realized that our lives are too different. Not just that he's an idol, though seeing him now perform on stage, hearing his name cried out by his fans, the circumstances of his life are so extraordinary as to seem unreal. But it is real, the success of his band and all the people whose livelihoods depend on them, as are the consequences. *She could ruin everything.*

Seeing the light of the subway exit up ahead, I hurry forward.

A hand grabs my shoulder, twisting me around.

I look up into Jaewoo's face.

He's wearing a ball cap that shadows his eyes, and a cloth mask over his nose and mouth.

The crowd parts around us, though a few throw curious glances in our direction. He takes my hand and we make our way out of the crowd, dropping it once we're clear.

Jaewoo must have a destination in mind because he walks without hesitation, leading me down an alley narrow enough that if I were to lift both arms, my fingers would skim the walls on either side. We climb a short flight of stairs, turn down a few more streets and alleys, and finally walk up such a long staircase that when I reach the top, I'm breathless.

We're in a small park that overlooks the city. It has a running trail, a few public-use exercise machines, and a children's play area with a set of swings.

"Want to . . . ?" Jaewoo asks, and I nod. We make our way over to the swings, each taking one of the single seats. We face the same direction, toward the ledge. Beyond the railing, Seoul spreads out for miles and miles, hundreds of thousands of bright lights, twinkling like stars.

I haven't been on a swing since I was in elementary school, so I kick off the ground, enjoying the rocking motion and the wind on my face. Jaewoo's legs are longer so he doesn't swing, leaning his head on the chain as he watches me. He's removed his face mask and taken off his ball cap, and though he's changed out of his performance clothes and washed the makeup from his face, he's so handsome, it's hard to look away.

I give one final pump of my legs and as I'm swinging forward, Nathaniel's baseball plops from out of my pocket onto the grassy floor.

Jaewoo leans down and picks it up. "Is this . . . ?"

I dig my feet into the ground, slowing my momentum. "Yes," I say, though now I'm blushing.

When Jaewoo says nothing, I look over to find him studying the ball, a contemplative look on his face.

"What?" I ask.

He shakes his head. Laughs. "This ball"—he tosses it up in the air, then catches it—"is the reason I broke my arm back in November."

I stop swinging altogether. "What?"

He grips the chain, grinning at my expression.

"It happened the last night of a long three-night shoot. We were filming in this warehouse, which we were warned had parts left unfinished, but we were feeling bored and stressed. During a break in the filming, Nathaniel and I decided to throw a baseball around. We were both in a little league, when we were younger."

"Oh my God, that's so cute," I interrupt. "Sorry, continue."

"So, yeah, we were passing it back and forth, having a great time. And then he threw it long, and I went for it. I felt the satisfaction of it hitting my glove just as I crashed into a plaster wall. The whole thing came down on top of me.

"The music video director was livid. He scolded us for an hour. He said that we weren't grateful, that we were a dime a dozen, that if we wanted to be successful we needed to take this seriously."

"I don't like that director," I declare. "I don't care how gorgeous the music video ended up being."

Jaewoo shakes his head, though there's a smile on his face. "We had to cut filming prematurely. Luckily we had an alternative ending, which was the one they eventually used. But still, I felt like such a disappointment. I broke my arm, and for what? A moment of fun. So after the shoot was over and we were at dinner, I excused myself from the table and just . . . left. I left the restaurant and walked and walked, until I saw the light of your uncle's karaoke bar."

He hesitates, and then says, softly, "I even saw you that night, laughing with your uncle as you sat on the barstool, your hair loose down your back."

I stare at him in shock, rearranging that night in my head. Not that it makes a difference on how the night eventually played out.

I press my foot against the ground, but I must push at a wrong angle because the swing rocks crookedly.

"Why did you leave, Jenny?" Jaewoo asks, and my heart stutters in my chest, even though I knew he would ask me eventually.

This is the end. Once we have this conversation, there's no reason to keep stubbornly holding fast to this connection between us. He needs to concentrate on what matters, his career.

And I need to get my act together and focus on what matters, my cello playing, the showcase, my future.

"For the same reason you left me the other day at the clinic," I say, and I'm proud of myself because my voice comes out steady. "Nathaniel more or less spelled it out." Jaewoo frowns. "It's because you have more at stake. I get it, really. Our lives are too different."

"Our lives *are* different," Jaewoo says, and my heart sinks, even though I literally prepared for this. "But that's not why I left."

My swing rattles, and I look up to see he's seized onto the chain of my seat, pulling me close. I have to grab onto his chain in order not to fall back.

"I do have more to lose than Nathaniel," he says, and the miserable feeling rises up. "After all, his heart's not at stake."

My breath catches. Is he saying what I think he's saying?

"I like you, Jenny," he confesses. "More than I've ever liked anyone before. It hit me that day at the clinic how much. And I did what I always do when I feel overwhelmed. I ran."

"And now?" I ask.

"I'm not running anymore."

With the hand that isn't holding my seat, he lifts my face to his and kisses me.

At first, it's a close-mouthed kiss, soft and sweet. But then he leans forward, and I feel my ball cap tip off my head as my lips part beneath his. I would collapse, weak-kneed, if I wasn't already sitting. He runs his hand through my hair, as I wrap one arm around his neck, holding him close.

I don't know how long we kiss in that park, with the city below us and the stars up above.

I don't know what this will mean for us going forward. Will we ever have a moment like this again? But none of that matters. I push it all to the back of my mind. Because tonight, the world is ours.

Twenty-four

The next day is Monday. I wake earlier than usual, rolling over in my bed to look across the room. Sori's already gone for her morning workout. She'd been asleep when I returned last night, otherwise I'd have asked her to wake me up. I'm not a huge fan of exercise any time before eight a.m., but I need an outlet for all the adrenaline coursing through my body. I hurry up and change into my uniform, waiting in the long line for the bathroom to wash and examine my face in the mirror. Do I look like a girl who'd been thoroughly kissed the night before? I glance around at the other girls, but no one is paying me any attention, too busy pulling out their hair rollers and catching up on what they did over the weekend.

Homeroom is much of the same. The teacher takes attendance and then leaves for a faculty meeting. Jaewoo isn't in class but he told me he wouldn't be. Last night, we'd caught a taxi to the academy, and though we hardly spoke to each other, our faces turned toward opposite windows, we held hands the entire way. He'd had the taxi driver drop me off at the back of my dorm, not leaving until I was safely inside, before heading to his own dorm.

I spend homeroom chatting with Sori about our weekends. I want to tell her about what happened with Jaewoo but not in a place where others might hear. I haven't told her before now because I wanted to respect Jaewoo's wish to keep whatever we had a secret, but now things are getting more serious, and I'd love a friend to talk to, especially Sori, who understands what it's like not only to be an idol but to date one.

Instead, I hold up her pink Kakao Friends mirror for her while she applies eyeliner and lip gloss.

"This is my morning workout," I joke.

"Stop shaking. Keep it straight."

Nothing can bring down my mood, not even Jina, who tries to take my head off in dodgeball.

At lunch, Sori joins Angela, Gi Taek, and me at our usual table. Neither Angela nor Gi Taek comments on this new development.

"You can sit next to me," Angela says, pulling out a chair for Sori, who sits primly at the edge.

"Why is the lunch line so long today?" I ask when I notice the line stretching out the door.

"They're serving macarons!" Angela exclaims. "It's the most popular meal item at SAA. The kitchen only gives one per tray. I've known people who've purchased two meals just so they could eat two."

As if to demonstrate, Sori picks up the tiny pink confection from her tray, placing it delicately between her lips. She bites down, chewing slowly, swallows, then sighs.

"You should do commercials for SAA," I say.

"She has," Gi Taek and Angela say at the same time.

"Is this seat taken?" Nathaniel pulls out the chair on Angela's other side.

There's similar movement beside me. I turn and gape. "I thought you said you weren't coming to school today?"

Jaewoo takes a seat. "Change of plans."

Last night we didn't exactly discuss what that kiss—*kisses*—would mean for our . . . relationship. We're no longer *just* friends—though it seems clear without saying that, whatever it is, we'll keep it to ourselves for a while longer.

Though I already know I'm going to be so bad at this. My face is turning red with just the thought of his kisses.

"Did you cut the line?" Sori asks suddenly.

Like all of us, Nathaniel and Jaewoo have trays with the coveted pastry.

"It pays to be nice to the lunch ladies, Sori-yah," Nathaniel says. Seeing as how last time they were in this lunchroom together they got into a huge argument, they're acting fairly civil. Sori rolls her eyes, while Nathaniel plucks the macaron from his tray and stuffs the whole thing in his mouth.

When he catches me looking, he says, "What? I have four older sisters. When I was growing up, if I left the good stuff for the end, it was stolen right off my plate! I'd never get to enjoy it."

"Our manager came early and waited in line," Jaewoo explains.

Poor Nam Ji Seok. "Is that in his job description?"

"Placating needy and hungry boys?" Nathaniel answers. "Yes."

Angela keeps sneaking glances at Jaewoo from across the table, probably assuming he's sitting with us because Nathaniel and Sori are.

"We're just here to eat lunch," Jaewoo says, "then we have to go back to the studio."

"You came all the way here to eat lunch?" This from Gi Taek.

"Today was macaron day," Nathaniel says. "We wouldn't miss it for the world."

As Nathaniel engages Gi Taek and Angela in a conversation about the merits of dining-hall food, Jaewoo shifts closer to me.

"You haven't tried the macaron yet?"

I'm a bit overwhelmed by his presence. The chairs in the dining hall are already pretty close together, and he's leaning toward me. I can smell his cologne, a subtle, fresh scent, like a sea breeze.

"I was saving it for last," I tell him, "but Nathaniel makes a good argument."

I reach for the macaron and bring it to my lips. I feel self-conscious, because he's watching me, but then I bite down and the sweet explosion of flavors in my mouth is incredible. The combination of the crisp outside and the soft and chewy inside, plus the raspberry buttercream in the middle.

I groan, "It's heavenly."

"Yeah?" Jaewoo laughs, a bit unsteadily.

With his chopsticks, he picks up his macaron and places it on my tray. "Have mine too."

I beam at him. He's giving me his macaron. It's like he's giving me his heart.

I look up to find Sori studying us, her expression unreadable.

"No, it's fine," I say. "You should eat it." I return the macaron to his tray.

"If you're not going to eat it, I will." Nathaniel reaches over, grabs Jaewoo's macaron, and pops it into his mouth.

That night, I'm sitting on my bed writing a paper for history class, when Sori abruptly turns toward me from where she'd been doing homework at her desk. I almost yelp in surprise because she's wearing a bright-red sheet mask

"So, you and Jaewoo." It's a statement.

"Me and Jaewoo, what?"

"Don't be cute with me." She looks away, taps her heel against the bottom of her chair, then returns her gaze. "You're not worried that I'll tell my mom?"

"Will you?" Honestly, it never occurred to me. She might be the daughter of Joah's CEO, but she's also my friend.

Still, she takes her sweet time in answering, taking off her sheet mask and using the tips of her fingers to tap the essence into her skin. She's wearing a Minnie Mouse towel headband to keep her hair from her face, which she adjusts.

"No," she says, after I've pretty much watched her preen herself for a minute and a half. "Before I was your roommate or even Nathaniel's girlfriend, I was Jaewoo's friend. He deserves this."

"He deserves . . . me?" I grin. "'Cause I'm so great?"

She rolls her eyes. "He deserves to be happy."

"Wow." I didn't think anything so cliché could feel so good. She thinks I make him happy?

She continues, "I don't want to say, 'you don't know him like I do.'"

"You just said it," I point out.

"Because I'm sure you're bound to know him way more intimately than I've ever known him . . ."

Oh. My. God.

"But his life hasn't been the easiest. Not that wealth necessarily makes things easier."

Spoken like a true chaebol.

"But Nathaniel's always been vocal about what he wants, while Jaewoo's more reserved, thinking of the group first before himself. Honestly, I'm surprised he even confessed to you, assuming that he has. It must have been hard for him, going after something he wants, rather than what's best for the group."

"Aww."

"Though I don't know why. It's not like you're worth it."

"Wow, Sori. I thought we were complimenting me."

"Oh, were we?" She grins.

"You don't have to worry about Jaewoo," I say. "I'll be sure to take care of his gentle artist soul."

"Yes, be sure to take care of his soul," she says, then adds, "and his body."

"Oh my God!" I throw my pillow at her. She sprints to her bed and grabs a stuffed animal. She has like a hundred. After we "became friends," they all started appearing out of seemingly nowhere. I think she'd hidden them beneath her bed.

I'm pelted with a Pikachu.

"Not fair!" I throw my arms up over my head, taking cover.

Then she's on my bed, pillow in hand. She goes for a headshot, but I tackle her and she collapses backward, with me on top. I can't breathe, I'm laughing so hard.

"You're heavy!" she complains, and I make myself like a log. "I hate this," she says, though she's laughing as hard as I am. And her laugh is louder than mine; plus she snorts. Our neighbors bang on the wall for us to be quiet, which only causes us to laugh more.

It takes another five minutes for us to catch our breaths, laying with our shoulders touching.

"Would you do it again?" I ask her.

I don't have to explain myself. She knows what I'm asking. If she turned back time and she had the choice of whether or not she'd date Nathaniel, would she do it all over again?

"In a heartbeat. Even after the scandal, even after the accusations and the heartbreak and the pain. He was my first love. I wouldn't give that up for the world."

Twenty-five

Spring means cherry blossom season and SAA's annual school camping trip to one of South Korea's national parks, which apparently was on the official academic calendar on the website. I hadn't known because no one mentioned it until a few days before we're supposed to leave.

"It happens every year," Gi Taek explained. "You're just"—he shrugged—"supposed to know."

"I'm a transfer student!"

"The school sent out an email."

"If it was in Korean, then I didn't read it."

"You really should work on your reading skills."

The night before we're scheduled to leave, Sori and I pack for the trip. It's a two day, one night trip, and each student is allowed to pack one small duffel bag.

"Are you going to be okay?" I ask Sori, who isn't exactly a minimalist.

"Shut up. Actually, can you pack my makeup case in your bag? Oh, and my face roller?"

"You don't need two sets of pajamas," I tell her, when I see her reaching for both her pink silk pj's and her LINE FRIENDS shorts and T-shirt.

She spears me with a look. "'Need is relative.'"

When she sees *me* packing my dad's old shirt, she eyes me judgingly. "Jenny." That's all she says. Just my name. Like it's a synonym for *disappointment*.

"What?"

"This is a two day, one night trip."

"Yeah, I know." I finally read the information page on the school's website, which had a translate option.

"As in, we'll be sleeping overnight somewhere with our classmates."

"Don't we do that anyway?" I ask. "I mean, we live in a dorm."

"As in, the girls and boys will be in the same building, likely a small house in the middle of nowhere, with little to no supervision. As in, Jaewoo will be there. As in, you can get into his pants or vice versa or both."

For someone who's super into Hello Kitty, she can be quite crass.

"Wait, he's going on the trip?" He hasn't been in school the past couple weeks. And I have no means of contacting him because his phone is still being monitored. I guess I could contact him through Sori, but I also don't want to get either of them into trouble.

"Jenny, no one misses this trip."

This sounds more ominous than excitement-inducing, yet

consider my excitement induced.

"Better," Sori says when I hold up a pajama set. Though, as someone who's stuffing a hairdryer into a twenty-two-inch duffel, her packing priorities don't exactly inspire confidence.

The day of the trip dawns dreary with rain clouds, but that doesn't stop every student at SAA, even those who don't stay at the dorms but with their families in Seoul, from arriving on time, duffel in hand, beside the long stretch of buses outside the academy.

Every student, that is, except for the members of XOXO.

"I thought you said they'd be here," I hiss at Sori.

"Maybe not." She doesn't look happy, her eyes scanning the crowd.

"Morning!" Angela calls, walking over arm-in-arm with Gi Taek. She's wearing a neon green rain poncho over a matching track suit set. Gi Taek's dressed just as stylishly in what is presumably a Japanese brand, if the kanji logo stitched onto the pant leg is any indication. They definitely took the lax dress code for the field trip and ran with it.

"Good morning," I say, and accept a hug from them both. As I step back, I have this weird out of body experience where I flashback to only a few months ago, walking onto the LACHSA campus. I never would have imagined hugging a classmate. And now, it feels so natural, so *damn heartwarming*, to greet Gi Taek and Angela in this way.

They both look at me strangely; I must have a weird expression on my face.

"Do you think we have assigned seats?" I ask, covering up my attack of affection with a question. "Or can we sit anywhere on the bus?"

"We probably just have assigned buses," Gi Taek says.

Of course, he's right.

Gi Taek, Angela, and I high-five when our homeroom classes are assigned to the same bus. We give our duffels to the driver who's stacking them neatly in the storage compartment beneath the bus. After boarding, we realize most of the seats in the back are filled so Sori and I take seats in the middle, with Gi Taek and Angela directly behind us. Our class monitors hand out food prepared by the cafeteria—bottles of water and gimbap wrapped in tinfoil.

I hold out hope until the last possible moment that Jaewoo might still show up. Seated by the window, I have a clear view of the curbside as the last of the students board the buses, until only the security guard remains, shutting the gates to the school. I turn from the window to see Sori craning her neck for a glimpse. Our gazes meet and she shakes her head.

After that, I try to resign myself to a fun field trip with my friends. It's never too early for gimbap, so I unwrap mine and eat it like a burrito. The smorgasbord of ingredients is like a symphony in my mouth—seasoned and sautéed carrots, spinach, and burdock root, plus imitation crab, yellow pickled radish, and bulgogi, neatly encased in rice and laver seaweed and sprinkled with sesame seeds.

"I wasn't hungry," Sori says, when I emerge from my food-bliss to find her staring at me. "But now I kind of am."

As we wind our way out of Seoul, Sori and I play phone games, and I take a selfie with Sori smiling prettily and Gi Taek and Angela making funny faces behind us to send to Halmeoni.

The chattering dies down as people plug into their music or settle in for a nap. I open my own music app, and soon Rachmaninoff and the drone of the bus on the road lull me to sleep.

Twenty-six

Sori shakes me awake an hour and a half later and I see that we've pulled into a rest stop. Half of the students have already disembarked, and there's no sign of Gi Taek and Angela.

"We have thirty minutes," Sori says. "Hurry up, I have to pee."

I quickly stand, letting Sori haul me off the bus.

Students from all the buses are making their way into a large single-story building, with cars and tourist buses parked outside it. Outside the rest stop, there's a few food carts—one selling hot dogs, slathered in batter and fried, another selling manju, custard-filled walnut pastries in the shape of husks of corn. There's also a coffee cart and several vending machines.

Inside the rest stop a food court offers a variety of ramyeon and udon to traditional Korean fare like bibimbap and hot soup dishes that you can order and pick up at different service counters. There's also a fairly large convenience store. I spot Gi Taek and Angela inside, loading up on snacks and bottled drinks.

"Hey," Sori says, "are you going to the bathroom?"

"No, I went before we left. Also my bladder isn't as tiny as yours."

She rolls her eyes and leaves in pursuit of the restrooms.

Most of the students are in the convenience store, with a few ordering hot meals at the counter. I'm still full from the gimbap, so I head outside in search of that coffee cart.

A few of the other people at the rest stop have the same idea because the line is long. Luckily, it moves pretty fast, and in about five minutes I'm at the front. I order a latte and reach for my wallet.

Which isn't on me, but where I left it, in my backpack on the bus. I don't have to look behind me to know that the amount of people has doubled from when I first got in line. Right after, a Japanese tour bus arrived at the rest stop, letting out a lot of caffeine-dependent adults.

The vendor looks at me pityingly.

"I'll pay for her."

I almost have whiplash, with how fast my head turns.

Jaewoo casually leans against the counter. He hands over a credit card. "I'm paying you back," he says, "for all that food you bought me in LA."

"Oh, is that what's happening?" I say, glad that my voice comes out normal, teasing, "Then I'd like to visit a few more stalls."

He's come. He's *here*.

And he looks so *good*. He's wearing a light-blue button-up

shirt, his hair swept back from his face, and slick aviators.

"Student," the vendor says, "your coffee?"

I turn to accept, blushing furiously.

Jaewoo and I leave the line, heading in the general direction of the buses. I'm suddenly overcome with a feeling of awkwardness. How am I supposed to act around him? The last time we were alone, we made out for half an hour on a swing set.

Of course right now we're not *exactly* alone. Our classmates are within sight, most chatting outside the rest stop, a few running around in an effort to get their muscles loosened before we have to get back on the bus for another two hours.

"So," I say, trying to act casual. "You're going on the field trip?"

He doesn't appear to have brought anything with him, a duffel or a backpack.

"Yeah, I was worried we wouldn't make it. We just flew back from Japan this morning."

"Do you do . . . promotions in Japan . . . often?"

A cry goes up behind us.

Outside the restroom, I spot Nathaniel surrounded by the group of Japanese tourists. He appears unfazed, throwing up peace signs and posing for selfies.

"Yeah," Jaewoo answers. "Jenny." He turns to me, a slight smile on his face. "I wanted to ask you—"

"There you are." Sori practically barrels into me. "I was looking all over for you. I was sure I'd find you outside one of the food stands."

"Ha, very funny."

"Oh, Jaewoo," she says, as if she'd just noticed he was standing right next to me. "I didn't think you'd show up."

"My manager dropped me off."

"That's nice. Well, Jenny and I have to be getting onto the bus. See ya!" She grabs my arm and pulls me away.

"Wait," I start.

"Act natural." Sori pinches my arm. "Look behind my left shoulder, what do you see?"

I follow her gaze despite being super annoyed with her. I haven't seen Jaewoo in a few weeks. You'd think she'd let me have a moment alone with him. What was he about to ask me? "I see Jaewoo."

"Oh my God, Jenny. Look farther." Concentrating, I look *beyond* Jaewoo to where Jina and her friends are grouped together outside the rest stop. Jina has her phone out and it's angled in our direction.

"Is she . . . ?"

"She could be taking photos, I don't know. But you have to be more careful."

I feel a chill run down my back. The idea that while Jaewoo and I were talking someone was watching us, *taking photos of us*, is disturbing, especially if the person is Jina, who for sure has only malicious intentions.

"Do you think she got any incriminating photos?"

"I don't think so. You two weren't standing *that* close. Plus I walked into the shot, and Jina wouldn't dare post a photo with me in it. She might target me at school, but if she posted a picture, my mother would get involved, and . . . even Jina doesn't want to piss off the CEO of Joah."

I take Sori's arm, squeezing. "I'm so glad you're on my team," I tell her. "You're like my ace in the hole," I add, in English.

"I have no idea what you're saying. Speak Korean." But then she adds in her cute accented English, "But, yes, I am ace."

A few minutes later, Jina and her friends board the bus, whispering to each other as they pass by me, then Gi Taek and Angela, followed by Nathaniel and Jaewoo. The rest of our class is already on board, and at the sight of them, a cheer goes up. Nathaniel bows, and Jaewoo's eyes scan the bus, as if in search of me. I sit lower in my seat. Can he *be* more obvious? Eventually they take seats in the front row, across from our homeroom teacher.

I wanted Jaewoo to come on this field trip, but now I'm not so sure. I thought leaving Seoul would give us opportunities to be together, but with so many of our classmates joining us, I think it might make things *harder* to keep whatever we have a secret.

Still, this is my first time outside of Seoul, my first time in the Korean countryside, and soon my excitement takes over and I push my worries to the back of my mind.

The landscape changes the farther we travel from the city. Beautiful swathes of farmland stretch for acres across a hilly terrain broken up by trees and country dirt roads. Farmers plant spring crops in the fields, shading their eyes with their gloved hands as they pause in their work to watch the train of buses rumble by.

An hour and half later we reach our destination. A sign that says National Park sits at the entrance of a large camping ground.

I'm surprised to see ten or so buses are already parked outside the campgrounds. It's not just SAA that has their annual field trip at this time and location, but other high schools as well.

I'm slow to disembark, mostly because Sori takes her sweet time and she's in the aisle seat. We're the last off the bus, accepting our duffels from the driver, plus a shirt from one of the class monitors. Apparently we're supposed to wear them during the trip so that our chaperones can keep track of us among the many other students present. Already kids are streaming through the entrance to the camping grounds, which is a nature reserve park with a dozen or so buildings and natural and historical sites.

A large map outside the grounds has a key with all the sites listed in Korean, Japanese, Chinese, and English. Besides the cabins, there's a restaurant, a museum, a recreational facility, a park services building, and a café. There's also a convenience store, because this is Korea.

The map also features drawings of a few landmarks. In the middle of the map is a bamboo forest and at the top right corner a blue oblong shape with cartoon reeds and frogs is marked with the words *Pond of Tranquility*.

"Let's go to the cabin," Sori says. She'd been studying the map alongside me, probably eyeing the hiking trails. "Floor space is limited. We need to stake our claim."

I'm not exactly sure what she means until we're standing outside our assigned cabin, which is more a one-story house built in the traditional Korean structure—or hanok—with a winged rooftop and sliding wood-paneled paper doors, than the log cabins of my childhood.

Similar to how our bus was grouped, our homeroom is combined with Angela and Gi Taek's homeroom, so the twelve girls of their class are rooming with the twelve girls of ours. Which means twenty-four girls on the floor of a single—albeit long—room.

"This has to be a fire hazard," I say.

From cabinets on the wall, we each pull out a bedroll and go about "staking our claim" to floor space.

Jina and her friends have already taken the spots closest to the door, presumably to make it easier for them to sneak out at night.

Sori on the other hand beelines for the window. Unfortunately for her, so does another girl. They eye each other before both diving for the same spot. It's like an episode of *Animal Kingdom*. I would have teased Sori if Angela and I hadn't joined in when we saw the girl's friends backing her up.

When the dust settles, Sori's by the window with me next to her and Angela horizontal right above our heads. The other girls are at our feet, *where they belong. Muahaha.*

"Jenny." Gi Taek calls me over from where he's standing by the doorway.

At his appearance, a few of the girls scream and cover their chests, though we're literally all wearing the same outfits we wore on the bus, with none of us having changed into our T-shirts yet. Gi Taek just rolls his eyes.

I head over. "What's up?"

"We have to sign up for activities. Wanna come with?"

I look over to where Sori is unpacking her duffel with Angela as an attentive audience, explaining each item as she pulls it out.

"Is that a humidifier?"

"Don't ask."

I follow Gi Taek out of the hanok into the small courtyard, then out onto a short, dirt path. According to the map, the students are all staying in the Folk Village, which is a replica of houses from the early Joseon period, separated by low stone walls.

"Boys are known to jump the walls at night to visit their girlfriends," Gi Taek explains, like he's a tour guide to Korean high-school life. Which I guess he kind of is.

The Folk Village is right next to the central area of the camp where the museum and the parks services building is located, as well as the convenience store and a fairly large outdoor stage.

The majority of the students are congregated here, and now I see why we were all given matching shirts. If it weren't for the bright-red shirts that are printed with SAA, we'd likely get lost amidst the students from all the different high schools.

A girl in a turquoise and magenta shirt walks by with SPAHS, for Seoul Performing Arts High School, printed on the back.

Another boy's shirt reads: Yongsan Music School. The theme seems pretty straightforward.

Gi Taek leads me to the activity table and picks up a clipboard with a sign-up sheet. After reading it, he hands it over and I flip through the pages. Besides checking in with our homeroom teacher at night and in the morning, we're pretty much free to do whatever we feel like. A few of the activities have a cap on how many people can go, like white-water rafting and cave exploring. But others, like a two-hour hike to a Buddhist temple, have an unlimited number of spaces.

There's also a sign-up sheet for a talent show, which will take place during the only mandatory activity, a barbecue dinner for all of the visiting schools.

Gi Taek puts his name down on the sheet for the talent show, with "Dancing" beneath the talent category.

"What about you?" he asks. "Any activities catch your eye?"

"The hike to the Buddhist temple seems pretty cool."

I hand Gi Taek back the sheet. As he's browsing, I let my gaze roam my surroundings. Most of the activities don't start for another hour, so most of the students are either unpacking in their cabins or heading out in groups to explore the nearby sites.

Outside the convenience store, I spot Jaewoo standing with Nathaniel and a few other boys from our class.

I glance around but when I don't see any sign of Jina, I start walking in his direction. I'll just ask him what activity he planned on joining. That's casual enough, right?

I almost make it before two girls dart in front of me. They're from another school, their T-shirts a flattering midnight-blue color.

"Oppa!" one says, and I narrow my eyes. I doubt she knows him well enough to call him oppa, a familiar term to address older male relatives or friends. "When I found out SAA would be on this field trip," she continues, "I was so excited. I'm such a big fan of yours. I'm a member of the Kiss and Hug Club."

All my annoyance *and jealousy* deflates.

She's a fan.

And I was about to do something embarrassing, like telling her to back off.

"Thank you," he says, then smiles.

I can practically sense the girl's heart stop, only to start beating again, faster, because I've felt that same way, when he's given me that very same smile.

I slowly back up, then turn around, sighing heavily. What if I go this whole field trip and the only time I talk to Jaewoo is at the rest stop?

"Jenny?"

I turn.

A boy stands behind me. At first I don't immediately place his face. Then I remember. Ian. I met him the first morning I ever spent in Seoul. He gave me his phone number, but with school and Jaewoo, I never got around to texting him.

What is he doing here?

Twenty-seven

"Ian, hi," I say, feeling at a little loss for words. Like a few of the students, he's dressed in a bright-blue shirt. Unlike the students however, he also wears a red armband.

Noticing the direction of my gaze, he explains, "I'm a Yong-san Music School alum so they asked if I'd join as a group leader, a paid gig. Gotta get that cash."

I remember now. He's taking the semester off to save up money before returning to college at the Manhattan School of Music.

"How are you?" he asks. "Getting used to the life of a Korean high-school student?"

"Yeah." I look around. "This field trip is pretty cool."

"They switch up the locations every year," he says. "When I was in my third year, we did an overnight stay at this huge Buddhist monastic compound in the mountains. A lot of praying and vegetarian food."

"Isn't there a temple here?" I ask. "I saw it on the sign-up sheet."

"Yeah, sort of. There's a shrine to the local mountain deity or sansin. The park pays for its upkeep."

"Oh, cool." Besides Korean school in the basement of the Korean church, I haven't been to any sort of spiritual place since middle school. It'd be fun to see the shrine.

"There's also a love story attached to the shrine. Apparently during, like, the Goryeo period, two lovers from rival families made the trek to pray to the shrine, then afterward, disappeared into these mountains and were never seen again."

I grimace. "That's bleak."

"Yeah, well, Koreans love a tragic story. Haven't you figured that out by now?"

I laugh.

"So, like," he continues, "at the shrine, you can pray to the sansin for general blessings, but most people who visit the shrine ask for something more specific." He waits, obviously drawing out the story for effect.

"Like what?"

"Love. It's a famous site for lovers because it's rumored that the couple actually survived and lived out their lives somewhere, together, protected by the sansin." He grins. "As you can imagine, it's a pretty popular spot with students."

Koreans love a tragic story, but what we love even more is a hopeful one.

He kicks a stone and it skitters a few feet before disappearing into a patch of grass. "We could go, if you want."

I blink, then blink again.

I don't know how to react. I don't know how to feel. I mean, I *know* how I feel. Flattered that he asked me, but also a little bit guilty. He must think I'm single. I mean, Jaewoo and I never talked about our relationship status after the kiss, but . . .

"Jaewoo-seonbae!" someone yells from close behind me. I'm tempted to turn, then I recall why I was walking away in the first place, so that I don't draw attention to Jaewoo and myself.

"Jenny?" Ian frowns.

"Sorry. Yes. I mean, I was thinking of signing up for that activity anyway, sort of like a counterbalance to spending all those hours on the bus. Don't you have . . . uh . . . prior obligations, like with your job?"

"We haven't been assigned activities. I'll request that one. I'm sure I'll get it. The other chaperones are teachers, and not a lot of them want to go climbing in the mountains."

"Okay," I say. When he continues to stare at me, waiting for more, I add, "I'll sign up for that one."

"Awesome. See you in an hour!" He waves, then heads off in the direction of the park services building.

"Who's the guy? He's cute." I nearly jump out of my sneakers. Sori's sidled up to me, her cat eyes zeroing on Ian's departure.

"An older man, Jenny?" Gi Taek's also appeared, giving his best impression of a smarmy sneer, wiggling his eyebrows.

"His name's Ian. I met him at a café my first day in Seoul."

"You're like a cute boy magnet," Gi Taek says, then pauses. "The cutest boy, of course, being me."

Angela giggles, having walked over with Sori.

"Yo, Jenny Go!" Nathaniel practically tackles me. I turn to see if Jaewoo walked over with him, but he's still standing with the girls from earlier, except now there are *two more girls* and a boy.

"Did you choose your activity for the day?" Nathaniel asks. "I was thinking of doing some white-water rafting. There's nothing like the thrill of drowning to complete a school bonding experience."

I sigh. "I was thinking of hiking."

"I'll join you," Sori says.

Nathaniel's eyes dart toward her, a small frown on his face, but then quickly lock onto Gi Taek and Angela. "Well, what about you two? Don't let me down!"

"It's not exactly my style," Gi Taek says, "but I guess I can give it a try."

"That's the spirit!"

"I *did* pack a swimsuit," Angela says, then glances at Sori and me, her expression guilty.

"Don't mind us," Sori says, her voice soothing. "We'll see each other at the barbecue."

Nathaniel narrows his eyes at Angela, clearly jealous that Sori is being so nice to Angela when she's always so snarky to . . . well, everyone else. If Angela doesn't watch out, she might find herself treading water during this rafting trip.

"What about Jaewoo?" Sori asks casually.

"Dunno," Nathaniel says. "He'll probably sign up for whatever his fans want. He's a sucker."

"Where are your fans?" Gi Taek drawls.

Nathaniel doesn't miss a beat. "According to online polls, I'm more popular with foreigners. Maybe it's my sex appeal and spirit of spontaneity."

Sori rolls her eyes.

"You're probably just too annoying for Koreans," Gi Taek says laughing.

An hour later, Sori and I are standing beside the entrance to the hiking path. A wooden sign staked into the ground reads: "Trail to Sansin." I stare enviously at Sori's hiking boots and a windbreaker, which she pulled from her seemingly bottomless bag of outfits, as I hug my LACHSA zip-up hoodie a little tighter. It may be school-disloyal, but at least it's warm.

"Attention, everyone!" Ian walks over, having changed into a loose jacket over shorts and carrying a large backpack. "Let me introduce myself. My name's Ian. I'm the group leader for this activity. We'll spend about forty-five minutes walking to the shrine, thirty minutes there, and about thirty minutes walking back downhill. If at any time, anyone feels light-headed or dizzy, please let me know. I have extra water bottles, energy bars, and bananas. I also have this." He holds up a walkie-talkie. "We can get a cart up here to take you to medical. Any questions? No? Then, lets—"

"Wait!" Two girls rush up the path from the campsite, on either side of . . .

Jaewoo! My heart swells. He's changed from the loose

button-up to the SAA T-shirt, which he wears beneath his own windbreaker. The girls I recognize as part of the group that was standing with him earlier.

"Okay, *now* I think that everyone's," Ian says. "Let's move out!"

I wonder if Nathaniel told him what activity I'd signed up for, and that's why he decided to join this one.

The students start to break into twos and threes to accommodate for the narrow trail. Immediately a boy from another class engages Sori in conversation, while even more girls encircle Jaewoo.

Resentment curdles in my chest. Even if he is here, it's not like I can walk up to him.

"Jenny." I drag my gaze away from Jaewoo to where Ian's hung back to wait for me. Resigned to my fate, I join him. "So," Ian says, as we start up the trail. "I checked my messages and noticed I never got a text from you."

That's an odd way of putting it, as if he *had* thought I texted him. How many girls does he give his phone number out to?

"Sorry, school started, and I . . ."—forgot, really—"wanted to concentrate on my music."

"Oh, yeah," he says, "SAA has a showcase at the end of the semester, right? I know a kid who was accepted into MSM immediately following his performance. Like, the rep in the audience came up to him and gave him a verbal acceptance."

"Seriously? Wow," I say. "That's amazing." My pulse quickens at the thought.

Though I feel a smidgen of worry. I haven't been concentrating on my music, not really, not to the extent that I had in LA. I've been distracted with school, and my friends, and, well, Jaewoo. But I resolve now that once we return to campus, I'll step up my game, sign up for more practice time, and maybe schedule a video session with Eunbi.

"Ian-ssi?" A girl calls over to him from where she and her friends are looking over a ridge. "What kind of plant is that?"

"I guess I should go do my job," Ian says, leaving my side to answer the girl.

As we make our way up the mountain the hike becomes a bit more arduous, the path taking us up a sharp incline and over grassy boulders, and once across a bustling stream, silver fish slipping over rocks that sparkle beneath the afternoon sun. Past the stream is a dense forest, the path harder to make out against the leaf-strewn ground, overgrown with moss and the roots of trees.

I'm up front, walking beside Sori, when the path we'd been heading up levels off, and there it is, a small shrine.

It's tucked against the side of a mountain, an elegant wooden structure, small in stature, painted predominantly green and red, with a single room and a gentle, sloping roof.

For how deep it is in the mountains, the shrine and its surrounding area is well-kept, the clearing swept of debris and all of the features of the building—the wood and paper doors, the little stone decorative figures on the rooftop—are intact. There's even the subtle smell of incense emanating from within the shrine, as if a visiting monk had only just left.

Everyone either rushes off to explore the area, taking selfies with the few stone statues that stand sentinel around the clearing, or collapses onto the ground out of sheer exhaustion from the last leg of the hike.

"I have to use the bathroom," Sori of the Small Bladder says as she makes her way toward a tiny building at the edges of the clearing. I look around for Jaewoo, but I don't spot him anywhere. The girls who'd been with him earlier are also looking around, brows furrowed.

Ian stands by the shrine, calling out instructions. "Let's keep the number of people in the shrine to two to three people at a time, four at the most." He then starts to turn in my direction.

In a sort of panic, I sprint behind the closest building. Crouching down, I glance around the corner to see Ian approaching. Oh my God, I feel ridiculous. Am I really *hiding* from him? Still crouched, I start to back up and bump into someone.

"Hey, watch it."

I twist around and almost fall over. "Jaewoo!" I hiss. "What are you doing?"

"I think . . ." he says slowly, "I'm doing exactly what you're doing."

From the other side of the shrine, I can hear the girls shouting. "Jaewoo! Jaewoo-oppa! Where are you?"

For a moment we just stare at each other, acknowledging the situation, both of us crouched down behind a mountain shrine while hiding from people who want our attention. I try to suppress a giggle, but soon find myself holding my hands over my mouth to stifle them. Jaewoo's no better, his entire body shaking with silent laughter.

"This is just like the photobooth," I say. "Why do we keep on ending up in these situations?"

"I don't know," he says, wiping the tears from his eyes.

I let out a snort and he holds a finger to his mouth. "Shh, Jenny!"

"I can't help it!"

Jaewoo smiles, clearly amused.

"Jenny!" Ian's voice is close now, moving around the side of the shrine.

"Jaewoo!" The girls are on the other side.

Curling his fingers over my wrist, Jaewoo pulls my hand away from my mouth. His eyes drop to my lips and I have a sudden realization what he's about to do.

My eyes widen. "They'll see—"

He kisses me, hard and fast. Then he's gone, rounding the side of the shrine.

"Jenny?" a voice says from behind me. I almost lose my balance. "What are you doing?"

I get up from my crouch and turn to face Ian. "N-Nothing, I just . . . thought I saw a fox. . . ."

Ian stares at me in disbelief. "We have to leave before it gets dark. You better have a look at the shrine now if you're still interested."

Ian must have had enough of me because he doesn't follow

me into the shrine. I'm only inside a quick few seconds, but it leaves a lasting impression. The afternoon light filters through the door, illuminating the far wall where a painting depicts an old man with a long white beard, presumably the sansin, sitting on a mountain beneath a tree and surrounded by tigers.

I throw a quick prayer the sansin's way before running down the path to meet the others.

Twenty-eight

It's dusk by the time we arrive at the center of camp and service staff are wheeling out large grills for the barbecue. Since it doesn't start for another half hour, we separate, heading off to our respective houses. I try not to feel resentful of my short time with Jaewoo, especially when Nathaniel enters the camp at the same time as us, soaking wet, having apparently returned from white-water rafting, tackles Jaewoo in a hug, and they go off laughing together.

Back at our house, a distinctly dry-looking Angela is sitting on the blankets, laying out two dresses.

"It's like you and Nathaniel participated in two entirely different activities," I say.

"Most of us didn't get wet," Angela says, deciding on the yellow dress, "besides a few splashes here and there. Nathaniel just fell overboard."

Angela wants to take a nap, so Sori and I walk over to the communal showers and quickly wash up, then head back to our house to use Sori's hairdryer, which I'm realizing was actually brilliant of her to bring. The other girls ask to borrow it after us, even bargaining with other items they've brought from Seoul—sheet masks, blister Band-Aids, mosquito repellant. Even Jina asks to borrow it. I expect awesome levels of petty from Sori but she hands the hairdryer over without a blink.

I must look surprised because she says, "Keep your friends close and your enemies closer" in English.

I put on one of the dresses I brought from home. Then I borrow mosquito repellent from one of our classmates and spray my bare legs so I smell kind of like medicinal oranges.

Afterward, Sori wants to do Angela's makeup, so after applying eyeliner and tint to my lips, I head out to explore the folk village a bit more. I glance through doorways into courtyards that are a lot like the one assigned to our class, boys and girls sitting on platforms chatting and practicing their acts for the talent show.

I'm walking by a hanok at the back of the village when I hear a familiar shout. I glance through the doorway to see Nathaniel and a few boys from our class kicking a ball around.

They're all shirtless.

Nathaniel's the first to spot me. "Boys!" he shouts. "We have an audience! Cover yourselves."

They all start to yell and run around in circles.

"Like she wants to see that." I hear Jaewoo before I see him, appearing from the side. He's zipping up his windbreaker but not before I catch a glimpse of his toned stomach and chest.

"Wait," I say, pretending to push him aside when he blocks my view. "I haven't seen everything I wanted to yet."

He scowls. "Everything you need to see is right in front of you."

I lean back, giving him a slow once-over. He doesn't break a sweat. He knows he looks good. Well, I don't look half bad myself. I flick my hair over my shoulder and watch as his eyes follow the movement.

"Aren't you going to dinner?" I ask.

"Soon," he says, though his attention seems to have shifted. Slowly he reaches out a hand. I go still, heart racing, as he brushes a strand of hair from my face.

"Jaewoo?" one of the boys calls out behind him.

He steps back. "Save me a seat?" Then he's turning back into the courtyard.

"What were you doing with Jenny?" I overhear the same boy ask, curious.

"She was just letting us know dinner's about to start," he says, casually.

I walk away, touching my face where Jaewoo's fingers had brushed my hair, my stomach all aflutter. I'm on cloud nine as I round a corner.

"At least it makes sense now, why you never texted me." I jerk my head around. Ian's leaning against the wall. "I mean, I get it. Why bother with a nobody when you could be with a K-pop star?"

There's a smile on his face, but his words have a cold edge to them.

"So," he says, "what are you, like, a super XOXO fan?" He laughs.

"What's wrong with that?" I ask.

His smile drops, "Jenny, are you serious? You said you wanted to go to the Manhattan School of Music."

"I do. And?"

"They only accept the best, people who are serious about their music, and now you're saying you're an *XOXO fan*?"

"Wow," I cut him off, "I didn't take you for a music snob."

He scoffs, "It's not being a music snob. It's having taste."

"Is this even about music?" I ask, channeling Sori at her most biting. "It sounds like you're just upset that I'm not into you."

He flinches and I don't care. He's a judgmental jerk.

"Whatever, Jenny," he says. "Have fun wasting your time on a fantasy."

With that he leaves, taking the last word with him. I'm so mad, but I refuse to let him ruin my night.

"Where'd you go?" Sori asks when I join her and Angela in the line for barbecue. She's looking gorgeous, as usual, in a silky sheath dress.

"Nowhere," I answer. "What's for dinner? It smells good." I peek up ahead to see cooks standing behind the grills as they turn over strips of galbi—marinated short ribs—as well as pork, and chicken, plus a variety of grilled vegetables. On the side is a banchan station, and beside that, huge industrial-sized rice cookers.

Sori looks like she wants to ask me more questions but then Gi Taek appears, looking chic in black. He must not have been in the courtyard with Nathaniel and Jaewoo, otherwise he would have come with them. A few of the students behind us grumble, but don't protest a second person cutting in line.

"How was white-water rafting?" Sori asks.

"A disaster." Gi Taek shudders. "Remind me never to go near a body of water with Nathaniel ever again. What about you two?"

"Our tour guide flirted with Jenny the whole time."

"Nice."

"We're not talking about him," I say sharply. Okay, so maybe I *will* say something.

I relay my conversation with Ian, how he said XOXO's music wasn't "real" music, and how I can't be a serious musician if I like them.

"He should announce that to *this* crowd," Angela says, nodding to indicate the hundreds of students from all the different music schools, many of whom are trainees or aspiring idols. "He won't get far with his limbs intact."

"Vicious, Angela," Gi Taek says. "I approve."

A thought strikes me and I feel the blood drain from my face. "Sori." I grab her hand. "Do you think he'll say something? About Jaewoo and me?"

I think back to earlier. What did he witness anyway? A bit of flirting, but it could just be one-sided on my part. It can't be a scandal if it's one-sided, right?

"You're fine, Jenny," Sori reassures me. "Ian's just a flirt who didn't get the girl for once. If he doesn't think K-pop is real music he wouldn't care about the life of idols either."

I slump in relief, trusting Sori's judgment.

"Why would he say anything about Jaewoo and you?" Gi Taek asks.

Whoops. Gi Taek's eyes narrow.

"Because we"—I brace for their reactions—"sort of have a thing."

"Jenny!" both Angela and Gi Taek shout.

Their voices carry and a few people turn to stare at us.

Lowering his head, Gi Taek hiss-whispers, "How? Why? Who?"

"What?!" Angela adds.

"Jaewoo confessed." I say, then cover my face with my hands because it's embarrassing.

"What?!" Gi Taek yells.

"That's what I said!" Angela grins.

"I'll take two of those, please," Sori says.

I lower my hands from my face and we all look at her. She's pointing to the sizzling galbi on the grill. Apparently we've reached the front of the line. The cook picks up two pieces of galbi with her tongs and places it on a paper plate, then hands it to Sori.

She glances over to find us all watching her. "What?"

We suspend discussion to choose what meats and vegetables we want from the grill, then move to the stand of side dishes to fill our plates with kimchi, green salad, braised potatoes, seasoned soybean sprouts, and spicy cucumber salad.

Angela manages to find us an empty picnic table. I thought I'd have a brief respite to enjoy my meal, but I underestimated Gi Taek.

"What does 'a thing' entail? Like hand-holding? Further than that? Hugs, kisses? What kind of kisses? Was there tongue?"

"Stop!" Angela covers her eyes.

"Your ears, Angela," Sori says. "Cover your ears." She picks up a slice of cucumber with her chopsticks and pops it into her mouth, then uses her same chopsticks to point to the edge of camp. "Oh, look. Lover boy."

We all follow her gaze to where Jaewoo stands with Nathaniel, having just arrived. They're both dressed now, in hoodies and sweats.

I wait for one or all of my friends to start teasing me relentlessly, but they immediately act super cool. Sori lowers her chopsticks, Gi Taek puts some of his food onto Angela's plate, and Angela stuffs a pile of rice in her mouth.

My heart fills in gratitude and amusement. Not teasing me is their form of encouraging me.

Across the campsite, Nathaniel meets my gaze. He says something to Jaewoo who looks in my direction. A smile spreads across his face, warm and dazzling.

"Heol," Gi Taek says in amazement.

"How can you not fall in love?" Angela sighs dreamily. "When he looks at you like that?"

Love? The word makes my heart tumble in my chest. That

can't be what I'm feeling. Not yet.

Nathaniel and Jaewoo get their plates of food. On the way to our table, however, a couple of fans intercept them, and by the time they arrive, they're accompanied by a whole group of them. We're quick to make room for everyone, and though I wish I could spend time with Jaewoo alone, to talk and flirt with him, I'm also happy to be here, surrounded by our friends, and the people who care about him. It just goes to show how wrong Ian is. Each person here is a musician, and their love of XOXO is *real* and, honestly, special.

The girl sitting next to me loves Jaewoo in particular because he wrote the song that she listened to over and over again when her brother passed away. I'm so moved by her that I share how music also helped me get through my grief. We exchange numbers to keep in contact after the field trip is over.

Halfway through dinner, there's a collective murmuring in the crowd as everyone turns their attention to where a boy and girl in color-coordinated outfits walk onto the stage.

"I'm Sung Minwoo," the boy says, "a Second Year from Seoul Arts Academy."

"And I'm Lee Yuri," the girl says, "a Second Year from Yongsan Music School."

"We're your MCs for tonight's talent show!" they say in unison.

An enthusiastic cheer erupts from the tables.

"We've taken the names on the sign-up sheet, cut them all out, and put them in this hat!"

The girl holds up a bucket hat. "We'll be calling acts at random, so get ready!"

"Where'd Gi Taek go?" Angela asks suddenly.

"Nathaniel's gone too," Sori says, though with suspicion.

On the stage, the girl pulls a slip from the hat. "First up we have a duo . . . Drumroll please." The boy taps the rhythm on his leg. "Year Three students from SAA! Hong Gi Taek and Lee Nathaniel!"

Angela screams and stands up on the bench. Sori groans and places a hand over her face, though she does shift slightly in the direction of the stage.

Fast-tempo music begins, blasting from speakers on either side of the stage. Nathaniel and Gi Taek run out and immediately start to dance in perfect synchronization, rolling their bodies and moving in step with each other.

I'm enthralled, and honestly, super impressed. When did they have time to practice? The track switches to XOXO's "Don't Look Back," and the crowd goes wild.

They perform a whole medley of songs as they switch from one song to another and another. They even throw in a few classics, like BTS's "Blood Sweat & Tears" and SNSD's "Gee," which are huge hits with the crowd, everyone knowing the iconic moves. Even though I'm not familiar with some of the songs, I still enjoy myself immensely and feel particularly proud when I recognize a few from when Uncle Jay plays K-pop at the karaoke bar.

I don't know what could top a performance like that, but

the next person pulled from the hat is an opera singer who belts out an epic power ballad that has people standing on their feet cheering. The rest of the night is a roster of amazing talent, of singers, musicians, and dancers. If this is a preview of the end-of-the-year showcase, it's going to be incredible.

Toward the end of the night, I glance up to find Jaewoo trying to catch my attention. We're sitting on opposite sides of the table with several people between us. Everyone's chatting so I can't hear him, though I can see his lips moving.

I shake my head, laughing. "I can't hear you," I mouth.

"Joo Jini?" The boy MC calls the final name in the hat.

"Joo Jini-ssi?" the girl repeats.

They lift their hands over their eyes, peering into the crowd.

"Did you go to bed already?" the girl sing-songs.

When no one approaches the stage, they look at each other, then shrug. "Well, that's a bit of a letdown," the boy says. "We have time for one more performance if anyone wants to close out the night? Anyone? Come on, friends. Don't be shy."

Jaewoo mouths more words at me, but I really can't hear him.

He stands.

"Ah!" the boy MC exclaims. "We have a surprise volunteer!"

"Our last performer needs no introduction," the girl says. "It's SAA's very own Bae Jaewoo!"

Jaewoo looks toward the stage, his expression one of surprise. The crowd laughs and then starts chanting his name. "Bae Jaewoo! Bae Jaewoo!"

When he starts moving toward the stage, a cheer goes up.

On his way, someone hands him a guitar. And by the time he's onstage, the MCs have set up a stool and mic.

The students quiet as he sits down, playing the opening chord of a song. Then it transitions into the melody of the first verse, and my heart goes still because it's *the* song, the one from the karaoke bar.

"Gohae."

"Confession."

"How can I tell her the words I want to say?" Jaewoo croons, his sweet tenor drifting over the campgrounds.

"When the world is against me, how can I tell her?"

Dressed in a hoodie, he doesn't look like the mega K-pop star that he is, but even so, his star power is undeniable; it's in his raw talent, his impassioned voice.

He sings with such sincerity and vulnerability, as if he means every single word.

Looking around at the crowd, everyone is spellbound, some even mouthing the lyrics along with him, their bodies swaying. This is what he does, and what makes him such a good musician. He brings joy to people; he inspires them.

He inspires *me*. He makes me believe I can have it all. I can have a solo in the showcase. I can have friends who will support me and love me. I can have *him*.

The music rises to a crescendo leading into the peak of the ballad, the final chorus, his voice full and strong, as he sings, *"Tell her, tell her, the words that I want to say, my confession. I love her."*

Twenty-nine

At ten thirty, one of the female teachers checks in on the girls to make sure we're all accounted for, then leaves the courtyard, closing the doors behind her. At eleven there's a loud thump by the wall and we all hurry outside to find Nathaniel on the ground, rubbing his backside. Then Gi Taek and the rest of the boys from our class climb over. Jaewoo's last, apparently having drawn the short straw for lookout duty. While the others scramble into the house, I wait for him, watching as he nimbly leaps over, landing on his feet. Catching sight of me, he pulls me close.

I wrap my arms around him, leaning back so that I can look into his face. "Earlier tonight, at the table, you were trying to get my attention." He nods, reaching out to pull a leaf from my hair. "Was it the same thing you wanted to tell me earlier, at the rest stop?"

"Yeah, I wanted to ask if we could talk. In private."

A muffled shout and laughter come from the hanok.

"I think this is as private as we're going to get."

He smiles, looking into my eyes. "I wanted to ask you if you'd be my girlfriend."

My heart swells. This feels momentous. I've never been anyone's girlfriend before. And it's Jaewoo, the boy I've practically been obsessed with since I first met him at my uncle's karaoke bar. I know that since I'm eventually going back to America, there's an expiration date on our relationship. And that even if there wasn't, he's an idol. His star is going to rise higher and higher. But still, I want to be with him here and now.

"Yes," I say, and seal it with a kiss.

In the hanok, Gi Taek and Angela are unearthing the snacks they'd bought at the rest stop, dumping bags of chips, cookies, triangle gimbap, packaged sausages on sticks, teas, sodas, and energy drinks. After all that trouble claiming floor space earlier, our pallets are haphazardly pushed against the walls and doors.

Everyone sits around in a circle and chooses their food from the pile. Jaewoo and I sit together, with our knees touching. At one point he grabs a blanket from one of the bunched pallets and puts it over us, with most of it on my lap and the rest on his. We hold hands beneath the blanket. I think I'm being sneaky, but I catch Sori's eye and she smiles before looking away.

It's one of the best nights of my life. We play Korean "drinking" games that I'd never heard of, let alone played. In one game, we have to pass a playing card around with just our mouths. If you drop the card, you have to take a shot of an energy drink. It's fun and ridiculous and I don't drop the card, though Jaewoo does, just once, our lips brushing.

Everyone jeers and teases Jaewoo as he takes the shot, but I remain seated, my face bright red, my lips tingling from his inadvertent kiss.

At six in the morning, the boys climb back over the wall, so that they'll be in their house in time to "wake up" in a half hour. It seems that we're not the only ones who've had an active night as most of the students at breakfast are bleary-eyed and non-talkative. Afterward Jaewoo, Nathaniel, Sori, Gi Taek, Angela, and I all sign up for a walk on the nature trail, which really is just an excuse for us to find a secluded field and take a nap in a pile.

With our classmates too tired from the night before to take much of an interest in anything besides sleep, Jaewoo and I decide to risk sitting together on the bus ride back to Seoul. Sori bullies Angela into sitting next to her, which leaves Gi Taek with Nathaniel. They gab the whole way back to SAA in the seats directly behind Jaewoo and me. But we don't mind, spending most of the bus ride slouched low and watching videos on my phone while sharing ear buds.

When we reach the academy, Jaewoo mouths, "I'll contact you," before heading over to XOXO's waiting manager with Nathaniel and Youngmin, who spent the majority of the field trip swimming in the lake. I don't exactly know *how* he'll contact me, since as far as I know his phone is still being monitored, but I trust that he'll figure out a way.

After spending so many hours with Jaewoo, I feel bereft. Sori has to strongarm me into going back to the dorms, where she insists we take "proper showers." Unfortunately, most of the other girls have the same idea.

"I refuse to go to sleep without bathing," Sori says eyeing the line of girls snaking all the way to the stairwell, and texts Angela. We meet up with her outside the dorms (she's on the second floor), then head over to the street where Sori motions for a cab.

"Where are we going?" I ask.

"Bathhouse," Sori replies.

While there are bathhouses in LA, I've never gone to one so I'm not entirely sure what to expect. But I quickly get into the fun of it as Sori, Angela, and I strip naked and take turns scrubbing each other's backs in a spa setting, complete with showers and multiple bathing pools. Afterward, we head over to a communal lounge area, dressed in oversized pajama-like clothing provided by the bathhouse. We get cold noodles in the restaurant and cucumber sheet masks from the small store, placing them on our faces and lying in a bed of cool stones, giggling at every little thing because we're functioning on very little sleep.

I don't get back to the dorms until right before curfew, at which time my phone pings with a text message in English— Hey, it's Jaewoo. I check the number and see that the text is from Nathaniel's phone.

I quickly text back, Hi.

The message is marked "read," then the little circles appear, signifying that he's typing. Like our first and only ever text exchange, I recall that he's a fast responder when he does have access to his phone. How was the rest of your day?

Good! I proceed to type out my first ever experience at a bathhouse, finally ending with: It was a lot of fun, though I think Angela and Sori have seen more of me than even my mom has in recent years. I send and then immediately regret my entire existence. Why oh why did I say that last part?

There's a significant wait time in which I close my eyes and roll around on my bed. Finally, my phone pings. I peek one eye open.

I wish I could have been there.

Oh. My. God.

I type up several responses, including We should go together next time and Wish you were there too, but end up deleting them all, overcome with embarrassment. I settle with How was the rest of your day?

We text back and forth for a little longer. This week he has more free time, but starting the following week, XOXO will be promoting the second single off their album, which means he'll be a lot busier. I feel a pinch of anxiety at the thought of things going back to the way they were, with Jaewoo ignoring me and me unsure about his feelings, but then quickly dismiss those worries. Things are good *now*, and that's all that matters.

Good night. I send, then add, I miss you.

My phone pings immediately with his response. Night. I miss you too.

"Jenny!" Sori shouts from her side of the room. "I'm going to murder you if you don't go to sleep *right now!*"

Thirty

Monday is another assembly day. Sori and I put on our blazers and hurry over to the concert hall. Though it's spring, it's still cool enough in the mornings that the blazer offers some warmth. By noon however, most students will be shucking them to eat their lunch beneath the afternoon sun.

Inside the auditorium, we take seats near the middle. I wave to Angela a few rows down, seated with a couple girls from her major.

Jaewoo, Nathaniel, and Youngmin aren't at the assembly. According to Jaewoo's texts, after the field trip, XOXO had a packed weekend of activities and their manager is letting them skip first period.

It's amazing how being able to communicate has done wonders for our relationship. If I ever need to talk to him, I can just text him. Though sometimes there's a lag, with Nathaniel acting go between.

At one point yesterday, after Jaewoo had sent me a particularly flirtatious text, I panic-texted him, What if Nathaniel reads this?

Oh, he replied, he for sure would.

What?!

So I delete them all before I give him his phone back.

"If you're not careful," Sori says, "one of the teachers is going to confiscate your phone." I'd taken it out of my pocket, almost unconsciously, to check if I had any new texts from Jaewoo. "Though maybe that would be a good thing," she muses.

I know she's only joking, but also there's truth to her teasing, and I don't want to be *that* friend. I put away my phone.

Like the first day of school, the principal walks out onto the stage once all the students are seated. We have to stand right back up to bow to her, but then quickly resume our seats.

She begins with the expectations for the second quarter and ends with logistics about the end-of-the-year showcase. We'll all have to audition individually according to our major. For example, with orchestra, each instrument has to audition for chair placement.

We can also submit a piece for a solo or collaboration, though only a few are chosen, the principal reminds us, and the competition level is high. She reiterates that representatives from all the major schools, talent agencies, and entertainment companies will be present in the audience.

Plus all our families. Which reminds me that I need to invite Mom and Halmeoni. For once, our schedules overlap and my mom should be at the clinic when I visit Halmeoni this Sunday.

As we're leaving the auditorium, Sori hooks her arm with

my own and gives me a sidelong glance. "I was thinking . . . after watching Nathaniel and Gi Taek's performance, which was ridiculous, let's be clear, but it gave me an idea . . ."

"Spit it out, Sori."

"What if *we* auditioned together, as a duo. You could still audition as a soloist," she says quickly, "but, like, I thought it would be cool. I remember you showing me your performance of 'The Swan,' and it reminded me of the ballet. We could do something similar. What do you think?"

"I think . . ." I say, pretending it's a hard decision to make as she bites her lip expectantly, ". . . that sounds like a great idea! I'd love to perform together with you." I've never performed a duet with anyone before, and the thought of doing one with Sori, who's such an incredible dancer, excites me as much as the thought of how much fun we'll have practicing together.

I'll still prepare for my solo audition, but this is something I really want to do.

"I'm so glad!" Sori beams. With our arms still linked, we make our way across the quad in time for homeroom.

Jaewoo doesn't show up to second period and I don't hear from him until lunch, when my phone vibrates in my pocket. Meet me in the 5th floor stairwell of the performing arts building.

"I'll see you guys later," I say without looking up.

"Have fun. Don't get pregnant," Gi Taek says as a farewell.

Practically sprinting to the PA building, I take the elevator up to the fifth floor. I guess I could have taken the *stairs* to meet Jaewoo in the *stairwell*, but I refuse to be sweaty and out of breath.

As the doors open, I'm surprised to find people in the hall. I feel self-conscious as I take the short few steps from the elevators to the exit door, like they *know* somehow I'm on my way to an assignation. The door is one of those industrial fire escape doors and I have difficulty pushing it open, finally stumbling out onto the fifth-floor landing.

I yelp as a hand grabs my wrist, pulling me into the corner. Jaewoo wraps his arms around me.

"Why here?" I say. "And why are we bunched in the corner like this?" Not that I'm complaining.

"Look up," he says.

In the corner of the ceiling, angled right above us, is a security camera.

"They have them all over school," Jaewoo says, "but of course there are some blind spots."

"And you know them all. You're like a spy, or a criminal."

"Yes, please continue comparing me to unlawful citizens."

I hook my arms around his neck. "What are we stealing?" I can feel Jaewoo's grin against my lips.

"Time?" he suggests. He must mean it as a joke, but it's actually the very thing we're trying to steal. Moments like this are so few and far between. Once XOXO starts promoting their second single next week, time with him will become even more precious.

Maybe it's the fear of that, the looming separation, that

makes every kiss that much more desperate.

When we finally break apart, Jaewoo gasps, "Are you free this Saturday?"

"I am," I say, equally breathless. "Why?"

He grins. "Would you like to go on a date with me?"

Thirty-one

I've never actually been on a date. I realize this the following Saturday when I'm supposed to meet Jaewoo and everything in my closet looks overworn and not special enough for the occasion.

"This is my moment to shine," Sori says.

"Yeah!" Angela agrees from where she sits cross-legged on Sori's bed with Gi Taek. As for Gi Taek, he's reading one of the smut manhwa from the hidden stash in the bottom drawer of Sori's side table.

"Sori." I grimace, when she pulls out a tight bodycon dress. "We're not going clubbing."

"You don't know that," she says, returning the dress to the rack.

"I doubt he'd take me to a place where he'd probably be recognized within minutes of stepping inside."

"You wouldn't get in anyway," Gi Taek says, not looking up from his book. "You're both underage."

"Didn't Bae Jaewoo tell you anything about where he's taking you?" Sori asks, exasperated.

"Not the location," I say, "but he did tell me the activity. We're going to watch a movie."

"Boring," Gi Taek and Sori announce.

"I love movies!" Angela beams, my only true friend.

"Well, what do *you* want to wear, Jenny?" Sori says. "You're partly dressing up for Jaewoo—I mean, it's your first date and you want him to lose his mind—but this is mostly for you. What sort of outfit are you imagining for yourself? What will you feel confident in?"

These are good questions and I think seriously before answering. "I want to wear something I wouldn't normally wear but is still me."

"Hmm," she looks at me contemplatively. "What about this?" Moving away from her rack, which holds most of her show-stopping outfits, she reaches into her closet and pulls out a little black dress. Except that it's not black, but a very rich dark brown. "Try it?"

I strip down to my undies and Angela squeals, though she's seen me naked. Gi Taek covers his face with his comic book. I step into the dress and pull the little cap sleeves over my shoulders. It has an attached choker, which I hook closed, and a sweetheart neckline. Finished, I move toward Sori's floor-length mirror, but she stops me.

"Put these on first so you can have the full effect." She pulls out a pair of knee-high boots.

I put them on in the entranceway so that I don't damage the

floor of the room. Gi Taek and Angela get off the bed to join Sori in crowding around me as I look at myself in the mirror for the first time.

"Wow," I say, and really that's all there is to say. The dress fits snugly over my shoulders and chest, flaring slightly out at the waist. The boots accentuate my long legs. "Are you sure I don't look overdressed?"

"You look hot, Jenny. And you should be overdressed. You're on a date. You're with a cute boy. Everyone should know it."

"Not really," Gi Taek says. "One clear picture sent to *Bulletin* of the two of you out together, looking all couple-y, and it's game over."

"*I'm* the one with experience in secretly dating a boy from XOXO," Sori says, "and I can say that you'll be safe with Jaewoo. He's the responsible one. I'm sure he's taking you somewhere he's already scoped out."

I feel a shiver of excitement go down my spine at the thought of spending so much time with Jaewoo. I'm nervous, not just about the date, but also about whether we can even have a real date without the fear of discovery, but I push those thoughts to the back of my head because I *want* to go on this date, and I want to wear *this dress*.

"You look great, Jenny," Angela says, and I smile at her through the mirror.

Gi Taek sighs. "What time is your date anyway?"

"Jaewoo says he's going to pick me up outside the dorms at two."

I'm taken aback by the look of shock on all their faces.

"What? Is that weird?"

Sori yells, "We only have a half hour to do your hair and makeup!"

I'm outside at the curb at two o'clock sharp.

At 2:05, Jaewoo hasn't appeared, so I walk down to the corner of the street to see if he's coming from that direction. I know he doesn't have Nathaniel's phone on him because he said he wouldn't, so I can't even text him.

Then a minute later, a sleek, blue car pulls up next to me, with Jaewoo in the driver's seat. Before he can get out, I open the door and slip inside.

I feel a warm glow as I see how he's drinking in the sight of me. "You look great."

"Thanks! I have questions though."

"Yeah, sorry I was late. There was traffic—"

"First of all, you can drive? And second, *you have a car?*"

He laughs. "Yes and yes. I got my license early this year. I usually keep my car parked in the garage of our dorms, but I have to drive it now and then to keep the engine fresh."

He eases away from the curb. He's not as dressed up as I am, wearing a hoodie and black jeans, but he's definitely put in some effort. There's gel in his hair and he's wearing a pair of stud earrings that are a deep red that sort of match my dress, which is completely coincidental but pleases me nonetheless.

"You want to play some music?" he asks. "You can sync up your phone to the car."

"Sure." I reach for my phone and open up Bluetooth. "I can play anything?"

"Knock yourself out."

I scroll through my song choices. Something about this conversation gives me a sense of déjà vu.

"That night at the karaoke bar, when I was looking for a song for you to sing. An XOXO song was listed in the book, wasn't it?"

"Yeah. It was one of the songs we released before our first full-length album."

"Imagine if I'd had you sing *that* song."

"I would have rocked it, obviously."

I don't have that exact song on my phone, so I instead play XOXO's "Don't Look Back," which is my favorite of theirs anyway.

Jaewoo shakes his head and I start laughing.

"I'm glad this amuses you."

"Don't tell me you don't listen to your own songs and sing along to your parts."

"To be honest, I don't . . ." He pauses. "I like to rap Sun and Youngmin's parts."

"Oh my God, you *have* to do it now."

"Only if you sing the vocal parts."

"You're on!"

I restart "Don't Look Back" from the beginning and this time sing the first verse. Then when it's Youngmin's rap break, I cheer Jaewoo along.

It takes us about an hour from the academy to reach our destination, a small city outside the Seoul capital area, all of which is spent singing and talking. On roads where there's less traffic, Jaewoo rests his right arm on the console between us so I can play with his fingers.

It's wild that we have to drive so far to watch a movie—when there's a mall with a theater one subway stop from our school—but it makes sense too. Out here, it's unlikely we'll encounter paparazzi.

"I already purchased the tickets for the movie," Jaewoo says, "so we have a half hour to kill."

"Okay," I say. "What do you want to do?"

"It's up to you," he says. "We could go over to the theater and see what's around there."

"That sounds perfect," I say as he links his fingers through mine.

Luckily, for a Saturday, the mall where the theater is located is not crowded, and most of the people are either older or with their families. No one pays us any attention. We naturally gravitate toward the small arcade outside the theater without either of us saying anything.

We spend some time playing this zombie shooting game, reaching the fourth level only to be killed in a splatter of gore. Then, before leaving, Jaewoo tries his hand at winning a plushie for me from one of the claw machines. He spends about ₩10000 on ten attempts with no success.

"It's rigged!" he yells, after the plush doll drops right next to the chute.

"It's okay," I say soothingly, holding back my laughter at how exasperated, and cute, he looks.

As we step away from the machine, a little girl hops up and slips in ₩1000, maneuvering the sticks lightly and pressing the Go button. The claw descends, picks up the plushie, and deposits it into the chute. Reaching in, she grabs the stuffed animal, blinks up at us, and then runs away.

"To be fair," I say after a long pause, "I'm sure an eight year old would appreciate that plushie more than I would."

"Maybe I can buy it off her."

"Jaewoo!"

He hooks an arm around me, and we walk side by side to the concessions stand.

"Since you got the tickets and paid for the arcade games, I'll get the food," I announce.

"It's fine. I'll get them."

"I insist."

"Jenny, I just signed an endorsement deal with Samsung." He grins. "Let me spoil you with popcorn."

"Wow," I say, "that's—that's amazing. Congratulations."

"Thanks. It wasn't just me. All the members signed the deal—it's our biggest so far."

He approaches the counter for the concession stand, scrolling through the manual ordering system.

I stand behind him, feeling suddenly overwhelmed.

He's likely a millionaire *at seventeen*. He owns an expensive-looking *car*.

I remind myself it's not like we're in this Cinderella

relationship. I'm not destitute. Though my mom's a single parent, she's a *lawyer*, and I've never *not* been able to buy what I wanted, especially after getting my part-time job at Uncle Jay's. But it's hard to shake the feeling that our lives are dramatically different.

"Should we get a combo?" Jaewoo asks. "Then we can try all the different flavors of popcorn."

"Okay," I say, though I'm not really paying attention.

The strange feeling doesn't dissipate until we've taken our seats and the movie starts to play. At first, it's weird seeing Korean subtitles at the bottom of a movie in English, but then I get absorbed in what's happening on screen and I completely forget about the subtitles.

By the time the movie's over, I'm feeling my normal self again. So what if he's rich and successful? I'm not comparing myself to him; it's not like I think I'm unworthy of him.

A glance at my phone shows it's a little past six. The plan was to make it back to the dorms by ten, which means we only have a few more hours.

"Want to grab dinner?" Jaewoo asks. "There are restaurants on the top floor."

"Okay," I say, taking his hand.

"Oppa," a voice says, from close behind us. "I thought that was you. What are you doing here? And who is *she*?"

Thirty-two

Behind us is a middle schooler, perhaps thirteen or fourteen, with a cell phone in her hand. This was a mistake. I should have never let him take me out on this date. I knew it was too good to be true. Now we'll be exposed and our relationship will end before it truly had the chance to begin.

"Joori-yah," Jaewoo says. "What are you doing at the mall so late?"

I'm so in my head that it takes me a moment to realize he's addressing her by name, which means he *knows* her.

"Jenny, this is my yeodongsaeng," Jaewoo says, placing a hand on her head, "Bae Joori."

His little sister. Now that I'm looking for a resemblance, I can see they have the same straight nose and narrow jawline. His handsome features look striking on her small face.

"Nice to meet you," I say.

"Nice to meet you!" she returns, then whips her head in Jaewoo's direction, one hand on her hip. "Are you coming home?

Is that why you're in the neighborhood?"

This is his *neighborhood*? No wonder he was confident bringing me here. He must know the area well. Though I thought he was from Busan. . . .

I must look confused because he says, "My mom and Joori moved to the city a year ago. I meant to tell you."

I narrow my eyes and he rubs the back of his neck, looking sheepish. Joori shakes her head and clicks her tongue.

"It must be nice to have them close," I concede.

He sighs in relief, then turns to his sister. "I don't know, Joori-yah. Mom probably hasn't prepared anything. . . ."

"She can order delivery! Please say you'll come."

When Jaewoo appears hesitant, Joori appeals to me. "Eonni." She addresses me as she would an older sister. "Will you come have dinner at our house, please?"

I smile, charmed. "I would love to."

We decide to walk the three blocks to Jaewoo's family's apartment, which is on the twenty-fifth floor of a residential apartment building, sprinting the last hundred feet when it starts to rain.

Joori texted ahead to let their mother know we're coming, and so when we arrive, the kitchen is already emitting delicious cooking smells—garlic, sesame oil, and soy sauce.

Joori follows Jaewoo into the kitchen while I take off Sori's boots. I pull down my skirt—I would have worn something more conservative if I'd known I was going to meet *his mother* today—and hurry to follow.

"Eomma," Jaewoo says, as a tall neat-looking woman in an apron embraces him. "You didn't have to prepare a whole meal." The small table in the kitchen is covered with side dishes, with only an empty spot in the middle.

"Of course I did," she says. "We have a *guest*."

Her eyes turn expectantly on me.

"This is Go Jooyoung," Jaewoo says, and I look at him in surprise that he remembered my Korean name. I'd only told him once, back in LA. "She goes by her English name, Jenny. She's my girlfriend."

"Yeochin!" Joori shouts. "I knew it!"

I stare at him, wide-eyed. I didn't think he'd introduce me as his girlfriend, but as a classmate. We'd kept it a secret at school, besides our friends who've figured it out for themselves, and it's surprising to be so open about it. Then again, this is his family, these are the people he loves and trusts.

"You're very welcome here Jooyoung-ah," Jaewoo's mother says, "ah, I mean, Jenny." She smiles. "We're just waiting on . . ." The doorbell rings. "There it is now!"

She opens the door and bows to the deliveryman who hands over a wrapped package. Bringing it to the kitchen, she opens the package and takes out a whole roasted chicken. She shoos Jaewoo away when he moves to assist her. "Why don't you show Jenny the apartment while I finish setting out the meal?"

The apartment is spacious, about twice the size of my grand-mother's.

"This is my room!" Joori says, pushing open the door nearest the kitchen. It's a medium-sized room with a full-size bed, a desk with in-progress homework, open books, and a computer. There are anime posters on the walls and a video console connected to a small TV.

"My brother spoils me," she says when she catches me looking. I'd noticed the massive flat screen in the living room earlier, and I wonder if he'd bought that for them too. Maybe even the entire apartment.

We skip Jaewoo's mother's room and go straight to Jaewoo's, next to the entranceway. As I enter the room, he closes the door behind us, and I realize Joori hadn't followed us inside. I turn away from him, suddenly nervous.

His is the smallest room in the apartment, which makes sense because he lives with the other XOXO members the majority of the time. It's sparsely furnished with a dresser, a bookcase, and a twin bed. I look away from the bed, blushing, and instead focus on the bookcase. There's mostly albums on the shelves, a few books, and two photographs. I pick up the first, a grainy photo of his family at the beach, his sister and mother standing on either side of him. Joori's adorable with a gap-toothed smile, no older than six years old, which would make Jaewoo around ten or eleven. Unlike his mother and sister, he's not smiling in the photo.

"We just moved back to Busan that summer," Jaewoo says. "After my parent's divorce, we lived in the US for a couple of years, so that my mom could escape the gossip, but ended up moving back to Korea when we ran out of money. It wasn't an easy time. I got in a lot of fights when I was a kid, nothing serious, just mad at the other kids saying stuff about my mom. You weren't far off when you called me a gangster." Though his last words are teasing, there's a wariness to them.

Lifting my hand, I trail my fingers across the photograph. On a closer look, I can see a bruise beneath Jaewoo's eye. And his arm is crooked at a slightly awkward angle. I look up. "Is this . . . ?" Back in LA, in the photobooth, I'd asked him if it had hurt, breaking his arm, and he'd answered, not as much as the first time.

He nods. "Soon after that photo was taken, I was scouted for Joah. At first, I refused. But they came back the following year and my mom forced me to go. I didn't know if I was doing the right thing, moving to Seoul. I always loved music, but I didn't want to leave my mom and Joori."

I place the photo back on the shelf. It must have been so hard for him, leaving behind his mother and sister when he'd spent so much of his childhood protecting them. Though I can see in his story how it was his mother who was protecting him by sending him away.

Reaching out, I pick up the second photo on his shelf. It's the boys of XOXO, though they all appear younger. Jaewoo and Nathaniel both scrappy fifteen-year-olds, Sun handsome and elegant even at seventeen, and Youngmin thirteen years old, flashing a peace sign. Unlike the photo on the beach, Jaewoo's grinning from ear to ear, his arm thrown across the shoulders of Sun and Youngmin on one side and Nathaniel on the other.

"It was actually Sun who convinced me to stay," Jaewoo

says, "when I thought about leaving. He told me that it was hard being an older brother, but with him around, I didn't have to be the strong one anymore. Then when Nathaniel came around, I had a friend my own age, someone who challenged me to be better, and then finally Youngmin. . . . He makes me want to be a role model, a hyeong."

I place the photo back on the shelf. I'm overcome with feelings, sadness for his childhood, happiness that he's found support and love with XOXO and the other members, and this ache inside me to protect him, to keep him safe.

"Wow," he says, rubbing the back of his neck. "I can't seem to stop opening myself up to you. It's been like this from the beginning. You do something to me. It feels similar to song-writing, but better."

"No, it's the same for me." I pause. "I can't believe I'm going to tell you this."

He laughs. "What?"

"The night we met, I had just gotten feedback from the judges of my latest cello competition. They told me I lacked spark. And so, when we first met in the karaoke room, I was annoyed about what they said, but also at you, 'cause you were annoying."

He laughs, shaking his head.

"But then we met again, on the bus, and then we went to the festival, and even though it was only supposed to be for one night, the more time I spent with you, the more I didn't want it to end."

"Are you saying . . ." Jaewoo says slowly, "that I was your spark?"

"I'm saying there was a spark between us!" I move to punch him playfully and he catches my wrist.

"And now?"

"I don't want it to end."

He lowers his head, his lips a breath apart from mine.

"Oppa?" Joori knocks on the door. "Dinner time!"

He moves upward and presses a kiss to my forehead instead, then grabs my hand and opens the door. In the kitchen, his mother is placing a large platter of the deboned pieces of chicken in the center of the spread.

Joori looks up from where she's already seated on the far side of the square table. "Eonni, come sit next to me."

I take the seat to her left and Jaewoo sits to my right, across from her, with their mother opposite me. The last time I sat down for a meal with my family was when I first arrived in Seoul. Being here with Jaewoo and the people who love him makes me miss the people who love me. Next time I see my mother, I'm going to ask if we can sit down for a meal with Halmeoni.

Jaewoo's mother is an incredible cook. Besides the chicken she ordered, which is apparently one of Jaewoo's favorites, Jae-woo's mother cooked every single dish of banchan.

At one point I turn to Joori and ask, "Do you want to be an idol like your brother?"

"Of course not!" she says, wrinkling her nose. "I want to be a video game designer."

Jaewoo winks at her.

After dinner, Jaewoo's mom cuts off slices of Korean melon, and we watch a BBC special on penguins on the TV as outside the rain comes down even harder.

"You parked at the mall?" Jaewoo's mother asks.

"Yes. If it doesn't stop in the next half hour, we'll take an umbrella and walk over."

Jaewoo's mother frowns. "I don't know if you should be driving in this weather, especially with Jenny. I'd feel much better if you stayed the night. Jenny, would that be okay with you? You can borrow my pajamas and we have a spare tooth-brush."

"Uh," I say, for a lack of a better word. I never expected to be in a situation where my idol boyfriend's mother asks me to stay the night after my first date with said boyfriend, and also after the first time meeting her. "Okay."

"Perfect! Call your mother?"

"I live in the dorms. I'll text my roommate."

I open my phone and message Sori. I'm staying at Jaewoo's overnight. Can you cover for me? The resident assistant checks rooms at around ten o'clock, but Sori can pretend I'm already in bed.

Sure, comes Sori's immediate response. Then, GET IT GIRL!!!!!

I quickly look up, but Jaewoo and his family have returned to watching the penguins fall over and get back up again on TV.

His mother doesn't want him driving in the rain, I quickly type out. Also, his family is so nice???

I'm expecting details when you get back, Sori replies, and I send her a zipper mouth emoji.

After the documentary, Jaewoo's mom goes into her room and returns with one of those long, and in my opinion very unflattering but comfortable dresses that I've seen older Korean women wear, complete with a clashing painted flower design. I put it on and Joori giggles.

Jaewoo deadpans, "Hot."

We spend the next hour before bedtime playing Mario Kart. By eleven o'clock, we separate to our rooms, Jaewoo to his, and Joori and me to hers.

"Thank you for sharing your room with me," I say, as I slip into the bed after her. I had to displace some stuffed animals to fit.

"I'm happy to. You're like my future sister-in-law, right?" she giggles, then turns to the wall and immediately starts to snore.

I envy her peaceful slumber.

It takes me much longer to fall asleep, the events of the day buzzing in my head.

While I finally manage to drift off, I wake with a start when thunder rumbles outside the window. The clock on Joori's nightstand say it's three in the morning. Careful not wake her, I slip out of bed. In the kitchen, I fill myself a glass of water and then walk over to the balcony off the living room. The door is unlocked, so I slide it back gently and step outside. Little potted plants rim the floor, as well as a drying rack, folded and placed against the wall. The balcony isn't open to the elements, but behind a pane of glass, where the water patters against it, like music.

"Can't sleep?" Jaewoo steps onto the balcony, sliding the door closed behind him.

"Yeah." I turn from him to look back out the window. Through the rain, I can see the city. A few lights glow in the fog, sparks of life in the mist-blue darkness. And beyond all the many buildings, like a beautiful backdrop, a seemingly never-ending mountain range.

"Korea is so pretty," I say.

"Yeah," Jaewoo says softly.

"I'm going to miss it."

"You'll come back."

Unspoken words lie between us. That I will leave. That our time together is limited.

"Jenny . . ." he begins.

"Let's go inside," I interrupt. It's a conversation we have to have eventually, but not tonight. "Before we wake your mom and sister."

He hesitates, as if he wants to say more, but relents. "Okay."

Inside the apartment, neither of us says a word, and yet we both make our way to Jaewoo's room.

I climb into his bed, and he wraps his arms around me.

We don't do anything, which is both a disappointment and a relief. I must drift off eventually, because only an hour or so later, he shakes me gently awake.

"Jenny." He kisses me, on my neck below my ear.

I wake, groggily, and stumble my way back to Joori's room, sliding into her warm bed and drifting into sleep just as light peeks through the window, sunlight after rain.

Thirty-three

The next morning, Jaewoo and I head over to the mall when it opens so that I can buy socks and sneakers as well as a sweatshirt to wear over my dress. We actually purchase matching "couple" sweatshirts with cute cartoon characters, which I know Gi Taek and Sori are going to tease me horribly about, but I think we look adorable.

It's Sunday, so instead of the dorms, Jaewoo drives us to the clinic so that I can visit Halmeoni while he goes to therapy.

Walking into Halmeoni's room, I'm surprised to find my mother sitting at her bedside. I'd forgotten that she was visiting today but after spending such a great evening and morning with Jaewoo and his family, I'm excited to spend more time with mine.

"Eomma," my mom says, as I approach the bed. Halmeoni looks up at me with an apologetic glance. I've apparently walked right into something. Mom doesn't even acknowledge me. "Stop being stubborn. The doctor tells me you could have had surgery a week ago, but that you refused."

Halmeoni pouts. "You weren't here a week ago,"

"But I'm here now. We could schedule it as early as next week."

"Why?" Halmeoni says. "You're here for another three months. Why can't we wait?"

"It'll take time for you to recover," Mom counters. "And . . ." She sighs, pressing her fingers to her temples, a clear sign she's stressed. "I need to go back to my life. *Jenny* has to go back to hers. I was thinking that if you had your surgery early, we could be in LA by the end of June."

My heart drops. The thought of leaving early never occurred to me.

"My showcase is at the end of June," I say.

"I can get the surgery after," Halmeoni adds quickly. "If I get it now, I won't be well enough to see Jenny perform."

We both wait expectantly as Mom mulls over our words. "Fine," she says, and I let out a sigh of relief. "You'll watch Jenny perform at the showcase, and then we'll leave as planned, soon after you recover."

While my mom checks a text on her phone, Halmeoni and I exchange a conspiratorial glance. Of course we want to spend more time with each other, but I also know Halmeoni wants the whole three months with her daughter. And I want that time with Jaewoo and my friends.

The rest of the morning is pleasant, though my mom spends a lot of it answering emails. She does tell me a little about the case she's been working on, which sounds incredibly complicated. My heart swells with pride at all the good work she's doing.

For lunch, Mom takes Halmeoni and me to a naengmyeon restaurant near the bakery. While slurping up delicious buckwheat noodles in chilled broth, Halmeoni asks me questions about the showcase.

"I'm auditioning for a solo," I tell her. "And my friend Sori and I are also auditioning for a duet together."

"Is Sori your roommate?" Halmeoni asks. "I'm so glad you're friends now!"

"What do you mean a duet?" Mom asks sharply.

I glance at her nervously. "It's a cello and dance piece. Sori's a dance major and . . ."

"So you're doing three auditions?" Mom interrupts. "For your ensemble, solo, and this duet?"

"Yes?"

"Jenny," she says. "Aren't the auditions in less than two weeks? How are you supposed to prepare for three separate auditions? Have you talked to Eunbi?"

"Soojung-ah," Halmeoni chides. "I think it's a wonderful thing for Jenny to perform with her friend."

"It's not about a nice memory, Eomma. This is about Jenny's future." She looks at me, disappointment written all over her face. "I'm starting to regret my decision to let you come to Korea. You should be concentrating on your music, not getting distracted by your friends."

If Sori is a distraction, I shudder to think what she'd say if she knew about Jaewoo.

Across the table Halmeoni takes my hand and squeezes. "She's only upset with you because of me."

That might be true, but Mom's not wrong either. Auditioning with three separate pieces is more difficult than if I had only two to concentrate on. But I'm determined to make it work.

For the next week, I do everything I can so that all of my pieces are a success. I book more time in the practice rooms, and Sori and I continue our late-night rehearsals in the dance studio. The only downside to all the time spent in practice is that I see less of Jaewoo, Though that's partly due to his own schedule, which has gotten busier since XOXO began promoting the second single off their album.

The following Wednesday, the program of the showcase is posted. I find my name on the list of soloists and my knees almost give out.

"Jenny!" Sori shouts.

She's pointing at the paper that lists all the collaborations.

"We got it?" I ask.

"We got it!" she screams. We hug and bounce around in a circle. Ours was the only duet that was accepted. It was a relief to get the solo, but getting the duet feels like a victory, one made even sweeter because I can share it with Sori.

"Oh my God," she says. "We have to think about outfits!"

The first person I tell is Jaewoo. One of the perks of the

Samsung deal was that he and the rest of XOXO were given the latest model of smartphones, paid for by the company. And more important, *not* monitored by their manager.

Guess what? I text.

He responds immediately. You got it?

Yes!

Congrats. I can't wait for your performances. You're going to be incredible.

You'll announce me, of course. Since Jaewoo and Nathaniel have already debuted, they've opted out of performing and instead are acting as the night's MCs. Jenny Go, cellist extraordinaire, and best girlfriend in the whole wide world.

Yes, I'll say it just like that. What are you doing after school on Friday? You want to hang out?

YES!

Meet me at Joah after school? I'll give the security guard your name and information.

I'll have to cancel one of my bookings in the practice room, which is slightly painful only because they're so difficult to come by now that the showcase is a little over a month away, but I've barely seen Jaewoo since our date. Skipping a single practice won't hurt.

I take a cab to the address Jaewoo texts me right after classes get out on Friday. I don't know what I expected the main building of Joah Entertainment to look like, but it's fairly inconspicuous, with a slate-gray industrial-looking facade. I pay the cab driver and step onto the street. As I approach, the young people loitering outside, girls dressed in school uniforms like me, stare at me curiously.

The guard in the small gatehouse glances up at my approach, but then looks back down at a laptop, where he's watching some sort of variety show.

I wave at him through the window. "Excuse me."

With a heavy sigh, he stands up from his chair. "What do you want?" he says through the plated glass.

"I—" Do I just tell him I'm here to see Jaewoo? I'm sure all these other girls are also here to see him.

"Well? Speak up, girl."

"My name is on the list? Jenny Go. J-E-N-N-Y-G-O," I spell out.

I'm relieved to discover that a list actually exists when he picks up a clipboard wedged beneath the computer. Written vertically down a piece of paper are names in Korean; the very last name is mine, scribbled in English. He points to it, and I nod.

"Tell whoever you're meeting to join you in the lobby."

"Thank you." I bow.

I hurriedly enter the building, hunching my shoulders to ward off the curse-filled eyes of the girls behind me.

The interior of the building is a lot nicer than the outside. The lobby is spacious, filled with natural light from upper floor windows. There's even an employee café to the right of the lobby.

"Jenny!" Jaewoo jogs over from the elevator bank. He looks

like he just came from washing up, his hair slightly damp, wearing a loose T-shirt that shows his collarbones.

I press my hands behind me so that I don't leap into his arms. As far as anyone can tell, I'm just one of Jaewoo's classmates, along for a tour. Because of the relationship between SAA and Joah, tours are common enough that people wouldn't think twice at my being here.

"Hey," I greet him. "I think I made all your fangirls outside explode with jealousy."

"There's people outside?" Jaewoo looks in the direction of the doors. "I should ask reception to hand out some water bottles. It's the hottest day this year, by far."

I follow him to the receptionist desk so he can make the request before we head over to the elevators.

"I thought we'd go on a tour of the building, and then maybe order takeout," he says, pressing the Up button. "Is there anything you're craving?"

"Hmm . . ." I lean back against the wall of the elevator. "What's around here that delivers to this address?"

"You name it, they deliver it."

I tap a finger to my lips. "I want a double-fudge sundae, waffles, and jjajangmyeon."

"Done."

The elevator stops on the third floor and the doors open. A short foyer connects to a large dance studio with floor-to-ceiling mirrors. Emblazoned on the back wall is the company logo and sign: Joah Entertainment.

"I've seen this room before," I say. "In your dance practice videos."

"You watch those?"

"You're my boyfriend. Don't think for a second I haven't seen all your videos, even the fan-made ones that point out all the evidence that you and Nathaniel are a couple."

"That's embarrassing," Jaewoo says. "And here I thought we were being careful."

We visit a few more rooms like this one on the same floor, though smaller. Some of them are occupied by sweaty kids, ranging from ages thirteen to sixteen. When Jaewoo and I walk in, they all stop their practicing to bow, calling him "seonbae."

They bow to me too, and I mimic Jaewoo, nodding politely.

"Trainees," he explains.

Afterward, we go down a flight of stairs to the second floor where he shows me a room with a long conference table used for company meetings. The last stop on the tour is the recording studio. Jaewoo pops out to order our takeout before rejoining me. The studio is fairly small, with a leather couch and low table. The majority of the room is taken up by a control panel that looks out onto a separate room encased by glass with a recording microphone hanging from the ceiling.

"When I'm not in the practice rooms, I'm usually here or in the room next door, which has all our instruments. Right before our tour this summer, we're releasing a special extended album and including a few new tracks. I can play you a sample from one of them, if you'd like."

"I would *love* that," I say, and he smiles.

He sits on one of the large chairs in front of the control panel and I take the one beside him, swiveling so that I'm facing him.

"Here," he says, handing me a pair of large noise-canceling headphones. He plays around with few controls on the panel and then music floods my ears.

I recognize the low, beautiful sound of a cello. I look up and Jaewoo nods, a smile on his face. The cello is soon joined by a whole symphonic orchestra, violins striking a powerful chord, then the electric guitar comes in at the same time as the drums, and my whole body shivers at the effect. And that's only the intro; it gets better from there.

The song is brilliant. It's going to be genre-breaking once the vocals are added, and I can only imagine how amazing the dance that'll be choreographed for a song like this will be.

When the sample finishes playing, I take off the headphones. "I love it," I gush.

"Yeah? I'm glad to hear you say that. It's a little different than our normal sound. I think it's because everyone took a part in creating it. Sun came up with the melody, I'm writing the lyrics while Youngmin's writing the rap verses, and Nathaniel's working with the choreographer. We've included Sun's interest in rock, Nathaniel and Youngmin's love of 90s K-pop, and my interest in experimenting with sounds and blending genres. It's a lot in one song, but . . ."

"It's incredible."

Jaewoo bites his lip. "Do you really think so?"

"Yes! It's already so good. I wish you could feel what I'm

feeling right now. I'm in shock. My heart is racing. I can't even imagine what it's going to be like once you've added the lyrics."

"I'm working on them now."

"Do I get a preview?"

He laughs. "I think I want to wait a bit, until the whole song is complete, and you can have the full experience. You'll be one of the first people to hear it, I promise."

Normally I'd be pleased at the prospect but my mind snags on what he's said earlier, that the album will be released *right before our tour this summer.* Will I even be here to listen to the song? I've been so busy lately with practicing for the audition. It'll get worse in the weeks ramping up to the showcase. And now he has to prepare for not only an extended album but a tour? How will we get any time together?

"To be honest," Jaewoo says, his eyes downcast as he slides his hand across the control board. "I was a little worried, since it was my idea to include a song like this. I was afraid that I was leading our group in the wrong direction. But . . ." He looks up, meeting my eyes. "I trust your opinion. If you like the song, then I can feel confident that I'm doing the right thing."

I catch my breath, feeling overwhelmed by a rush of emotions. Because I want to be there for him when he needs support, to witness him in moments like these, when he's on the verge of creating something brilliant.

Just as I want him to be there for *me*, for my ups and downs, whatever they may be.

But how can we be, when we live in different countries? When we're pursuing such different dreams, he an idol in a band that's about to be a global sensation, me a concert cellist? And I don't even know if I'll achieve that since I'm canceling practice times to be with him.

"Where are the restrooms?" I ask abruptly.

He blinks, leaning back from where he'd sat forward in his seat, as if he couldn't help moving closer to me, even with the cameras in the room. "Out the door and down the hall to your left."

"I'll be right back." I swivel the chair around and hop out, following Jaewoo's directions.

In the bathroom, I splash cold water onto my face, staring blankly at my reflection.

What is wrong with me? Why am I getting so emotional?

It's just that, I can *feel* myself falling harder and harder for Jaewoo, and at the same time the countdown clock is ticking, for the showcase, for Halmeoni's surgery, for when I leave Korea. I just feel so overwhelmed.

When I get back, Jaewoo's no longer in the room. Instead, Sun sits on the leather couch.

I hesitate, unsure if I should leave.

"Why are you standing by the door? Come inside. Sit down." He says the words politely, in jondaemal, but his tone sounds more like a command than a request.

I sit down on one of the swivel chairs across from him.

"Jaewoo went down to pick up the food," he explains.

I nod, placing my hands on my knees. Silence ensues, with him just looking at me, his expression unreadable. Of the four members, he's the one I know the least about.

"I'm Jenny," I say, scrambling to fill the silence. "We've never met formally. I'm a classmate of Jaewoo's."

"Jaewoo's never brought a classmate to the studio before. You must be special to him."

Usually such kind words would be accompanied with a smile, but Sun's expression gives nothing away.

"He's been a good friend to me," I say carefully. "I transferred to SAA from a school in LA because of a family situation. It would have been hard to adjust to a new school, if it weren't for him."

"Jaewoo's a good kid. Responsible, kindhearted, besides being incredibly talented."

I nod vigorously.

"He means so much to a lot of people," Sun continues, "not just to his family, of course, but to everyone here at Joah. He started training at the company when he was twelve years old. It's been difficult for him, away from his family for all those years. But he kept on working hard. He'd spend hours in the studio training his body and voice.

"Everything he has now, he's earned through hard work and dedication. He's in a good place, and his talent will only bring him more opportunities, bring him more fans who will support him. He has a bright future ahead of him. It would be a shame if he lost it all now.

"And he could, if he's not careful. It only takes one mistake."

I can hardly breathe; it's like my whole body has frozen over.

"A few months in Korea," Sun says. "What a fun time for you, an adventure. It'll be a good memory when you return home."

Standing, he nods at me. "XOXO was meant to record a radio show today, did you know? But we had to cancel because Jaewoo said he couldn't make it. How odd, that he'd back out of something we'd scheduled weeks in advance. I have to go make apologies on behalf of the group. Of course that's my job as the leader, to protect the members. I'll always protect them, even from themselves."

By the time Jaewoo returns, Sun has left. I follow him to where he's laid out the takeout food on a table in the kitchen. He's ordered everything I'd asked for: jjajangmyeon, a chocolate-fudge sundae, and both breakfast and dessert waffles because he wasn't sure which kinds I wanted.

A few trainees walk in and join us for the meal. I listen and laugh and pretend like everything's fine.

Afterward, Jaewoo walks me to the lobby.

"Thanks for coming by today," he says. "It was good to see you. Sorry I haven't been around—"

"Jaewoo," I interrupt, Sun's words still ringing in my mind. "I don't want you to . . . pass up opportunities because you, I don't know, think you're being a bad boyfriend."

"What are you talking about?"

"Like today. You should have gone to the radio show."

He frowns. "How do you know about that?"

"I just don't want you to . . . to risk your career because of me."

"What are you . . . that's not . . ."

He reaches for me and then realizing what he's doing, drops his hand. Across the lobby, the receptionists are watching us. A look of frustration passes over his face. "I don't know what this is about, but you don't have to worry about my . . . career. I know what I'm doing. I know what I want."

My heart is racing and I feel on the verge of tears. "I'll text you when I get back to the dorms, okay?"

He watches me a second, and then finally nods. "Okay."

I leave before he says anything more, catching a cab and crying the whole way back to the dorms.

Thirty-four

After taking a long, hot shower, I text Jaewoo on the way back to my room. Sorry for leaving like that. I had a great time with you today.

Jaewoo responds immediately. Don't worry about it. Thanks for texting me that you got back safe.

For the next few weeks, Jaewoo is more attentive than usual, constantly checking in, sending me his schedule every morning, and calling me at night. I try to put the conversation I had with Sun out of my head, but it worries me to think Jaewoo is messing up his own opportunities because of me. I know that I've canceled practice sessions to be with him. It's just that with the showcase and Jaewoo's packed schedule, I feel like I'm having to choose between Jaewoo and my future more and more and I feel . . . overwhelmed.

Since my cello instructor at school has to spread her time between students, I schedule a private lesson with Eunbi over video. After playing my solo for her—"Vocalise" by the Russian composer Sergei Rachmaninoff—I listen as she makes corrections and tells me which parts need a bit more finessing.

As our lesson is finishing up, she says, "Before I let you go, I wanted to tell you about an email I got this morning. The LA Philharmonic is interested in featuring soloists from the local high schools. It's by invitation only and was sent out to all the teachers in the area. The audition is the last Saturday of June."

That's a week after the showcase.

"I was hoping to enter you," Eunbi says, her enthusiasm evident through the screen. "I really think you should come. It's a great opportunity. Jenny, is something the matter?"

"No, I—" I paste a smile on my face. "Thank you for telling me. Can I have some time to think about it?"

That night at dinner, Sori and Angela notice my lack of appetite.

"What's wrong, Jenny?" Angela asks. "Tteok-bokki's your favorite."

We're back at the Korean restaurant outside SAA's main gate, sharing a hot plate of the spicy cylinder rice cakes.

When I tell them what Eunbi said, they're quiet for a few seconds.

Then Sori asks, "Are going to do it?"

"I'd have to leave Seoul a month early."

"But it's, like, the opportunity of a lifetime."

"I don't have to do the Philharmonic as long as the showcase goes well." Though it's not the same. A solo performance at the showcase will be great for my resume, but a spot on the LA

Philharmonic for the entire summer? That *is* an opportunity of a lifetime.

"Is it 'cause of Jaewoo?" Angela asks softly.

And I know what she's asking. Is it because I don't want to leave him?

Only a few weeks ago, I told him I didn't want him to pass up on opportunities because of me. Shouldn't I say the same for myself?

Sighing, I reach for my wallet to pay.

"What's that?" Angela asks.

I follow her finger to where she's pointing at a small corner of plastic peeking out from one of the wallet's inner pockets.

I pull out the sticker photo, the one Jaewoo and I took in the booth back in November. I place it at the center of the table and Angela and Sori crowd around it.

"Oh my God, it's you and Jaewoo!" Angela exclaims.

"Where was this taken?" Sori asks.

"In LA."

"And you keep it in your wallet?" Angela beams. "How cute!"

"Emo!" a loud voice shouts from behind us, calling the restaurant worker. Startled, I look up to see Jina and a friend of hers sitting two tables down. I'd been so caught up in my own head, I hadn't been paying attention to my surroundings.

But if Jina heard any of our conversation, she doesn't show it, ordering a plate of tteok-bokki for her table.

"Does Jaewoo have this same photograph?" Angela asks.

"Don't sticker photos get printed in pairs?"

"The printer of the machine broke when printing our photos so I'm the only one with a physical copy. Which reminds me, I should send it to him again."

I hover the camera over the sticker photo. As I press capture, a text message appears.

Are you free? I'm parked behind the library.

"It's Jaewoo," I say, grabbing the photo from the table and stuffing it into my pocket. "I wasn't expecting to see him this week. He's been so busy . . ."

"Did you forget?" Sori asks. "I booked one of the practice rooms for our rehearsal."

Dammit. I forgot. "Can we reschedule?"

"Are you serious? You know how difficult it is to secure practice rooms."

"Don't be mad, Sori-yah," Angela attempts to intercede. "Jenny hardly ever gets to spend time with Jaewoo."

"God, this is reminding so much like how it was with Nathaniel. You're not his beck and call girl, you know? You don't have to drop everything just because he comes around."

"He's the one with the schedule," I say defensively.

"*You* have a schedule too. We need to practice or we won't be ready for the showcase. I thought you said you needed something unique to stand out in your portfolio. Are you really going to blow your chances of a future, a long-term one, for a guy who can never, and I mean *never*, put you first?"

Sori's voice breaks on the last sentence, her eyes never

leaving mine. I know part of her frustration comes from her concern for me, but also a part of it is stems from her history with Nathaniel.

"It's okay," Angela says softly. "When's the next time you'll get this chance? You should go, yeah? Every moment is precious." I give Sori an apologetic look and then get up from the table.

Guilt gnaws at me for abandoning Sori as I run through the school gates and across the lawn toward the library. She's not wrong. I *should* be practicing for the showcase, since a great performance will help my portfolio stand out from all the others applying to music schools next year. That's what I should be thinking about, next year, my future, not *this moment,* running toward a boy who I know can never truly be mine. But I can't help myself, we hardly get to see each other as it is, and after the showcase, I'll only have a month left in Seoul. I need to take advantage of every moment we can grab together.

Jaewoo's car is parked where he said it was, right at the curb of the street behind the library. The passenger door is unlocked and I jump inside. He's already facing me, a warm smile on his face. I fling myself across the console and kiss him soundly on the lips.

He laughs when I release him. "It's good to see you too."

"How long do you have?"

He grimaces. "Not long. We're filming an episode of *Catch Me If You Can* this weekend. We already filmed the Seoul portion, but we're leaving soon to film the rest. If I head out in a half hour, I should make it in time."

A delivery van drives close by us down the street, honking at a few jaywalking students.

"Do you think we're too exposed here?" I ask.

"Yeah." He shifts the gear into drive. We take a few side roads to a small parking garage where Jaewoo leaves his car, grabbing a ball cap out of the backseat.

The street outside the parking garage is empty, the few open businesses a chicken shop, a beauty store, and three karaoke places with bright neon signs.

Jaewoo and I look at each other, clearly having the same idea.

We pick one at random and go down a flight of stairs into the basement of the building. It's about half the size as Uncle Jay's place, with six small rooms on either side of a poorly lit hall, overseen by a crone-like woman sitting on a low stool watching a K-drama.

She gives us a narrow-eyed once-over as Jaewoo hands over cash, paying for an hour in the room even though we have less than thirty minutes.

Once in our room Jaewoo takes off his baseball cap and picks up the controller to queue in a few songs. I glance at the door, where there's a small window, glazed over from age and debris. Then the first of the songs begins, and I don't know who moves first but we're suddenly in each other's arms, kissing like we can't get enough of each other. The backs of my knees hit the edge of the seat and we break apart only for me to scoot onto the faux leather, with Jaewoo climbing over me.

Slowly he lowers his body, watching me closely, to make sure this is okay.

I nod, almost imperceptibly, bending my arm to wrap my hand around his forearm. His muscles are taut as he holds the majority of his weight off me. I close my eyes just as his lips reach mine, and they're soft, and gentle, and achingly sweet. Everything that was rigid and nervous inside me melts with the touch of his lips.

The music he'd queued up earlier transitions into another song as I kiss him back, a bit more aggressively, moving my arms to circle his neck, my legs gripping his waist. His hands tremble as he unbuttons my shirt, while I pull his shirt from his waistband.

When his fingers brush against my rib cage, I gasp, and his eyes immediately flit to mine. "Are you all right?" he asks. "Is this okay?"

This is the farthest we've ever gone, and though I'm nervous, the answer is "Yes," as I reach for him. "Yes."

We don't stop until we realize it's silent in the room, the songs on the queue having run out.

I look to the monitor to see the timer displays 29:00 minutes.

"We should go," I say, sitting up. My whole face is flushed. He's no better.

"I could be late," he says with a groan. "I'll just be late."

I edge off the seat and stand. "*I* don't want you to be late.

And also . . ." I blush, "I want more time, for this, for us."

"Yeah." He joins me, a crooked smile on his lips. "I do too."

We each tidy up the other person. He buttons my shirt and I smooth down his hair and put on his cap, flipping it forward so that the bill shadows his eyes.

Outside, the karaoke room owner inspects us closely, but we must pass the test because she doesn't say anything.

Five minutes later, Jaewoo drops me off outside my dorm.

In my room, Sori's not back yet. I try to do my history homework, but it's hard to concentrate, replaying those moments with Jaewoo over and over again.

When Sori does finally show up, she doesn't say a word to me, sitting at her desk and putting in her earbuds.

I really want to talk to her, to process what happened, but she's giving off scary vibes. At ten, she leaves her desk and shuts off the light. Facing the wall, she goes to sleep.

Thirty-five

In the following weeks I pour myself into practicing for the showcase, which includes extra orchestra rehearsals and hours with Sori trying to nail down our collaborative duet. We've perfected all the technical aspects of the piece, but when our respective advisors—my orchestra director and her dance instructor—come to critique our performance, both point out the same glaring truth: we're not in harmony. Which isn't surprising. It's difficult to be in harmony when one of us is not speaking to the other.

I'm walking across the quad the Saturday before the showcase, when a familiar voice calls out my name.

I turn. "Mom?" It takes me a moment to register that she's actually here, on campus. For the three-and-a-half months I've been at SAA, she hasn't visited. I know she's been busy, but I wish she'd found time to visit at least once.

Still, she's here now. I walk over, smiling. "When did you arrive? You should have texted me you were coming."

"Jenny, we need to talk." My heart drops into my stomach. "Is there some place quiet we can sit?"

"There are tables outside the library." I lead her to a table that faces the quad, shaded by a large tree. "I usually sit here when I have study hall, especially now that it's warmer."

She perches at the very edge of the circular seat.

"Can I get you anything?" I ask. "There's a coffee vending machine—"

"Why didn't you tell me about the opportunity to play with the Philharmonic?"

I blanch. Eunbi must have told her. I hadn't because I was still holding out that the showcase would go so well that I wouldn't *need* the Philharmonic. I could spend one last month in Seoul, as planned.

Mom watches me, waiting for an answer.

"I didn't think it was possible," I lie. "School doesn't end for another month."

"Is it because you have a boyfriend?"

I must look startled because she says, "Your halmeoni let it slip by accident." Standing, she brushes imaginary dirt off her skirt. "I already spoke to your teachers here at SAA, and they said you can take your finals online. And once you turn in your English and history papers, you'll have met all the requirements for LACHSA. You can leave Seoul as early as next week, in time to audition for the Philharmonic."

Next week? "But—but what about the showcase?"

"The showcase is next Friday, isn't it? Your return flight isn't until the following Sunday."

I gape at her. "You already bought the tickets?"

"Yes. You'll do the showcase, which Eunbi says will be pivotal for your portfolio, and then leave, like I said."

I can't believe this is happening. Today is Saturday. I have a little over a week in Seoul, in Korea.

"I can't just *leave*," I say. "Halmeoni still hasn't had her surgery yet."

"Don't make that an excuse," she says sharply. "She's not your mother, she's mine."

"Then why aren't you spending more time with her?" I think of Halmeoni, the last few times I've visited her, the sadness in her eyes. "She misses you."

I miss you.

"I didn't come here to argue with you. I came to tell you what our plans are moving forward."

"What *your* plans are for me." I'm getting all mixed up, my emotions making me raise my voice. My mother looks around, grimacing at the attention we're receiving. "You're not even asking me what I want."

"What do you want?"

"I want to stay in Korea."

She narrows her eyes. "Because of a boyfriend?"

"Because I love it here. I have a life here. Friends." Family, though I don't say that.

"Jenny." My mom sighs, and she genuinely sounds tired. "Don't jeopardize your future because of a few wonderful months in Seoul. I understand how new experiences can feel exciting, but they're just temporary. Don't prioritize short-term moments over long-term goals. I know you're unhappy now, but once you're back home in LA, you'll see it was all for the best."

I race to my dorm room and call Jaewoo the minute my mom leaves.

He doesn't pick up, so I text him.

Where are you? I need to talk.

He texts back immediately, which means he saw my call but couldn't answer: Sorry, I have a taping in a few minutes. I'll call you later tonight.

At six, I text: When are you calling?

At seven, he answers: I'm sorry. We're being rushed to another event. I can still call you though, when it's over. It might be late.

It's fine. I'm okay, I text back. I don't want him to worry. Yet, even as I send the text, tears start forming at the corners of my eyes.

At eight, I hear the sound of buttons being pressed and the door unlocking. Light from the hallway filters into the room, where Sori stands backlit.

"Jenny?" she says, flicking on the light switch. "Why are you sitting in the dark?"

Catching sight of my face, she drops her bags on the floor and hurries to my bed. She gathers me into her arms, as if we hadn't been not speaking for weeks, as if none of that matters anymore. "I'm sorry. I've been such a brat. This must be so hard for you. It was hard for me and Nathaniel, but I knew what to expect."

She thinks I'm crying over Jaewoo, and I am, partly, but it's not just that.

She gently pushes back my shoulders, looking me in the eyes. "We need to get you out of this room," she says.

I nod. Right now, I'd do anything to chase away these feelings.

"How do you feel about going to a K-pop concert?"

Is it considered cheating if you go to the concert of a boy band that's not the idol group your boyfriend belongs to?

This is not a question I ever thought I would ask myself. Yet here I stand, outside a concert venue, staring up at the poster of nine beautiful boys.

Their group is called 95D or 95 the Dream, which apparently stands for 9 High-Five the Dream.

"I've seen them before," I say. "At EBC. They were in the lobby."

"Are there any that catch your eye?" Sori asks, her expression serious.

I point to the one in the middle, who of the nine, looks the most like someone I might meet on the street. "He's pretty cute."

"Jo Jisoo," Sori says. "He used to be a trainee at Joah, but then switched companies and debuted with 95D as their youngest member. He's cute, but he's not my favorite. *Him*." She points to the guy second from the right with red hair. "Jun-oppa. I love him."

I turn to stare at her. Sori usually looks gorgeous, but tonight, she's gone all out. Her hair is in a high ponytail that swings when she walks, plus a leather bustier and vinyl joggers.

"You love him," I repeat. Just to be clear. She's never said this about Nathaniel, who was her actual boyfriend.

"Yes, I love him." She says the words without inflection, like she really means it. And . . . I guess when you're a fan, you really do mean it.

I turn back to the poster, where Jo Jisoo looks at me as if, with him, I really can high-five my dreams. "Then I love Jisoo."

When I turn back to Sori, she gives me a single nod. "Okay."

We buy light sticks at the merch booth inside the stadium. Only then, outfitted properly, do we head into the arena, which is already packed to the rafters. Sori's pulled some strings so our "seats" aren't seats at all but access to the standing floor in one of the sections next to the stage. The concert hasn't started yet, but music blasts through the speakers. On either side of the stage are huge screens showing clips from the band's music videos. Beside me, Sori waves her light stick whenever Jun's face appears, even if only for a quick second.

At 9:05 the lights dim and a chant rises up from the crowd.

"Nine! Five! Dream! Nine! Five! Dream! Nine! Five! Dream!"

I turn around in a complete circle, gazing up at the sea of

colors in the stadium, as the light sticks, synchronized and controlled backstage, change from white to pink to baby blue.

Then the stage erupts with fire and all nine members of the band appear, as if by magic, though probably from a lift beneath the stage floor. The music starts and I recognize the song from when they performed it at *Music Net*. The choreography takes over and I get lost in the total, all-encompassing experience.

I don't re-emerge until two hours later, when 95 the Dream performs their last song, called back onto the stage by the crowd for an encore performance.

"That was incredible!" I say as Sori and I stumble out of the stadium into the humid night. My heart is still racing, and it's like I can still feel the beat of the music vibrating beneath my feet.

Pressing closer to Sori, I confess, "I think you might be the best friend I've ever had. I'm glad you're my roommate."

"Me too," she gushes. "I'm glad you're my roommate. I'm going to miss you so much when you go back to the States."

"I love you, Sori. More than Jo Jisoo."

"I love you, Jenny!" She pauses. "Not as much as Oppa, but close."

Thirty-six

On the morning of the showcase, I receive a text from Jaewoo. For the past couple of days, he'd been promoting in Japan, and though we've been texting every day, it's been sporadic, only a quick "good night."

> On my way back now, but probably won't get to the school until right before the showcase starts. If I don't get to say it in person, you've got this!

Gi Taek and Angela are in the room, having slept over the night before, Gi Taek and Angela in Sori's bed and Sori and me in mine. I told them about leaving Korea earlier than planned and they'd been attached to me like barnacles since.

"Can't you try convincing your mom again?" Gi Taek asks.

"You don't know my mom. When she thinks she's in the right, there's no convincing her otherwise."

"What was Jaewoo's reaction?" Angela asks as she rolls one of my shirts in a tight bundle, handing it over to Gi Taek who lines it up alongside others in my suitcase.

I don't respond immediately, instead taking books down from my shelf and placing them in a box. I'll mail these, along with my heavier items, back to the States.

"You haven't told him yet, have you?" Gi Taek says.

"He's been promoting in Japan. I didn't want to . . . worry him."

"Jenny, your boyfriend needs to know you're leaving the country two days after he gets back."

"I'll tell him," I say. "After the showcase. I just don't want it to ruin tonight."

The keypad outside the door sounds, and Sori comes inside carrying a bag of Subway sandwiches. She distributes one to each of us in turn, then sits down at her desk, spinning to face me.

"Did Kim Jina say anything to you?"

I frown. I haven't thought about Jina in a long time. Once our little friend group formed, she'd left us mostly alone. Bullies don't like a difficult target.

"No, why?"

"Someone told me she was in the bathroom, talking crap. Not exactly sure about what."

"Why do girls like to gossip in bathrooms?" Gi Taek asks, plucking out the tomatoes in his sandwich.

"I don't," Angela says. "I use the restroom for a different kind of crap."

"Angela!" we all say together.

"Hmm . . ." Sori drinks diet soda from her eco-straw while

slowly spinning around in her chair. "As long as we can keep an eye on her and squash any rumors she starts, it should be fine."

"No one hurts my Jenny!" Angela shouts, reaching into my underwear drawer.

"Angela, you don't have to fold those," I say.

"I guess that's one pro about going back to the States," Gi Taek muses aloud. "You don't have to worry about waking up to a front-page article on *Bulletin*."

We all laugh uneasily and Sori shakes her head. "I'm sure it's fine."

An hour before the showcase, I slip on my black wide-legged jumpsuit. It's my favorite outfit to wear for performances or recitals when black is a uniform requirement. The wide-leg pants, worn with heels, give the illusion of a skirt when I walk. And most important, I don't have to worry about flashing the audience when I have to tuck my cello between my knees. To complete the outfit, I wear just one accessory—a red ribbon, a gift from my father. When I was little, he used to tie my hair up with it, but tonight I wrap it around my wrist, end over end, like a good luck charm.

The orchestra opens up the showcase, so I head out before Sori and the others. Already the doors to the music hall are open to the public and people can be seen streaming from the gates across the lawn. I scan the crowd for Mom and Halmeoni, but I don't see them.

"Eonni!"

A young girl calls across the lawn, and though the term could literally address any "older sister," I turn toward the voice.

Jaewoo's younger sister races across the lawn, stopping short of colliding with me.

"Joori," I say. "Hi!" I look behind her to where Jaewoo's mom approaches and bow to greet her. "Did you come to see Jaewoo? That's so nice of you."

"We did come to see Jaewoo . . . but also you!" Joori shouts. "Jaewoo says you're performing three times!" She holds up the program, where my name is indeed listed three times, among the cello section of the orchestra, next to Sori's name as a duet, and then as a soloist toward the end of the program.

"Are your parents here?" Jaewoo's mother asks.

"It's just my mom and me," I say, "and she should be here soon, if she's not already inside. She's bringing my halmeoni."

"Oh, yes. Jaewoo mentioned you're close with her."

"Yes." I smile, then offer, "She's scheduled for surgery soon."

"How wonderful!" Jaewoo's mother says. "Your mother must be so relieved."

"I—yeah." I hadn't thought of that.

I've thought about how Halmeoni feels about Mom and how I feel about her, but I've never thought about how *Mom feels*. It's just that she never seems to have any feelings, which I guess is unfair. She's a daughter too.

Maybe I *can* convince her to let me stay in Korea another month. I didn't try because I knew how'd she answer. But maybe it'll be different if I tell her, honestly, how I feel—that

298

this is the happiest I've been in a long time and I feel rejuvenated, a better musician, a better person.

I've decided. After the showcase, I'm going to talk to her.

Beaming, I bow to Jaewoo's mom. "See you inside!" She and Joori smile and wave me off.

Behind the auditorium, where the orchestra students are moving their instruments to backstage, I catch up with Nora, my stand partner. She's brought my cello from the music room along with hers.

"Thanks," I say, retrieving it.

We head inside, moving onstage from the right wings, where stagehands have already set up the chairs and stands in a half circle, with the conductor's podium front and center.

Settled in our seats, the conductor has the first chair oboe play an A note, and we all tune our instruments to match hers.

Muffled through the closed curtains, we can hear the sounds of people in the auditorium, their voices a loud murmur.

For the hundredth time, Nora reaches out to fiddle with the music. Then silence descends. Everyone sits a little straighter in their seats. The curtain parts, and Jaewoo and Nathaniel walk onto the stage.

I'm supposed to keep my eyes on the conductor, but I can't help gazing after Jaewoo. He's wearing a suit perfectly tailored to his lean body, with a thin tie and classic black leather shoes. He's let his hair grow longer in the past few weeks and though it's mostly swept back from his face, one strand is left to dangle rakishly over his eyes.

"Jenny," Nora hisses and I wrench my gaze from Jaewoo, focusing on the conductor who's lightly tapping his baton against the podium.

From behind him, Nathaniel and Jaewoo begin their opening words, welcoming the audience and highlighting a few key students in the ensemble. When Nora's name is mentioned, she stands and bows to the audience. Though Jaewoo and Nathaniel are reading from a teleprompter, their banter and lighthearted-ness appears natural, the audience laughing at the appropriate moments.

"And now," Nathaniel says, "the Seoul Arts Academy Symphonic Orchestra will play Stravinsky's 'The Firebird.'"

The conductor raises the baton and Nora and I both lift our bows to the strings.

Twenty minutes later, I'm rushing off the stage. I have thirty minutes until my next piece, and in that time I have to change and do my hair and makeup.

In the hallway I run into Sori, who has my dress in a garment bag.

"I watched the whole performance from the back of the audience," she says. "You were incredible."

"It was an ensemble," I say. "You couldn't have picked me out."

"No, you were incredible. Accept my compliment." She hands over the garment bag. "Twenty-six minutes and counting."

We rush to the bathroom. We don't bother with the stalls, stripping down next to the sinks. She's wearing her outfit beneath her regular clothes, so it's just a matter of throwing them off with a magician's flourish. She then proceeds to help me shimmy into my dress, which is a floor-length ballgown she'd had Joah's stylist procure from the company closet. While the skirt poofs out, the top of the dress is fitted to my chest, leaving my arms and shoulders bare. She carefully gathers up all my hair and pins it into a neat ballerina's bun to match her own. We each do our own makeup and then, turning to the mirror, we stand side by side, me in my red ballgown with rhinestones dotting the skirt, her in a red leotard with a sheer skirt, also festooned with rhinestones.

We look good; in fact, we look beautiful.

Slowly Sori raises her arm, cell phone in hand, and takes a mirror selfie.

We make it to the stage with five minutes to spare. I grab my cello and quickly tune before hurrying to the left wings.

After the trio of violinists before us finish to loud applause, the lights dim and a stagehand quickly rushes out onto the stage and places a chair and music stand to the left of the stage. The applause quiets as I walk forward, one hand tightly gripping the neck of my cello, the other holding up my skirt so that I don't trip.

I make it to the stool and sit down, arranging my dress around me before placing my cello neatly between my knees.

"And now we have our only duet of the program." Nathaniel's voice can be heard announcing us. "A collaboration from two students from Year Three. Dance major Min Sori is a trainee at Joah Entertainment. She holds national champion awards in rhythm gymnastics, classical jazz, and speech and debate. Though coldly beautiful on the outside, on the inside, she's a bucket of marshmallows."

The audience chuckles, and on the far side, a few teachers exchange glances. Apparently Nathaniel had gone off script.

"Our second performer," Jaewoo says, his voice strong and warm, "is classical cellist major Jenny Go, a Korean American transfer student from LACHSA." From this vantage, I can see the teleprompter. It ends there, but he continues speaking. "Jenny is also an honors student, a loving granddaughter, and a phenomenal dancer, though she might disagree." The crowd laughs appreciatively, with one loud guffaw from the back, presumably Gi Taek.

"She's planning on attending music school after graduation, where she'll continue to grow her incredible talent and share her music with others."

On the sidelines, I can see the teachers trying to get Jaewoo's attention, but he continues, his voice resonating throughout the auditorium. "Though her time at SAA has been short, she's left a lasting impression on many of us, especially those of us whom she'd call her friends."

A gentle spotlight finds me on the stage. I drag my gaze away from Jaewoo and take a deep breath. I press my left hand to the fingerboard and bring my bow level with the strings.

As I begin to play another spotlight materializes right of the stage, and I know with the murmuring of the audience, that Sori has appeared. She sways and leaps to the sound of the music, which is a classical arrangement of a popular K-pop song. It's a blend of both of our interests, a true collaboration. I put everything into the performance because it's not just for me, but for Gi Taek and Angela, whose friendships have meant the world to me, and for my mother and Halmeoni listening somewhere in the audience, and for my father, who can't be here as he should be, but still *is here*, because I am.

I play for Jaewoo, who, while everyone watches, enraptured by Sori's movement, never takes his eyes off me.

And lastly for Sori, who in these short few months has become my very best friend.

After the song ends, the hall explodes with thunderous applause.

"Jaewoo?" Nathaniel says. "Wasn't that something else? Hello, Jaewoo? Come in, Bae Jaewoo."

"Oh, sorry," Jaewoo says, startled, and the audience laughs.

I pick up my cello and walk toward Sori. She meets me halfway, at the center of the stage. She takes my hand, squeezing, and we turn to the audience together and bow, letting the roar of their applause wash over us. Then, still holding hands, we rush off stage, laughter in our throats, adrenaline rushing through our veins.

Backstage, I barely have time to place my cello on its stand before Sori grabs me in a fierce hug. "We did it! We really did it!"

I hug her back, just as tightly. "Thank you. I couldn't have done it without you."

We hold each other for a few more seconds before she lets go. "You have to get ready for your solo!"

"And you have to get ready for your group routine." She and Angela are both performing in a contemporary group number.

As I turn to my cello, I feel a soft vibration in the pocket of my dress. I reach into the voluminous skirt and pull out my cell phone.

"You brought your phone onto the stage?" Sori says, aghast.

"I put it in there as a joke, to be honest, when I found the pocket, and totally forgot about it." I open up my phone. "It's a text from my mom."

"Maybe she's congratulating you on the performance."

I pull up the message and start to read.

Jenny, I'm so sorry. I had to leave early. I've gone to Severance Hospital at Sinchon. Halmeoni was taken to emergency—

I don't finish. Grabbing the edge of my skirt, I rush out the door.

Thirty-seven

I race across campus, the voluminous skirts of the ballgown making it difficult to sprint full-out. Past the gates, I spot a taxi that's dropping off late arrivals, catching the door and sliding inside. I don't even have my wallet, but the taxi driver takes pity on me, especially when I tell him my destination: Severance Hospital at Sinchon.

He drops me right outside and I stumble through the automatic doors. It's hectic in the lobby but everyone still stops and stares at the sudden arrival of a teenager in a red ballgown. I pick up my skirts and hurry to the nurse's station.

"My name is Go Jenny. I'm looking for my grandmother. She was rushed to emergency surgery."

"What's your grandmother's name?"

"Kim Na Young."

The nurse picks up a tablet, checking the screen. "Eighth floor. Elevators are on the left past the station."

I don't wait for her to finish, reaching for my skirts. Outside the elevator, an incoming call appears on my phone. Jaewoo. I accept the call just as the doors to the elevator open.

"Jenny?" Jaewoo says, and it's hard to hear him with the roar of music in the background. "Are you all right? Where did you go?"

Before I can answer, the call drops and the elevator arrives at the eighth floor.

Just as I'm stepping out, my cell phone pings with a flurry of texts, the topmost from Gi Taek: Jenny, where are you?

At the hospital, I quickly type back and send.

"Go Jenny-ssi?" A woman in teal scrubs stands before me. "The nurse downstairs called and said you were coming up."

I pocket my phone. "I'm looking for my halmeoni. Kim Na Young. Is she okay? Is she all right? I was told to come immediately."

The nurse's eyes widen. "Oh, yes, she's fine. Your halmeoni is actually out of surgery now."

"She's . . . fine?"

My knees give out and I collapse to the floor. The nurse crouches down beside me, one hand on my shoulder. "Poor child, you must have been so frightened."

I sniffle. "Is she allowed visitors? Can I see her?"

"Yes. Your mother is with her."

I let the nurse help me to my feet.

"Room 803," she says and I nod, taking the last few steps on my own. Outside the room, I pause. The door is slightly ajar and I can hear Halmeoni and Mom talking softly inside.

I press my hand to the door only to hesitate when I hear a sob. It takes me a moment to realize it's my mother. She's . . . crying, something she hasn't done since Dad passed away.

"You didn't come," Mom says. "I needed you, and you didn't come."

"Nae saekki," Halmeoni is saying, "my baby. Eomma is sorry. I should have been there for you. I did wrong. Forgive me, forgive me."

My mom is sobbing, heaving sobs, harder than I've ever seen her cry.

"You—You didn't have the means to come, and I didn't help you. But it's been so hard, Eomma. I had no one."

"You have me. You will always have me. And your daughter. Your beautiful daughter."

"I'm so scared, Eomma. I drive Jenny to be stronger but sometimes I think I'm pushing her away. I just want to protect her."

"Like I protected you? You've seen what a terrible job I did. Keeping out the people you love isn't protecting them, Soojung-ah. Loving them. Trusting them with your heart. That's all you can do."

I step away from the door.

My phone buzzes in my pocket for the gazillionth time and I finally take it out. *Why* are my friends texting me so much? I'm grateful they're concerned, but I'm a bit *busy*.

Gi Taek: Jenny, why aren't you answering your phone?

Angela: Are you okay?

Sori: Which hospital?

Jaewoo: I called the clinic. I'm on my way.

Gi Taek: Jenny, this is serious. Are you somewhere safe?

I frown. *What* is he talking about? Then a series of links appear in quick succession, sent from each of them.

Angela: "BREAKING NEWS: K-Pop Idol Bae Jaewoo's Secret Girlfriend."

Gi Taek: "XOXO's Bae Jaewoo Dating Scandal."

Sori: "Bulletin Reveals XOXO's Bae Jaewoo in a Relationship with Classmate"

With shaking hands, I click on the last link. It jumps to a popular gossip site, where the top trending article is this very one, complete with a huge, blown-up picture of Jaewoo and me.

I'd expected to see a paparazzi shot of one of the times Jaewoo and I were together in public, on the field trip, our date to the theater, or that afternoon at the noraebang. But instead it's . . .

The sticker photo.

Unlike the article of Nathaniel and Sori's, my face isn't blurred, but visible, if not super clear due to the quality of the photo.

A text pops up.

Jaewoo: I'm here. Where are you?

I rush to the elevator, pressing the button for the ground floor. Luckily no one gets on and it goes straight to the lobby. The doors open to chaos. Security guards are yelling as a dozen photographers with huge cameras point them at a single person standing at the center of the lobby.

Jaewoo.

He turns as the elevator fully opens, catching sight of me, slowly lowering the phone he holds to his ear.

The paparazzi follow his line of sight and it's like the hounds scenting their prey, surging forward, held back only by the hospital guards.

Jaewoo walks swiftly in my direction. He's still dressed in the suit from the showcase, though his tie is loosened and his hair is a mess, as if he's run a hand through it multiple times.

Reaching me, he pulls me into a fierce hug, which I return with equal force. Behind us, the elevator closes, cutting off the noise from the lobby. Jaewoo releases me only to press the button for the highest floor.

"Are you all right?" he asks, his eyes searching mine. "How is she, your halmeoni?"

"She's good. She was rushed into emergency surgery, but it went well."

He sighs with relief, leaning against the elevator wall.

The numbers of the elevator increase as we ascend. Twenty-five. Twenty-six. Twenty-seven.

"I'm so sorry," I say quickly, my words tumbling out. "I had the photograph in my wallet, but I must have dropped it. I was careless. It's all my fault."

"It's not your fault," Jaewoo says. "None of this is your fault."

The elevator stops. We've reached the top floor of the hospital. Jaewoo takes my hand and leads me to the stairwell, up a single flight, pushing open the door to the rooftop.

The night air is balmy. A dry wind sweeps across the open

space, catching the loose strands of hair that have fallen out of my bun.

Jaewoo takes off his suit jacket, and then loosens his tie entirely, slipping it over his head.

He moves to the edge of the roof, safeguarded by a wall and railing. I join him, looking down to where news vans are packed in among ambulances and other vehicles.

"You'd think they'd have more respect," Jaewoo says, his voice bitter.

"How did the paparazzi manage to show up at the hospital so quickly?"

"They were waiting at the school and followed me when I left. I almost lost them—my cab driver had a bit of a daredevil streak—but they caught up to us near the hospital."

He drags his gaze from the scene below. "Are you sure you're all right?"

"I—" The answer isn't so easy. My mind is a blur, my emotions all tangled up, and then a realization hits me.

"I was supposed to play a solo tonight."

Jaewoo looks stricken. "There's still time for you to do it."

"No," I say. "I can't." By now, they would have passed over my slot in the programming, and there was an intermission—people will have read the article. My solo was my ticket into MSM; now I *have* to go back to the States. The Philharmonic is my last chance. "It's over."

"Jenny—"

"What happens now?" I ask.

He must follow my train of thought because he answers,

"My company will release a statement."

"They'll deny it, won't they? Like with Sori and Nathaniel."

"I—I'm not sure. But I'll do everything I can to protect you."

"Don't," I say sharply. *Protect.* It's that word again. But I don't want the people I care about to protect me, not when it hurts them. Jaewoo. Mom.

Jaewoo had been taking a step toward me, but he stops now, his expression one of hurt and confusion.

"Don't protect me over the people you should be protecting, your bandmates, your family, yourself. Think of the people who have been in your life in the past, who will be in your life in the future."

"Jenny, you *are*—"

"I'm leaving, Jaewoo. In two days. Less than that now."

There's a short pause, then he says, softly, "When were you going to tell me?"

And I know, suddenly, what I have to do, what I was trying so hard not to accept. I *am* leaving, and even if I leave in two days or a month from now, the end results will be the same.

Jaewoo's too good, he'll never break up with me, especially not after this scandal. He'll do everything in his power to protect me.

If anyone's going to look out for his best interests, and mine, it'll have to be me.

"Does it matter?" I say coolly. "We would have broken up in the end."

He winces. "Is that right?"

"Jaewoo, there was a reason it took so long for us to get together. Our lives are too different. You're famous, an idol, and I want to go to music school in New York City."

I think of my mother's words, just a few days ago. She was right. I just didn't want to hear it. "I'm going back to my life. You should go back to yours."

"You make it sound so easy," he says harshly.

Now it's my turn to wince. "I'm sorry about the photograph. If your company can just deny it, as long as there's no other evidence—"

"And damn, someone should have told me our breakup was inevitable from the start, then maybe it wouldn't hurt so much."

"Jaewoo . . ."

"I didn't ask you to be my girlfriend because I thought our relationship would end in a few months. People don't begin relationships thinking they'll end."

"No, people end relationships when they know they should have never begun in the first place."

"Do you really believe that?"

No, I want to say. I want to tell him that these past two months with him, these past four months in Seoul, with all of our friends, have been wonderful.

But I'm in too deep, it already feels like I'm tearing out my heart to say these words, but I have to, because I'm leaving, and it's better to hurt him now than to tell him what I really want to say, that I think I'm in love with him.

"Yes."

The door to the rooftop opens.

"Jaewoo." His manager stands silhouetted by the light inside. "I've been looking all over for you. Why didn't you answer your calls? It's a circus downstairs. Security is giving us an escort out the back. We have to go."

Ji Seok notices me then. "It's best if you leave alone."

Jaewoo picks up his jacket, where he'd dropped it on the ground. As he passes by me toward the door, he pauses. I look up into his face, holding back my tears.

"I meant to tell you earlier," he says with one last devastating smile, even though I just broke his heart and mine, "you were beautiful tonight."

A few seconds later the door shuts with a bang, and he's gone.

Thirty-eight

In every K-drama, the penultimate scene usually involves a chase, the throwing away of all inhibitions and fears, when the heroine and her greatest love unite, and all is well in the world.

But no one comes running through the airport to stop me. And on Sunday, I board the plane and fly home.

Thirty-nine

It's a wonder you don't have an SNS profile, Gi Taek texts at two in the morning, which is six at night Korea Standard Time. Though maybe that's a good thing. . . .

I've been home a week and would have gotten over the jet lag if it weren't for the group chat Gi Taek started with Angela and Sori the minute I landed at LAX. He'd titled it "FWOJ," which stands for "Fun Without Jenny."

Sori: I would hurt anyone who came for you on SNS. I'd be
　　in the comments, belittling people.

Gi Taek: You'd make things worse.

Sori: How dare you.

Angela e-laughs: ㅋㅋㅋ

Maybe it's *because* I don't have any social media profiles that the backlash from the scandal hasn't been completely awful, at least on my end, but also it could be because no one knows the identity of Bae Jaewoo's rumored girlfriend. The photograph that was released shows my face, but my features are blurred, and I kind of look like a strange alternate version of myself who, if released from the photo, will come to murder me and take my place.

Anyone who knows me can tell that it's, well . . . me, but otherwise none of my personal information was released, including my name.

I think a part of it is that I am a minor, but it's more that Joah's lawyers are working around the clock to protect Jaewoo, and by extension me.

The Monday after the scandal broke, while I was somewhere over the Pacific, Joah released a statement declaring that the members of XOXO's private lives were, exactly that, private. It was a hard stance, neither an admission nor a denial. But the message was clear—Jaewoo would have the full support of his company. I was surprised, since I assumed they'd cover it up, like with Nathaniel and Sori, but maybe Sori convinced her mother to set a new precedent.

On XOXO's official SNS, Jaewoo released an apology for the inconvenience to the hospital staff and patients the night the article was released, not explaining why he was there, but accepting responsibility for any disturbance he might have caused. The comments below his apology are filled with support from his fans, condemning the paparazzi for following him into the hospital and endangering his life by chasing him.

Though there are a few hostile comments, calling him ungrateful for his fame, selfish for hurting the band, and a hypocrite for "acting" like a prince but "behaving like a pauper."

Seeing these comments, I have a mind to channel Sori and leave scathing replies, but I know, ultimately, that won't help.

Sori: It'll calm down in time. Anyway, your news is boring. Did you see the news that Lee Jae Won and Lee Tae Ra are engaged! Lee-Lee couple! I knew their chemistry in Rebel Heart was real.

Angela: I'm so happy for them!!!

Me: You guys, it's 2 in the morning here. I'm going to bed.

Angela: We miss you!

Me: Miss you too.

I close out of our chat, but instead of sleeping, open up a browser out of habit. It's only been a week, but I move by rote memory, clicking on XOXO's profiles on all their SNS platforms and checking to see if there are any updates, and then logging onto their fan sites to see their daily schedules.

I can't exactly tell, but it seems they're just as popular post-scandal as they were before, if not more so. XOXO also released their tour dates for the All the World's a Stage tour, kicking off in Seoul for two nights of concerts, and then traveling through Asia, Europe, and finally, the US.

They have a stop in New York City.

The same day as my audition for the Manhattan School of Music, which I already have plans to fly out for.

Not for the first time, I check the availability of tickets. But nothing's changed since they sold out in the first twenty-four hours. The only ones left for purchase are re-sale tickets at exorbitant prices.

I groan and fling my phone across the bed. Why am I even *looking*?

It's not like I'll go.

Or maybe I will. I'll purchase one of the tickets so far in the back you need binoculars to see the stage and I'll just watch him from afar. That seems like a very specific and cruel punishment that I rightly deserve.

My phone blinks with a message and I hurry across the bed, knowing it won't be from Jaewoo, but still . . . hoping.

It's from Mom:

We visited the hospital today and they said Halmeoni's made a full recovery, which means I'll be coming home on time after all! I'm sorry, for a lot of things. I think we should have a long talk when I get home. I love you, Jenny.

Love you too, Mom

Why are you awake? Go to sleep!

Laughing, I drop my hand to the bed and look up at the ceiling. It only took Halmeoni surviving a major surgery for my mom to open up. She was only a *little* bit angry that I didn't get the spot on the Philharmonic orchestra, oh, and that I was involved in a K-pop scandal with an idol. Luckily, instead of getting angry at me, she started calling up her colleagues who specialize in privacy law, only calming down when she saw that Joah had a handle on things.

Our relationship isn't the same as it was before Dad passed but we're talking, and it's a start.

I close my eyes, but I know I'll have difficulty sleeping, so I do what I've been doing since I got back from Korea. I open my music app and press repeat on XOXO's album.

Their music is the only thing that can calm me enough to go to sleep.

I don't know why it's been so hard to adjust.

Maybe it's the jet lag, or maybe it's that I miss him.

The week before senior year starts, Uncle Jay and I fly across the country so that I can tour East Coast colleges. I also set up a live audition at each school I visit. I could have set up a video call, but I really wanted to audition in person.

Uncle Jay generously offered to cover the costs as my "early graduation present." And since Mom has a big case coming up, he's the one taking me, which is fine for him because, as he put it, he wanted to "check out the karaoke scene in New York's Koreatown" anyway.

"I'm sure it's exactly like LA," I say.

"No, no. These East Coast Koreans do things differently."

It's the third and last day of our trip and we're sitting having lunch at a restaurant that overlooks Times Square. I've already visited and auditioned for the Boston schools, and Julliard just this morning. I have the audition for the Manhattan School of Music in an hour, the audition that will determine whether I'll attend the school I've been dreaming of going to half my life.

But it's hard to concentrate.

XOXO is here.

In New York City.

They were in Europe for a week, and they arrived at JFK sometime in the past twenty-four hours. I know because I follow one of XOXO's dancers and she regularly updates her status, which the fans use to track down the members' location.

"Why aren't you eating?" Uncle Jay asks, tapping my tray of burger and fries. "Are you that nervous? You have nothing to worry about. You crushed your auditions at all the other schools."

He's right. I've already received a verbal acceptance from Berklee.

"I'm not nervous," I say, letting my gaze wander outside the window where hundreds of people make their way across a busy junction, billboards flashing above them, bright even in the daylight.

One catches my eye. A Broadway ad for the newest hit musical. Uncle Jay and I didn't have time to watch one this trip, but *when* I'm back in New York City, it's going to the top of my bucket list.

Then the ad switches to a commercial, with a few people on the street stopping to watch: XOXO Live Tonight at Madison Square Garden for the All the World's a Stage Tour, Doors Open at 7.

"Isn't that the kid you dated?"

"Uncle Jay!" I hiss, looking quickly around at the other restaurant goers, but none of them are paying us any attention.

"Is he performing in the US or something?"

"He has a concert at Madison Square Garden."

Uncle Jay whistles. "Damn. Did you really meet him in my karaoke bar? I should have gotten him to sign something. That would have been great for publicity."

"I met him the night you told me to get a life."

"What?" Uncle Jay has the audacity to look offended. "I would never say that."

"It literally was the catalyst for all my insecurities!"

"Whoops." He shrugs. "Sorry."

While I fume, he takes a bite of his BLT. Outside, the ad begins to play on another billboard. I'm tempted to take out my phone and record the ad just for myself, especially the part where Jaewoo appears on the screen, with his name and position in the band listed.

On the street beneath the billboard, a couple of tweens have stopped in their tracks, pointing at the screen and fangirling.

"So you took my sage advice to heart, huh? How mad would you be if I did it again?"

I look at him warily. "Just say it."

He leans back in the booth. "It's more of a story."

I sigh. "As long it's not a movie quote."

"It won't take that long. You eat, while I talk."

I comply, if only because I refuse to waste food.

"When your dad and I were around your age, this new girl moved into town."

I narrow my eyes, not sure if I want to hear a story about one of my uncle's many exes.

"Naw, hear me out. She was a new student at our school,

from Seoul. Really pretty, and of course she wouldn't give your dad and me the time of the day, some scrappy kids from LA's K-town. I gave up pretty quickly—there were a lot of people who wanted my attention."

I roll my eyes.

"But your father, he was determined. He'd write her letters and walk her home from school. Then he got sick . . ." I remember. He was first sick in college, later he would relapse. "And so he started to pretend he wasn't interested in your mom. . . ." He pauses. "We're talking about your mom, by the way."

I laugh, tears in my eyes. "I know."

"But by then, she was in love with him. And so though he tried to push her away, she pushed back even harder, visiting him in the hospital, writing *him* letters. After he got better, they graduated and got married, and had you, and they were happy. For a long time."

"I miss him," I whisper.

Uncle Jay doesn't have to say anything. He misses him too.

"You're like both your parents, Jenny. You're stubborn and loyal and good, and when you love, you love with your whole heart."

I stare at my uncle, who isn't my father, or related to me by blood, but who's been there for me every day of my life.

"What are you saying, Uncle Jay? You have to tell me in Jenny-speak."

"I'm saying, people do strange things to protect their hearts. But when you're afraid, your heart is closed, and it's never the right time, but when your heart is open, and you're willing to be brave enough to take a chance, the time is always right."

"I think I made a mistake, Uncle Jay, and I don't know how to fix it."

"That's not true. You know exactly what you need to do. You just gotta . . . go."

"Jenny, after your audition and reviewing your portfolio, we're pleased to offer you a verbal acceptance into the Manhattan School of Music."

I gape at the admissions director, who's watching me with a warm smile of understanding. I'm sure she's used to witnessing a similar shocked expression on the faces of the students she delivers happy news to. This is the culmination of all my hard work, everything I've ever wanted.

"Professor Tu, our cello professor," she continues, "is taking a few students to dinner in a few minutes, if you'd like to join her."

"I—what time is it?"

She blinks, glancing at her wristwatch. "It's a little past five thirty."

"Then I'd be honored to join the professor for dinner."

The dinner is at an Italian restaurant on the Upper West Side. It's served family-style, much to my excitement. I'm already in awe of Professor Tu, who besides having taught in Asia and Europe, has also been a member of award-winning ensembles.

The students also seem really cool, especially the girl seated next to me who's a sophomore studying contemporary cello and the boy across from her who wants to be a composer.

The conversation at dinner flows and, honestly, I'd have lost track of the time if I wasn't so conscious of it. Six o'clock passes, then seven. At half past seven, I'm chomping at the bit, literally chomping on a piece of garlic bread. Everyone's having a great time. The few students who are old enough are on their second bottle of wine. When the waiter comes over, the professor asks to see a dessert menu.

"Are you all right?" The sophomore girl has a concerned look on her face.

I stand up abruptly. All eyes at the table turn toward me. "I'm sorry," I say, "but I have to go."

"Of course, Jenny," Professor Tu says. "Do you need someone to ride with you back to your hotel?"

"I'm not going back to my hotel," I say, and I don't know what possesses me to further explain, but I add, "I'm going to a K-pop concert."

"You should have said sooner!" Professor Tu exclaims. "Concerts wait for no one."

"Is it XOXO?" the sophomore girl asks. "I love them."

I stare at her, then the rest of them—every expression is either warm or curious. I remember Ian and the way he'd made me feel as if my love for Korean pop music meant I couldn't be serious about attending the Manhattan School of Music.

"This isn't . . . weird?" I ask.

"Weird?" Professor Tu looks genuinely shocked. "No, why would it be? It's music and we're all musicians. You'd better hurry. You don't want to be late!"

"No, you're right." I smile at her, then at the rest of the students in turn. "I don't want to be late."

I rush out the door, waving my hand vigorously for a cab, leaping inside when one pulls over.

A single thought repeats over and over in my head.

Please don't let me be too late.

Forty

Traffic is at standstill outside Madison Square Garden, so I abandon the taxi at 36th and 7th and run the last few blocks.

In the cab, I'd sent a message to FWOJ:

On my way to Madison Square Garden. Wish me luck.

The replies come in from my friends, hyping me up:

Gi Taek: AJA! AJA!

Angela: JENNY! Fighting!

Sori: Get your man!

I check the time on my phone. It's 7:40, which means XOXO goes on in twenty minutes.

I try to call Jaewoo but his phone must be turned off because it goes straight to voicemail.

Hurriedly, I text Nathaniel, who I haven't contacted since the night Jaewoo and I broke up:

I'm at Madison Square Garden. Is there any way you could get me inside?

Even with twenty minutes to showtime, there's a huge line

outside the stadium, slowly pouring through the doors where staff are checking tickets and guards are checking bags.

Without a ticket, I'll never get in.

I open my phone to call Nathaniel and it immediately powers down. I was so exhausted from traveling last night that I forgot to charge it.

I estimate around fifteen minutes until showtime. Or at least, when they're scheduled to start. If this concert is anything like 95D's concert in Seoul, it won't begin on time.

I circle around the building, looking out for something, anything.

There! A side area cordoned off with a single guard. Visible behind the rope is a door, a separate entrance for the road crew.

I hurry over.

The guard, a burly Latino guy with a beard eyes me with suspicion. "The line for entry is on the other side of the building."

"I need to see XOXO."

"Yeah, you and the twenty thousand other people."

"No, like, I *know* them. I'm a classmate."

"Sure you are."

"Seriously, ask Nam Ji Seok. He's their manager."

"Nice try. Now if you'd step back . . ."

No, this can't be how it ends, foiled by a security guard. My eyes dart behind him.

I can't give up *now*. I need to see Jaewoo, to tell him that I'm sorry, that I was wrong and afraid and . . .

"Jenny?"

Someone approaches from behind the security guard from where they exited another one of those sleek black vans. My heart lifts, then immediately sinks.

It's Sun.

"What are you doing here?" he asks. He's already dressed to go on stage, in a sparkling dark-blue jacket that probably cost a million dollars, his long hair falling elegantly over his shoulders. He's absolutely beautiful, and the last person I wanted to see.

"I came to see Jaewoo."

"Ah." He bites his lip, and I can see him thinking.

"I know you don't like me," I blurt out, and he raises a single, well-groomed eyebrow. "I know you think I'll only distract Jaewoo, that his career will suffer from being with me. But I think you're wrong. Jaewoo can't help taking care of people—he's too good-hearted—but he doesn't have to take care of me. Because the truth is, I don't need him. I have a whole life that's separate from his. But I still *want* to be with him. I want to be there for him when he's unhappy just as much as I want to be there for him when he's happy. Though I hope he's never unhappy because it physically hurts when he's unhappy, you know?"

"I know."

I'm so startled by his response that I immediately shut my mouth.

Sun turns to the security guard, who's been watching us

with a quizzical expression. Unless he can understand Korean, he has no idea what I just said.

"Excuse me, sir." Sun holds up a card on a lanyard he's wrapped around his wrist. Speaking in broken English he says, "I am one of the artists. She's"—he gestures vaguely in my direction—"VIP."

A piercing scream comes from behind me. "Sun-oppa!"

He's been spotted. Soon, more screams join the first, and the ground literally appears to shake with the rush of pounding feet.

"Damn." The security guard reaches for his radio to call for backup. "Take her inside. Hurry."

I bypass the rope and follow Sun to the side entrance. The cries of "Sun-oppa" can be heard, cutting off as the door shuts behind us.

"Thanks," I say, catching my breath. We haven't gone far, but my heart's still racing from the adrenaline. "I—I didn't think you'd help me."

"I'm not helping," he says, completely poised. "I'm just choosing not to stand in the way."

"That's helping."

He shrugs. Pivoting, he starts walking down the hall, and I hurry to follow. We pass by a few crew members who bow to him and wish him a good show, while glancing at me curiously.

"You and I both have different views on what's best for Jae-woo," Sun says, glancing down the corridor to check that no one's watching, then returning his gaze to me, "but it's his life. He should be the one who makes the decision that he thinks is best, don't you think?"

"Has anyone told you that you're wise?"

He smirks, then turns with a flip of his long hair, calling over his shoulder as he leaves, "They don't call me the leader of XOXO for nothing."

I walk swiftly down the corridor. I don't know what time it is, but Jaewoo's somewhere nearby, I just have to find him.

"Hey, stop right there!" Another security guard; this time one of XOXO's crew, as he speaks in Korean. "Do you have clearance to be down here?"

Dammit! I'm so close. The corridor hooks at the end. Should I make a run for it?

"Don't mind her," another voice interrupts, one I recognize. "She works for the venue."

I glance over my shoulder.

Youngmin engages the man in friendly conversation. His hair is dyed bright red and he's wearing a black outfit with chain-like accessories. Catching my gaze over the man's shoulder, he winks.

I seize the opportunity he's given me, racing down the corridor, rounding the corner, and running smack-dab into Nathaniel.

"Hey, Jenny, isn't this a surprise." Nathaniel's wearing a paisley jacket over loose trousers. He's also bleached his hair since I last saw him, to a brilliant-white color, a stark contrast to his dark eyes. "What are you doing here? Last I checked, we weren't in Los Angeles."

"I'm auditioning for a place in programs for cello at a few New York universities."

"Nice. How'd you do?"

"I got into my top choice."

"Congrats!" He raises his hand for a high-five and I raise mine instinctively.

"Wait!" I scowl. "I'm not here to make small talk with you. Where's Jaewoo?"

A small crease forms between his brows. "I don't know.

"What do you mean you don't know? Isn't your concert about to start?"

He sighs, scratching at his cheek, careful not to mess up his makeup. "You know Jaewoo. When he's feeling overwhelmed, he likes to be alone. Just—uh—not a great time to go disappearing. I was actually on my way to ask Sun if we should push the show back another thirty minutes. It's 8:05 already. We're supposed to go on in ten minutes."

Jaewoo's *missing*. A feeling lodges in my chest, not so much worry but determination. "You go find Sun. I'll get Jaewoo."

Nathaniel watches me for a few seconds, then nods. "I leave him in your care."

We part ways, him back down the corridor I just passed, and me down the hall that branches to the left, opposite where I'd run into Nathaniel.

Where does one find a lost K-pop star ten—*now*

nine—minutes before he's supposed to perform live?

All the doors in the hall are closed. I go to the nearest and wrench it open. Four crew members with cup noodles lifted to their mouths turn to stare at me.

"Sorry!" I apologize, bow quickly, and close the door.

I'll never find him, if I go door-to-door. Think, Jenny!

The lights in the hall are dim, the roar of the stadium reverberating through the floors. Light filters from beneath each doorway, suggesting activity within.

Except for the last door on the right. No light penetrates from beneath the crack. I start walking toward it, then jogging, then full-out sprinting.

You know Jaewoo.

I do know him. The first time we met, I found him in the karaoke room, sitting alone in the dark with his eyes closed.

Reaching for the doorknob, I find it unlocked. As I twist and press it open, the light from the hall cuts through the darkness. Jaewoo looks up from where he's seated on a couch at the back of the room.

"Jenny?" He stands. "What are you—" He falters. "What are you doing here? Is everything all right?"

I step through the door. "Everything's fine."

Now that he's here, in front of me.

Like the others, he's dressed like he walked straight out of a fashion magazine, in a dark blazer with a shirt underneath that has a deep-cut V. I have to force myself to keep my gaze on his face, and not his exposed chest. His outfit also has a few chain motifs, to match Youngmin's, including a light strand that rings his neck.

"Jenny?"

"Sorry, I was distracted. You're very . . . distracting."

His face, which held a measure of confusion smooths out, and his lips twist in a rueful smile. That's when I notice he holds something in his hand.

"Is that . . . ?"

The sticker photo. I'd thought it was lost for good.

He nods. "Turns out someone from our school found it on the lawn and sold it to a local gossip magazine, but she'd only sold a photo she'd taken of the original."

"Was it Jina?"

He frowns. "Kim Jina? No, this girl was a First Year. She was only thinking of making a bit of cash. She returned the picture and apologized. I accepted her apology. By then, the scandal had blown over anyway."

"I'm sorry," I blurt out. Then repeat the words deliberately, "I'm sorry."

Jaewoo doesn't say anything, just waits patiently for me to continue.

"I'm sorry for leaving like that, right as everything was happening. I was . . . afraid. It sounds silly now, but I was afraid of how much I cared about you, and I was scared that it would destroy me when we did break up. It's ironic that it did destroy me, but it was my own doing."

I take a deep breath. "I was wrong to begin a relationship

with you thinking it would fail in the end. I should know better. I'm a musician. You don't practice in order to give a bad recital. You work hard, you put in the time, energy, and passion, and you give a beautiful performance."

Jaewoo watches me for a second, his expression giving nothing away. Then he says, deadpan, "I'll be your partner for this beautiful performance."

"Oh my God!" I groan. "You're totally messing up my metaphor."

He starts laughing, his whole body shaking, tears in his eyes.

I scowl. "What time is it? Don't you have your own beautiful performance to get to?"

He stops laughing. "Oh shit, you're right. I forgot about that."

"You forgot about it!"

He grins, which is completely unfair, because with his makeup and that outfit, it's like a cupid's arrow to my heart. "My girlfriend that I was in love with who broke up with me on a hospital rooftop three months ago in Seoul shows up right before my concert in New York City. Yeah, I forgot about it."

In love with!

"You almost made me forget why I was in here in the first place . . ."

"Oh yeah, why were you in here?"

He smiles shyly. "I was nervous. I am nervous. This is the biggest concert we've ever given, and our first in the US."

"You're going to do great. You've prepared for this. And you have bandmates who will support you, even if you do make a mistake, which you're not going to," I add hurriedly, "but you know what I mean."

Wow, I suck at pep talks.

"You're right," Jaewoo says. "I think I'm ready now." I reach out a hand to him, and he takes it. Together, we hurry from the room, rushing back to the junction where I last saw Sun.

The rest of the members of XOXO are all there, waiting.

"Jaewoo-hyeong! Jenny-nuna!" Youngmin shouts.

"Oh, look," Nathaniel says with a teasing smile, "Jenny's brought him back to us."

"I just needed some time," Jaewoo says, rubbing the back of his neck with one hand, while keeping a tight hold onto mine with the other.

"Yeah, we know," Nathaniel says, but gentling his words with a wink.

"Are you all right?" Sun asks. "We can stall a bit."

"I'm fine."

"If you get overwhelmed up there, Jaewoo-hyeong," Youngmin says, "just make this signal." He raises his pointer finger and scratches the underside of his jaw. "I'll do something silly and distract everyone."

Jaewoo grins. "Thanks, Youngmin-ah."

I start to tear up. How can you not, witnessing this moment?

It's just so beautiful, the care they have for one another. The trust, love, and belief. It's remarkable and just so *wholesome*.

"Jenny-nuna?" Youngmin asks. "What's wrong? Why are

335

you crying?"

Jaewoo releases my hand, only so that I can wipe the tears from my eyes. "I'm just . . . I'm just a big *fan*."

They all laugh.

Jaewoo turns toward his bandmates. "Are we ready to do this?"

"Yeah!" Youngmin pumps his fist in the air.

Nathaniel grins. "Let's give them the show of a lifetime."

"Everyone put your hands in," Sun says, and they all put their right hands in, from oldest to youngest on the top. "Who are we?"

They press down on their hands together, then lift up. "XOXO!"

Recipient: Jenny Go, The Manhattan School of Music

Jooyoung-ah~
Happy New Year!

Thank you for the gifts you sent my mother and sister. Joori has been bragging to all her school friends that she has a cool eonni in the US. Both she and my mother can't wait for you to visit Seoul for the summer. It's all they talk about. But that's all right, it's all I can talk about too.

Wishing you luck on your final exams—this postcard should arrive before then—I know you're gonna rock it. Because you're great at practicing.

I'm great at practicing too. Let's practice a lot the next time we see each other.

I know we spoke just last night, and I know that whatever I tell you in this postcard you'll have known for however long it takes for you to receive this, but I still wanted to write down the words, that I'll say to you in person, this summer.
사랑해.
XOXO, Jaewoo

Acknowledgments

To my agent, Patricia Nelson, who I depend upon in all things publishing, and who lifts me up and challenges me to be the best writer I can be—thank you.

To the Three C's that made *XOXO* possible: to Camille Kellogg, I'm so grateful for your early belief in me; to Catherine Wallace, *XOXO* would not be the book it is today without your brilliant notes; and lastly, to Carolina Ortiz, I'm so happy to have you on Team *XOXO*!

To all the people who make me look so good: to my copyeditor, Jill Freshney; proofreader, Lisa Lester Kelly; production editor, Nicole Moreno; production manager, Sean Cavanagh; and so many working behind the scenes—you are truly appreciated.

To the team at HarperTeen and Team Epic Reads, special shoutouts to Shannon Cox, Sam Benson, Keely Platte, Aubrey Churchward, Jennifer Corcoran, and Cindy Hamilton. It's an honor to work with all of you!

To the talented artists behind my cute and romantic cover: designer, Jessie Gang; and illustrator, Zipcy. Thank you for giving me the cover of my rom-com dreams!

To the authors who showered *XOXO* with such beautiful words—Gloria Chao, Maurene Goo, Sarah Kuhn, Lyla Lee, Emery Lord, Emma Mills, Aminah Mae Safi, Kasie West, and Julian Winters—thank you!

To the Tree chat, who wrote together with me throughout those first turbulent months of spring and summer 2020: Akshaya Raman, Erin Rose Kim, Katy Rose Pool, Maddy Colis, and Amanda Foody. Without your daily encouragements, this book would not have been written.

To my very talented and supportive critique group: Alex Castellanos, Amanda Haas, Ashley Burdin, Christine Lynn Herman, Claribel Ortega, Janella Angeles, Mara Fitzgerald, Meg RK, Melody Simpson, and Tara Sim—I'm so honored to call you critique partners and friends.

To all the friends who continue to support me in all things, thank you: Kristin Dwyer, Stephanie Willing, Candice Iloh, Michelle Calero, Devon Van Essen, Gaby Brabazon, Olivia Abtahi, Cynthia Mun, Sonja Swanson, Ashley Kim, Michelle Kim, Ellen Oh, Karuna Riazi, Nafiza Azad, Lauren Rha, Veeda Bybee, David Slayton, and Michelle Thinh Santiago.

To my BFF, Lucy Cheng—I'm not sorry for dropping you off for classes while blasting SHINee's "Ring Ding Dong."

Finally, I want to thank my family: my mom, who used to bring me to the Korean store to buy CDs and the Korean rental store for VHS recordings of music shows; and my dad, who supported my K-pop addiction wholeheartedly! My cool older cousin Jennifer, who I will forever associate with H.O.T. and my silly and loving older cousin Adam, who always sends the best BTS-themed gifts! Katherine, also known as the author Kat Cho, but who I call eonni, my writer BFF, and noraebang partner—there is no one I would rather sing BTS's "Spring Day" than with you. Sara, Wyatt, Christine, and Bryan—trips to Korea are better when you're around. Heemong Samchon, for buying me every single Fin.K.L album when I was eleven and Heegum Samchon—I miss visiting you in LA, but visits to Korea are fun too! Bosung, Wusung, Eugene, and Daniel—I still have that G-Dragon sweatshirt. Emo and Emo Boo, thank you for all the wonderful summers spent at your home in Seoul. My loving grandmothers—even now, the sound of Korean voices on the TV gives me warm memories of watching K-dramas over your shoulders. My older brother, Jason, who began my love of Korean music in truth. And lastly, my younger sister, Camille, my K-pop concert buddy and favorite person in the world—I love you!

And to all my cousins, aunts, uncles, nieces, and nephews in my very large, boisterous, and loving family: love you, love you, love you!! Shoutout to Seojun, as always.

And special thanks to Toro, my sweet pup, who must listen to the same K-pop songs on repeat while I'm drafting.

Last but not least, to all my readers, thank you! Your support means the world to me.